SKINNY LEG

SUZETTE BRUGGEMAN

SWEETWATER
BOOKS

An imprint of Cedar Fort, Inc.
Springville, Utah

What others are saying about *Skinny Leg*

"Suzette tells her story with flair. She incorporates a humorous, light touch that results in my favorite style . . . fun to read! Even though she deals with some heartache and drama, it's done in a way that keeps the enjoyment needle bouncing up throughout."

—T. C. Christensen, film director of *17 Miracles* and *The Fighting Preacher*

"A wonderful and inspirational book for anyone who loves dogs, dog mushing, a challenge, or an adventure. Throw in a boy who has his own challenges, and you have tales the likes of the Iditarod Trail!"

—Doug Swingley, four-time Iditarod Champion

Dedication

To Mrs. Poulsen, my high school English teacher, for poking the beast that clambers around in my head at all hours of the day and night and brings me such joy.

Some of the text in this publication was quoted from Jack London's *The Call of the Wild* (United States: Dover Publications, 2012).

This is a work of fiction. The characters, names, incidents, places, and dialogue are products of the author's imagination and are not to be construed as real. The opinions and views expressed herein belong solely to the author and do not necessarily represent the opinions or views of Cedar Fort, Inc. Permission for the use of sources, graphics, and photos is also solely the responsibility of the author.

ISBN 13: 978-1-4621-3807-4

Published by Sweetwater Books, an imprint of Cedar Fort, Inc.
2373 W. 700 S., Springville, UT 84663
Distributed by Cedar Fort, Inc., www.cedarfort.com

LIBRARY OF CONGRESS CONTROL NUMBER: 2020942529

Cover design by Wes Wheeler
Cover design © 2020 Cedar Fort, Inc.
Edited and typeset by Valene Wood

Printed in the United States of America

10 9 8 7 6 5 4 3 2 1

Printed on acid-free paper

Chapter 1

The sideline of a football field has to be the loneliest place in the whole known universe. I should know. I spent enough time there back in fifth grade.

Two years ago, for the tenth Saturday in a row, I stood next to Coach Decker at the forty-yard line, my fingers drumming away on my thigh pad. For three and a half quarters, I'd stuck to him like a wad of gum on the bottom of his shoe while he followed the game up and down the sidelines. Aside from a, "Hey, Spence, refill this water bottle, will you," in the middle of the second quarter, he'd hardly acknowledged my existence.

The shriek of a whistle cut through the ruckus, silencing my little drum solo. I shot Coach another glance out the corner of my eye, terrified I'd been forgotten.

"Offensive line, stay with your blocks!" he yelled to my classmates lining up behind the ball.

The four mini gridirons chalked onto Jaycee Park's yellow grass were buzzing with Grid Kid football. A 5-pump squirt from my Super

Soaker in any direction would've nailed some lucky dog blocking, running, or tackling—basically having a blast.

I bent to pull up my black knee sock that had slid down around my ankle again. Could a leg be more scrawny and pathetic? My scoff made a white puff of air. My stupid calf muscle didn't even have enough bulk to keep a sock in place, let alone to launch me across a football field. I jerked the ribbed top up over the weird purple fishnet pattern of blood vessels that glimmered through my skin, strangling the life out of that leg.

I have a rare birth defect in the veins of my left leg, so it doesn't grow as much—*Cutis Marmorata Telangiectatia Congenita*. Try saying that three times fast. Try saying it once flawlessly.

Flawless.

Flawed.

Less than.

Loser.

Mom had said to me at least a million times, "You may have a skinny leg, Spence, but you have a big brain, and a big brain will serve you much better in life than sports ever will. You're the lucky one. You'll see."

Thing is, I didn't want a big brain. I wanted a tackle! Even more, I wanted a quarterback sack. Who cared about the smart kid? No one! The only kids who mattered at school were the fast kids, the kids that could throw a ball and score points for the team. The *athletes*. The rest of us, we were nobodies. *I* was a nobody. My skinny leg had seen to that.

Out on the field, Max snapped the ball to Nico, and Cory, our star running back, broke left. He caught Nico's pitch at a dead run. In two strides, he was past the linemen and blitzing the linebackers. I straightened up, eyes glued on Cory. He cut right, juking the corner-back, and suddenly there was nothing but fifty yards of empty space in front of him.

"Go, Cory!" I yelled, jumping up and down and sending my sock into another nosedive.

Cory was tiny. But just like a hummingbird, he was also super quick. As I watched him fly down the field, legs churning, ball tucked against his side, a fireball of jealousy formed in my gut. I'd never be in his league, never run as if shot from the barrel of a gun, never be cool like that. Not only is my left leg skinnier than the right one, it's shorter too. I don't run, I galumph.

Cory blasted into the end zone. Cheers erupted from the parents scattered along the sidelines while our team went wild, whooping and high fiving each other. Cory held the ball high above his head. His face mask couldn't hide his Grand Canyon grin. Twenty to zero! A burst of excitement doused the jealousy burning through me, and I broke into a big grin too. We were headed for a Team Decker shutout!

The offense trotted back to the sidelines together, chatting and laughing and all piling up on Cory. They jostled me between their shoulder pads on their way to the orange Gatorade cooler, while I picked at the grass with the toe of my cleat.

"Two minutes left in the game," yelled the high-schooler referee.

Coach briskly rubbed his hands together. "One more series, defense," he said then waggled his fingers for us to huddle up around him. "Listen, boys. A defense's pride is in keeping the other team from scoring. So, let's go out in glory for our last game! What do you say!"

Everyone cheered.

"Dairy Queen Blizzards for a Team Decker shutout!"

We all cheered again.

"Bruggeman!"

My head snapped up. Coach was looking right at me.

"All in for this series."

My heart made a rabbitty leap.

"Defensive end. Watch for the sweep to your side, okay," he barked.

I jerked a nod at coach then stole a quick look at my dad who'd been prowling along the sidelines the whole game. Football's in my DNA. Apparently, Dad was some big high school football god back when dinosaurs roamed the earth. He likes to brag how his picture still hangs in his high school locker room. He played defensive end on "the most feared D-line in Montana high school football history" and has a State Championship trophy to prove it.

Then there's my brother, Chase. At six foot two, two hundred pounds of muscle, he's a starting defensive end for his high school's football team. I have his team roster with all the players dressed out in their green and gold jerseys and looking fierce tacked to my bedroom wall. They all have such thick necks.

Jaw set, Dad gave me a fist pump in the air.

"Go, Spence!" Mom hollered from her lawn chair as she reached for her camera.

I pulled on my helmet, and my world shrank. Wiggling in my mouth guard, I headed out onto the field. I wore a specially made lift in my shoe to help even me out. But even with the extra inch, I still ran like a three-legged dog.

I lined up just to the outside of their tight end and got into my stance. My heart beat high and suffocating up in my throat. I pulled in a steadying breath while I waited for the snap. *Come my way, come my way*, I chanted in my head.

"Hut!"

In a flash, the ball was in the quarterback's hands. He dropped back as if to pass, then threw a quick power-toss to the tailback. The tailback went left, stumbled against one of his O-linemen, bounced off him, then reversed direction and swept back toward my side. I ran as hard as I could to the outside.

In seconds he was so close I could hear the breath huffing out his nostrils, could see the Black Mamba look in his eyes. Just three more steps and our paths would intersect. No way would I let him get around my end. He was all mine!

I put on a burst of speed.

His wind ruffled the little hairs on my arms as he blew right by me. With a gasp, I whipped around. *Pull him down from behind!* thumped my heart. My arms shot out and dove for his legs.

You know those slow-motion scenes from cartoons where the character's voices get all stretched-out and deep? I swear that happened to the world as the ground rose up to meet me. I made a final, desperate grab.

Air—that's all I caught before pancaking myself on the turf.

Whoops and cheers from the opposite side of the field broke through the pounding in my ears. I slowly lifted my head. I pulled the grass out of my face mask while I watched the rest of my team chase the runner all the way to the goal line. To my horror, my eyes filled with tears. I blinked three times, and they were gone.

After the game, Cory's mom handed out snacks while the parents chatted. I had zero interest in the snack line—less than zero, actually—so, I skipped it and slunk toward the Gatorade cooler where we'd all dropped our pads.

"Graham Crackers suck," I heard Nico say as I passed the picnic table where he sat with Max. "Wish that gimp wouldn't've ruined it for us."

Max gave a snort of disgust. "My sister could've made that tackle."

Hot lava rushed to my face. I dragged the hood of my sweatshirt up over my head and hunkered into it.

"Wish he wouldn't have come out for football at all," Nico scoffed.

Max crushed his empty juice box. "Too bad they gotta let everyone be on a team that wants to play," he said, shooting it into the nearby trash can. "It's a stupid rule."

Their words hit me like kicks and punches. I forced myself not to break into a run.

"Yeah," Nico grumbled, "the *stupidest*. Losers shouldn't get to play. They bring the rest of us down."

I suddenly felt like puking. I snatched my pads and helmet off the grass, then made a beeline for our Suburban, chin planted on my chest to avoid an outright sprint; barely seeing, barely hearing, barely not imploding.

Mom and Dad caught up with me halfway to the car. As we hustled across the park, the cold November wind kicked up with a fury, swirling leaves into mini tornados, slapping trash against tree trunks and car tires, and washing us in a wave of grit.

When we got to the Suburban, Mom reached out a hand and smoothed my hair. "You want to go get something to eat somewhere? Mexican maybe? Spicy salsa," she cajoled.

I had the mortifying urge to burrow my face in the crook of her neck and bawl. I shrugged away from her, embarrassed to be treated like a baby. "No thanks, not hungry," I muttered, throwing open the door. I tossed my pads onto the seat and climbed in. All I wanted was to go home and disappear—

Disappear into the pages of a book.

Chapter 2

At the first step upon the cold surface, Buck's feet sank into a white mushy something very like mud. He sprang back with a snort. More of this white stuff was falling through the air. He shook himself, but more of it fell upon him. He sniffed it curiously, then licked some up on his tongue. It bit like fire, and the next instant was gone. This puzzled him. He tried it again, with the same result. The onlookers laughed uproariously, and he felt ashamed, he knew not why, for it was his first snow."

"We've gotta leave in ten minutes, Spence!"

Mom's voice reached underneath my bedroom door and jerked me back from the wilds of Alaska. Groaning, I flopped over onto my belly and buried my face in my pillow. Now that Grid Kid football was over, Mom made me swim on a club team. I *despised* swim team. I despised it more than putting my coat on over a long sleeve T-shirt and having the inside sleeve roll up to my elbow, watching the 5th grade puberty video with the girls, bran cereal (get a job, bran cereal!), and burning my tongue on hot chocolate combined. Like Nemo, I have a bum fin and am about as worthless at swimming as I am at running.

"Exercise is as good for your mood as it is for your body," Mom had said to me at least a million times. "It chases away all the little black rain clouds in your head."

I growled into my pillow and pummeled it with a fist. Sometimes my mom drove me crazy! Why did she make me torture myself? I'd had it with team sports. I wanted to walk Team Sports to the end of the plank at sword point, poke it in the back, then watch it step off into shark-infested waters and a bloody demise. I let out another muffled growl. If only Mom would let me stay home and read *The Call of the Wild*. Life hurt a lot less all alone in my room with a book.

The Call of the Wild. A little thrill buzzed through me. I flipped back over and ran my thumb across the glossy gray and white Siberian Husky on the cover, then poked my nose into the pages and inhaled.

Reading was the best part of my life. When I cracked open a book, my neon sadness instantly faded to a dim glow in the back of my mind. Actually, everything faded into the background. Books didn't judge me or demand anything of me—besides returning them to the library on time, of course. And they'd never let me down—except for *Where the Red Fern Grows*. Now there was a downer if there ever was one. And *Bridge to Terabithia* too, come to think of it—though once in a while it was nice to be sad about something other than me for a change. For a while, books made me something different, something better. Besides my dad, books were my best friends.

Last week I'd checked out *The Call of the Wild* by Jack London at school. Once I'd gotten a taste of the first chapter, I scarfed up the whole story in one big bite. It was candy for my mind. I didn't want to swim dumb laps. I wanted to lay on my bed and breathe the cold Alaskan air and listen to the Huskies howl while I reread the adventures of the dog named Buck who was stolen from his family in California and sold into the life of a sled dog. No other story had grabbed hold of me and wouldn't let go like this one had. I couldn't get enough of Buck's fight for survival in the Alaskan wilderness. Not nearly enough.

"Let's go!" Mom hollered.

I rolled my head and cast a sour look at my mesh swim bag. "Yeah, yeah," I muttered under my breath as I rocked out of the dent in my mattress.

That afternoon, sled dog fantasies fueled my thirty laps up and down the pool. I barely even noticed when Maggie, a girl two grades under me and half my size, lapped me on the breaststroke. Okay, fine. Twice; the little humanoid lapped me twice, and if you're thinking things couldn't get much worse than that, you're wrong.

11:37 a.m. the next day found me sitting at the end of a crowded cold-lunch table in the school cafeteria swamped in the buzz of a hundred voices. I was arranging the contents of my insulated lunch bag in front of me—PB&J, baby carrots, single-size pack of Sour Cream & Onion Pringles (rated 3rd tastiest in a blind taste test of 16 different Pringles flavors), and bottle of Sunny-D—when a shove to my shoulder sent juice splashing all over my "Never Trust an Atom—They Make Everything Up" T-shirt.

"Hey, *loser*," sneered a voice at my back, "you owe me. You cost me a Blizzard on Saturday."

While I scrambled for a napkin, a hand reached around me and snatched the Pringles from my food lineup. "Hey!" I snapped, shooting a glance over my shoulder just in time to catch Nico's ugly smirk before he turned and walked away.

Fuming, I stabbed him in the back with my eyes as he swaggered toward the athlete's table. *Nico The Mosquito.* The thought was such a good one, it came with a snort. Nico definitely had a lot in common with the biggest jerk of the insect world. Annoying. Noxious. Mean. Even an entomologist, the biggest insect-lover, would slap a mosquito without thinking twice.

As he squeezed himself in next to Cory, I conjured a mental Pixar short of a winged and six-legged Nico sticking his long proboscis into my bare bum and sucking my blood until he was so fat he exploded like a water balloon. That made me feel a little better.

But the good feeling didn't last because the next day Nico snagged my Pringles again on his way past my cold-lunch table. "Knock it off!" I snapped, swatting at his hand and missing by a mile.

"What are you going to do about it, gimp?" he scoffed. "Chase me down and take them back?" Knees spread wide, he started clomping his feet up and down and flopping his bent arms around like an imbecile.

My face burned like a marshmallow held too close to a campfire. I shot a quick, panicked glance around the table. A bunch of people had turned to watch, food held suspended in mid-air. Across from me, a girl named Hazel snickered behind her Cheetos bag, and it was like every sound in the cafeteria stopped but that one. An excruciating second passed, followed by another. Then all two hundred kids were on their feet, pointing at me, and shrieking with laughter.

Flawed. Failure. Less than. Loser. Heart pounding, I blinked hard to chase away the daymare, then dropped my gaze to my PB&J as the normal cafeteria buzz rolled back over me. I let out a shaky breath.

"Didn't think so, freak." Nico scoffed. "Too bad though, 'cause everyone loves a good laugh." Then he sauntered away, the crunch of Pringles trailing behind him.

The rest of the afternoon, I felt like poo on a shoe. For the first time ever, the clock on the classroom wall was way more interesting than a chemical vs. physical changes of matter lesson in science or even a subject-verb agreement game during English. I wished I could put a saddle on the minute hand and spur it into a gallop. I couldn't get to my bedroom, and *The Call of the Wild*, fast enough. Then I'd read myself to smithereens.

The next morning, my body felt so heavy I could hardly drag myself up the stairs. When I shuffled into the kitchen, Mom looked up from the griddle and nearly blinded me with a smile. "Good morning."

I scowled. What the heck was so good about it? Not this horrible stomachache I'd woken up with. Not Mom's whole-grain, mashed banana, and walnut pancakes. *Gag.* And definitely not the fact it was another school day.

I rubbed her smile from my eyes. "I'm going to eat hot lunch today."

Mom flipped a pancake then gave me the side-eye. "You hate hot lunch."

"No, I don't," I snapped, crossing my fingers behind my back.

"Spencer . . . " Mom said my name in her "where were you the night of the murder" voice.

"The menu says pizza today. I *love* pizza." I widened my eyes and nodded for effect. Crust made from recycled shoe boxes. Lumpy, green cheese. Grease so deep on top you needed a scuba mask to eat it. *Ugh. I'd rather eat a rat carcass.*

"Okay . . . " Mom said in her "I believe you as far as I can throw you" voice, but I went to school with money in my backpack.

At lunch that day, I sat at the far end of the hot lunch table nearest the aide's table and within smelling distance of the fumes that wafted from the toxic sludge in the bottom of the garbage barrels. Nico didn't find me, and by the end of the school year, I swear that spot bore a permanent imprint of my butt cheeks from hiding out there every day.

Too bad avoiding the Mosquito wouldn't prove as easy as greasy pizza.

Chapter 3

One afternoon in November, about a week into my hot lunch purgatory, I stood at our dining room window staring at the mountains fifty miles of wide-open prairie away. We live in Great Falls, Montana. My town looks nothing like the majestic mountain/crystal lake duos pictured on those Montana tourism calendars. Nope. It straddles the Missouri River out on the plains looking drab and sullen. *Oh, give me a home, where the buffalo roam*, and all that. Instead of pine trees, we have wheat; instead of grizzlies, plain ole boring cows.

I pressed my palms to the cold windowpane, imagination firing bright enough to drive all the crummy school stuff from my head. There wasn't any snow in our yard yet, but the tallest of those mountains, the one called King's Hill, wore a white cap, and did for six months every year. With my eyes narrowed on that snow, the thoughts of Buck and his sled dogs that had been smoldering in my mind for days flared into a full-blown bonfire.

"Go out and get the eggs before it gets too dark, Spencer," Mom called from the kitchen, breaking my trance.

"Going," I mumbled, casting a last long look at King's Hill.

Vibrating with a new energy, I bounded out to the chicken coop. When I rounded the barn, my mind mapped out the space by the hitching post for dog boxes. Passing the trailer Dad used to haul his bird-hunting dogs, I mentally added a few more compartments and filled them with sled dogs. I could practically hear them barking now. Since our closest neighbor was half a mile away, nobody would complain about the noise. *Except for Mom,* taunted my annoying inner voice. I wanted to punch it in the mouth.

After I collected the eggs, I went over to feed and water Dad's hunting dogs without being asked. They each greeted me with paws to my chest and wet nose to my nose. While I filled their bowls, the freezing wind bit at my cheeks and turned my fingers into little cherry popsicles. But I barely noticed and even got satisfaction from scooping the poop.

"What was that for?" Dad asked when he got home from drilling teeth at his dental office and found the dog chores already done.

I shrugged nonchalantly, afraid to put voice to the hunger growing inside me. I wanted sled dogs so bad I felt it as an ache below my ribs. But I knew that the moment my dream was out of my mouth, Mom would shoot it down and that would be the end of it.

Six horses, two mules, two bird dogs, a cat, a miniature parrot, a hedgehog, a tarantula, two peregrine falcons, homing pigeons, and chickens rounded out our menagerie. "No more pets!" Mom had said eleventy thousand times. "We've got ourselves a Noah's ark situation developing here."

The Unsaid always saves room for possibilities. Plus, Hope is a hundred times sweeter than the disappointment of a big, fat No. So, I kept my dream locked inside where Mom couldn't obliterate it.

"Thanks for taking care of the dogs, bud," Dad said. The smile lines that fanned out beside his eyes crinkled down at me. When he knuckle-rubbed my hair, I felt like I'd swallowed some sun.

The days wore on. School, Mosquito evasions, chores, stupid swim team, homework, hot lunch rubbery mystery meat—everything in my life became background noise to thoughts of dogs and sleds and that snow on King's Hill. At night, I lay awake thinking about sled dogs, not sleeping, not even wanting to. And when sleep would finally drag me under, endless ganglines of sled dogs throwing up wings of snow as they ran looped through my dreams.

One evening when me and Mom were coming up our driveway after another worthless swim practice, I blurted, "Mom, it would be so cool if we had a dogsled team!" No warning. It just popped out.

Mom hit the brakes so fast the Suburban slid to a cockeyed stop, flinging me forward and spitting gravel against the underbelly. I cringed, wishing I could shove the words back in and swallow them whole.

Her head whipped around. I could practically hear the whistle of the incendiary bomb headed my way. I shrank down in my seat and braced for the blast.

"You've been talking to your dad," she accused.

"No, I haven't," I shot back. "What are you talking about?"

"Yesterday he said the same thing to me about wanting a dogsled team. He just finished reading a book about the Yukon gold rush in Alaska, and he's obsessed. You know how your dad gets when he's obsessed with something."

At that unexpected bit of news, I felt a little electric jolt and sat up straighter.

Mom jabbed a finger in my direction. "You guys are conspiring against me."

"No, we're not."

"Dad has too many hobbies already," she said. "When would we have time for a bunch more dogs?"

Fly fishing. Camping. Falconry. Triathlons. Mountain climbing. Archery. I ticked them off in my head, feeling less hopeful as the number grew.

"Do you know how much work all those dogs would be?" Mom said.

"I'll do it all!"

"Uh-huh."

"Really, Mom, I will!"

Mom made a quick shake of her head. "It doesn't matter. It's never going to happen, so quit ganging up on me."

"We're not ganging up," I said defensively.

Mom blew out a long breath. Then she turned and stared out the windshield, hands gripped on the steering wheel. "You really don't know anything about Dad's book?"

"No!"

"You two didn't talk about this already, hatch some devious plan behind my back?" "No." My voice sounded so whiney.

"Huh," she murmured, and this weird stillness came over her. Up ahead, our house, crowned by the sinking sun, stood like a red brick island in a sea of prairie grass. I watched an arrow of geese shoot through the enormous fiery ball of energy without getting incinerated while Mom just sat there thinking about who knew what.

Inside the sealed vacuum of the car, the suspense spread like deadly gas until it got hard to breathe. Finally, Mom turned in her seat to look at me. I tried to swallow but couldn't get it down.

"Well . . . " She rolled the single word around on her tongue. Then one side of her mouth curved up. "Maybe something else is at work here. Let's have a family meeting tonight and discuss it," she said, and I felt like I'd swallowed more sun.

Chapter 4

About this dogsled insanity . . . " Mom began from the couch across the room.

I shot a quick look at Dad's face, hoping to find a clue there, but it was buried in a fly-fishing magazine. I dug my fingertips under my kneecaps as my heartbeat revved up. I'd come to the family meeting prepared to beg, to barter everything—including my birthdays and Christmases—to promise whatever it took. My life had come to this moment.

Mom bounced a fist on her thigh. "I doubt that there's a sport that would suit you better, Spencer."

My whole body went stiff as I waited for the "but." There's always a hippo-sized *but* in the important stuff.

"From what I can tell, mushing is as academic a sport as it is physical. It might be just the thing for you. *But*—"

"Hey, Mom," Chase cut in from where he sprawled on the carpet harassing our dumb cat. "Did my package come today?"

There it was—those three little letters that spelled *H-E-Double Toothpicks No!* dangled from Mom's lips. I glared at Chase like he was responsible for Ebola, then looked down between my feet feeling as if a hole had been punched in my life.

"Yes. I left the box sitting on the table by the front door," Mom said to my ignoramus brother, who popped up off the floor and padded out of the room completely oblivious to my misery.

Mom unglued herself from Dad's side and crossed to me. A wrinkle creased the space between her eyes. "Come here." The dip in the cushion as she sat tilted me against her. I tried to squirm away, but she snaked an arm around me and pulled me in close.

Ugh. I hated mush.

"Dogsledding might be just the thing for you, Spence. *But,*" my head bobbed with the shrug of her shoulder while that word hung between us like tighty whities with skid mark stains pinned to a clothesline.

I squeezed my eyes shut and went limp inside.

"I really don't know much about it," Mom went on. "I think it's definitely worth looking in to. See if you like it as much as you think you will before we make a big commitment."

My eyes shot wide. Was that a *yes*! It sure sounded like one to me! I ventured a peek at Mom's face to see what was happening there. She was shining a little smile down on me. I gaped at her. I'd come prepared for a fight, and she hadn't even brought a weapon. She'd simply given in.

My grin stretched so wide my face hurt. The way she was looking at me, it was pure magic. Then her eyes went glassy and understanding seeped all through me. My mom wanted a bunch of dogs like she wanted permanent diarrhea. But she was worried about me, so she was willing to do something undesirable to make things better—kind of like Harry Potter in *Deathly Hallows* when he accepts that he must die at Voldemort's hand before Voldemort can be killed.

Chase reappeared in the doorway, an empty box wedged in his armpit. "If you can beat me in a hot pepper showdown tonight, I'll be your dog handler when you race," he said, holding out a little bottle of Bud's Wicked Tickle Ghost Pepper Powder.

Racing! I thought, feeling full of Pop Rocks at the prospect. "You're on!"

"And Mom can be my handler," Dad said, flashing her a wicked grin.

"When Hell freezes over," Mom shot back.

"That's what we're counting on. Right, Spence?" Dad said.

"Yeah, we're gonna need a ton of cold and snow to run our dogs!"

From across the room, Dad's eyes glowed at me like a kid's on Christmas. "Come on, Spencer. Let's go google Montana mushers and see what's out there."

I shot up off the couch.

An hour later, Dad was in his study making a dogsledding call on his cell phone (!), and me and Chase were sitting in the kitchen with a gas station chicken sandwich on the counter between us. Me and my brother love spicy food. More specifically, we love to see how many Scoville Heat Units (SHU) we can handle without . . . well, dying.

The Scoville Scale is the measurement of the firepower—the concentration of the chemical compound capsaicin—in chili peppers. Tabasco sauce, rated at 3750 SHU, and the jalapeño, at 10,000 SHU, are near the bottom of the Scoville Scale, while the Carolina Reaper, at a whopping 2,000,000 SHU, is at the tippy top.

For the past few months, we'd been eating our way up the Scoville scale. We were building up a superhuman heat tolerance because . . . hmmm . . . because inflicting nuclear pain on ourselves made us feel cool, I guess. That, and according to the book *The Adolescent Brain: Learning, Reasoning, and Decision Making* I'd found on Mom's bookshelf, the prefrontal cortex—the rational part of a boy's brain—isn't fully developed until the age of twenty-five. Boys do dumb stuff, what can I say, *and* we can't be blamed for it because it's totally backed by science.

Anyway, so far, we'd survived the Rooster Spur, Ring-O-Fire Cayenne, and Devil's Tongue—basically every chili pepper up to the Red Savina Habanero which, at a head-exploding 580,000 SHU, had turned us into fire-breathing dragons a couple of weeks before. Our ultimate goal was to face the wrath of the Carolina Reaper without a trip to the emergency room. But not today. No way, José! We may have been stupid, but we weren't *that* stupid. Yet.

Today we were going up against the Ghost Pepper which *only* has a measly 1,000,000 SHU. Measly, my foot (scoff)! I was an experienced fire-eater. The anticipation alone of those measly one million SHU hitting my mouth made me pee a little in my pants.

Chase took the top bun off the sandwich and started shaking Bud's Wicked Tickle Ghost Pepper Powder over the patty while I poured a tall glass of milk and set it beside the sandwich. Chase kept on shaking . . . while I started shaking in my boots. When the patty resembled a chunk of Australia's famous Simpsons Desert (google it), Chase turned to me with palms lifted high above his head and whooped, "Are you ready to ride the heat wave!"

I echoed his whoop and slapped his hands a couple times while we made all sorts of Neanderthal sounds to pump each other up. Then Chase threw his head back, beat his chest and howled gorilla-style while I sucked in a big lungful of air, put my game face on, and turned inward for strength.

"I'll go first," Chase said, picking up the sandwich. He took a bite. I watched riveted while he chewed and hummed and nodded thoughtfully. Then, smirking and waggling his eyebrows, he handed the sandwich to me.

Mind over matter. Mind over matter, I chanted in my head. I licked my lips. Took a bite. Began to chew.

The first bite was actually kind of sweet and innocent. *A big bad wolf in grandma's clothes*, I thought. But I was no Little Red Riding Hood. I knew what was coming. And this sensation of a tomcat chasing a mouse around inside my stomach, it was part of the fun.

I handed the sandwich back to Chase. When he took another bite, his eyes teared and bugged out a bit. "Oh, that tickles," he said, a hand flying to his mouth.

Boy, did it ever.

Bite number two, the heat kicked in with a vengeance. With shocking speed, it spread through my mouth until it was a 5-alarm fire. When I swallowed, flames flowed to the back of my throat, down through my esophagus and into my stomach leaving a blistering trail. I fought to keep my face blank. "Mmmmm," I said, giving my bro a grin while I blinked furiously to keep my own sudden tears inside.

Chase tore off another bite. "Oh, baby . . . that's hot! That's really, really hot!" he panted as he chewed. His face had turned the color of a beet. I watched his mouth form a big O, and he blew out a few huffs of air before snorting a high-pitched laugh. "This pepper's no joke!"

Another bite, another explosion of heat. Saliva flooded my mouth in defense. I slurped my own spit as I sucked in cool air to fan the white-hot coals inside my mouth. It was all I could do to hold back a whimper. "Meh," I said, shrugging nonchalantly as I chewed. "No big deal."

"You're a big fat liar," Chase scoffed, then threw back his head and opened his mouth in a silent, red-faced scream.

A hysterical giggle bubbled up out of me.

Back and forth the sandwich went. One minute in and my heart was already galloping away in my chest. All my waterworks were turned on full blast. Tears streamed down my cheeks, snot gushed from my nose, and sweat had sprouted up all over my forehead.

Chase screwed up his watery eyes and made three slow pounds with a fist against the countertop. "Mo-ther," he whimpered, then exploded off the barstool. He ran around the counter and grabbed the fire extinguisher from under the sink. "I hate the world! I hate that I ever existed!" he bellowed. He stuck the nozzle in his mouth and mimed pulling the pin and spraying the foam. "The struggle is real!"

I doubled over in laughter, tears of hilarity mingling with the pain tears streaming down my face.

Chase yanked up his T-shirt and looked down at his bare chest.

"What are you doing?" I gasped around the ten million hot pins stabbing my tongue.

"It feels like my nipples are going to spout fire!"

We howled with laughter.

Chase started bouncing around the kitchen on the balls of his feet punching the fridge, the cabinet doors, my shoulder. "If I make it through this," he panted, "I'm going to love everyone in the world! I'm going to love you *so much*, little bruh . . . You'll see."

Nope. I wouldn't see because I wasn't going to make it through. I was drowning in a vat of molten lava. This hurt was its own kind of evil. My face was melting off my skull. My eyes felt like they were popping out of their sockets. I cast a longing look at the glass of milk before my eyeballs plunked to the floor and rolled beneath the fridge and went dark forever. Tutting, Chase shoved the scrap of sandwich into my hand.

We were both panting like racehorses. I forced in another bite. Began to shake. My body was in full freak-out mode. This was about the time it told me to keel over. "Dy-ing . . . " I whimpered, toppling off the barstool and onto the floor.

Chase was dancing around the kitchen again making all sorts of angry noises while I writhed on the tiles. Growling, he slapped his palms against the pantry door with a loud crack. "I can't take it." He spun around. "That's it. I'm tapping out."

When he made for the glass of milk, I swear the heavens opened and a heavenly choir sang the Hallelujah Chorus in my head.

At the last second, Chase's hand swerved sharply. "Kidding," he sing-songed, grabbing the sandwich instead. He took a bite and beamed a wicked grin down at me.

Whimpering, I pulled my knees to my chest. My mouth and the back of my throat were burning too hot for me to tell my brother how much I hated him. The pain from my lips to my guts was so intense I thought at any second I would spontaneously combust into a pile of ashes. *Maybe Mom will keep me in a tiny ceramic jar on the mantle.* The absurd thought sent me into another excruciating fit of giggles.

Chase held the last hunk of sandwich out to me. "Focus, twerp," he barked, shoving me with his stockinged foot.

Mutely shaking my head, I pushed to my hands and feet then clawed my way up the barstool. "Un-cle," I whispered, lunging for the glass of milk.

Then it was at my lips. Oh glorious, delicious, avenging dairy product! As the cold milk filled my mouth and flowed down my pipes, the heavenly angels started to sing again. Surely nothing had ever felt so good in the history of mankind.

"How do you know how heavy a red-hot chili pepper is?" Chase asked as I guzzled.

I looked at him out the corner of my eye as my throat worked furiously.

"Give it a weigh, give it a weigh, give it a weigh now," he sang in that famous tongue-tripping staccato.

My choke of laughter at the hit 90's song punch line sent milk spraying out my nose and all over the front of his shirt. "You . . . you, fecal face!" I spluttered, swiping milk from my chin with my shirtsleeve.

With a triumphant smirk, Chase grabbed the gallon of milk from the countertop. I collapsed back into a heap on the floor.

Chase nudged my head with his foot. "Good effort, soldier," he said then strolled out of the room, milk jug swinging at his side.

"Don't get cocky, moron," I called to his retreating back. "You haven't won 'til the ghost pepper makes its exit."

Mouth smoking, I lay there curled up on the cold kitchen tiles. Outside the wind raged and pummeled the windows with needles of ice, but with my brother's deep voice singing "burning ring of fire" echoing down the hallway, and my sled dogs more hologram than dream, I felt the earth was an especially great place to be alive right then.

Chapter 5

The setting sun was spinning cotton candy clouds across the sky when we pulled into a snowplowed parking lot at King's Hill the following Saturday. A link on a Montana musher's website had listed mushers willing to introduce others to the sport. Dad had called a man named Terry Adkins during the infamous ghost pepper showdown, and he'd invited us for our first ride.

The bed of the truck we parked beside was fitted with little compartments arranged like a wall of post office boxes, with doors that opened to the outside. Behind each door, a dog lay in a tiny bed of straw. Several sets of paws dangled out from between the vertical slats of the metal grates on the doors. I even caught sight of a few sets of eyes glowing out at me from the dark insides of the boxes. I could hardly stay in my skin.

I jumped out of the truck and stood there for a second, just taking it all in: the towering Christmassy trees all decked out in white, the crisp, glittery air, the calm of the twilight, the anticipation fizzing through my veins à la Cherry 7-Up. It was a moment that would stay in my mind for at least a thousand years.

A man wearing dirty Carhartt overalls rounded the front of the truck. Snow white hair poked out from beneath the earflaps of his red flannel cap. "You must be Spencer," he said, thrusting out a gloved hand to me. "I hear you've caught the mushing bug."

"Yes, sir," I said, pumping his arm with my best grip.

Dr. Adkins (we'd learned he was a veterinarian) unlatched a compartment, and a dog leaped down. It was a blonde, short-haired, pathetic excuse for a husky. Dr. Adkins clipped a short chain from its collar to a line attached around the bottom of the truck. The dog stretched leisurely, sniffed in a circle, then lifted a leg and peed on a tire.

The second dog Dr. Adkins pulled out was black with yellow legs, muzzle, and eyebrows. It was small and rangy and . . . well, a bit of a letdown too, to tell you the truth. It followed the same stretch, sniff, and pee routine.

Dad unhooked a latch and a sleek, chocolate-brown Anubis-looking dog straight from an Egyptian pyramid painting emerged from the box. *Wait! What the?* Not one of these dogs looked like the majestic Siberian Husky on the front cover of *The Call of the Wild*. Real sled dogs had bushy tails, triangular ears that stood straight up, and cool Batman masks on their faces. These were a bunch of mutts.

Dr. Adkin's looked at me scowling at his dogs and chuckled. "I bet you were expecting big Malamutes or Siberians."

I nodded, feeling the balloon of anticipation inside me deflate a little.

"Everyone does at first," he said, pulling out a pure white dog with ears that flopped forward. "These are Alaskan Huskies."

Dad sidled up. "Alaskan Husky is obviously not a pure breed."

"Nope. But don't let their scrappy look fool you. They're engineered for speed and endurance rather than hauling power."

I screwed up my nose. "Engineered?"

Dr. Adkins nodded. "During the Yukon gold rush in Alaska, there was suddenly a big shortage of draft dogs, so miners brought dogs of every size and breed with them to haul their stuff. When the gold was gone, they turned them all loose. Alaska Natives bred the best of those dogs to their powerful, freight-pulling Malamutes and Siberians to add specific qualities like speed and stamina, balanced bodies and tough feet to their teams. That's how we got the strong Alaskan racing type we have today," he tipped his head toward the dogs clipped along the bottom of the truck, "and why you can see hints of labs and collies and hound breeds in them. Alaskan Huskies are really nothing more than successful mixed-breed mutts."

"More a concept than a breed then," Dad said.

"Exactly. When mushers talk huskies, we're describing a dog based on the way it *performs*, not how it looks."

Grinning, Dr. Adkins shifted the chain from one hand to the other while the white dog danced around at his feet. "Alaskan Huskies are the most remarkable athletes on the planet. An exceptional sled dog can run a hundred miles in a single stretch, and after a hot meal and a few hours' rest, it's begging to go again."

My eyebrows shot up.

His grin widened. "Sled dogs have extraordinary stamina and this incredible ability to recover quickly that scientists are still trying to figure out." He made a slow shake of his head. "I've spent forty years with them, and my wonder never ceases. Pound for pound the sled dog is the most powerful draft animal on earth, capable of maintaining average speeds of eight to twelve miles an hour for hundreds of miles. They're just that remarkable."

Wild! Dogs with superpowers!

"One Alaskan Husky might look different from the next," Dr. Adkins glanced at me with a gleam in his eye, "but they all have an insatiable need to run. You'll see." He held out the dog's chain. "Here, son. Put Spook next to Jax."

Feeling incredibly important, I clipped Spook on the link, then crouched down next to her. She skittered under the trailer. I pulled off a glove and held out my hand to her, palm down. "Hey, girl," I said gently. I was answered by a low growl, not of anger, I decided, but of shyness and suspicion. I accepted it as a personal challenge. For the next several minutes, I held very still, crooning soft words to her, ignoring the cramps forming in my legs and the cold nipping my bare skin.

It happened by degrees: the emergence of her nose, the stretching out of her neck, the quick sniff of my hand and speedy retreat, the gradual reappearance of her head. All the while I kept on talking soft to her, telling her all about Buck and his team, how excited I was for my first dogsled ride, and how bad I wanted a team of my own.

I was only halfway aware of Dad and Dr. Adkins working above and beside me, letting down dogs and readying gear, talking back and forth in deep voices that flowed over me like a slow-moving river of warm honey. Then Spook pushed her snout up under my palm, and the whole world narrowed down to me and this dog. I inched my hand up and burrowed my fingers into the thatch of hair between her ears. When she didn't flinch away, I gave her a tentative scratch, relishing the feel of her.

"You've got a friend there, young man," Dr. Adkins called over his shoulder. "You must have some crazy, powerful mojo. Spook won't let anyone but me touch her—not even my wife."

I eased my arm around Spook's neck. "You like me, do you," I murmured into her ear. She leaned into me, and I leaned right back, hiding my wild grin in her ruff.

Beside us, Jax frog-squatted and dumped a steaming turd in the snow. Dr. Adkins dropped a flimsy little rake and a pan with a long handle in the snow at my feet, breaking our spell. "You get poop patrol while your dad helps me harness the dogs," he said, jerking an elbow toward a 5-gallon bucket lined with an outdoor garbage bag. "Then it's time for the fun part."

But I was already having the time of my life.

Chapter 6

D r. Adkins straddled a dog between his knees. When he slipped its head through the padded neck-hole of the harness, the dog automatically lifted one leg and then the other and stepped into the openings of the heavy nylon strap that ran along its breastbone. Then he tugged the top of the harness over the shoulder blades and down to its tail while the dog stood as still as a mannequin.

Dad watched once, then got busy harnessing the dogs on the other side of the trailer. In no time, twelve dogs were harnessed, and the 5-gallon bucket was half full of crap. The last of the sunlight had faded away, and a gold-medal moon balanced on the hills. Dad and Dr. Adkins flicked on the headlamps strapped around their foreheads and dragged two sleds from the trailer. Dad seemed to know just what to do. He's like that with everything.

They tied the one sled in front of the other, then tied the back sled to the grille on Dr. Adkin's truck, and stretched a long gangline out in front of them. When they started bringing dogs over from the trailer and hooking them on the gangline, all hell broke loose.

The moment each dog was clipped in, it went nuts—slamming into its harness, kicking snow behind it like a charging bull and screaming in high-pitched yelps. Soon the racket was earsplitting. But it was a happy noise—a wild frenzy that opened my adrenaline valve, flooding my system with excitement. Within minutes, the parking lot was absolute mayhem with twelve dogs on the line, all jumping and yelping and frantic to run.

Dr. Adkins motioned to me. "Get in the sled bag," he shouted through the pandemonium, gesturing to the sled in the front with an elbow. I tossed the rake and pan into the back of the trailer and scurried over.

I scrambled into the blue canvas bag which was fitted to the dimensions of the sled basket with a big zipper running its length. Dad pulled the hood of my parka up over my head and tugged the zipper to my chin, then stepped on the runners behind me and grabbed the handlebar.

There was an urgency to all our movements now. The sled wobbled and jerked with the frantic hammering of the dogs against their harnesses. This close, I could see the energy rattle through their legs, into their chests, and out their open mouths. The rope leading from the sled into the gangline was taut and quivering with the enormous amount of power just waiting to be unleashed.

Dr. Adkins climbed onto the sled behind ours. Sensing we were about to leave, the dogs' howling and lunging reached a fever pitch. It was intense and thrilling, and all that harnessed energy seemed to gather right in the middle of my chest making it hard to breathe.

"Hike, hike!" Dr. Adkins shouted and pulled the quick release on the cable. The sled jerked, lurching me forward. I made an involuntary whoop as I ricocheted back against the handlebar, which was both a backrest for me and a place for Dad to hold on above my head.

It was as if someone hit an off switch on the noise. The instant the dogs began to move they went perfectly silent. Their tails lowered, their ears flattened, and they threw their shoulders into their harnesses as we rocketed out of the parking lot and into the trees. It was one of the biggest *WOW* moments of my life!

The light from Dad and Dr. Adkins's headlamps illuminated our path like a single headlight. Everything went by in a blur. Up ahead, the trail split. "Gee!" Dr. Adkins called out. The lead dogs veered to the right so sharply, our sled tipped up on one runner as the team whipped around the turn. I whooped again, then threw back my head and laughed.

The trail cut through a corridor of trees stretching away from us, dissolving into the darkness. The dogs flew toward the abyss, and my soul flew right along with them.

"I was the only veterinarian in the first Iditarod back in 1973." Dr. Adkins's statement to Dad punched through my awe.

No way! I'd read all about the Iditarod. The iconic 1000-mile race across Alaska was the Super Bowl of dog sled races! My ears perked up.

"I caught the bug and went back the following year to run it with a team of my own," Dr. Adkins continued. "I started the race with only twelve dogs—sixteen's the standard—and most of them were rejects from other teams or dogs right out of the pound." He chuckled softly. "I wouldn't recommend that—running with dogs that aren't prepared. But I managed to take all twelve all the way to Nome. After that, I changed from an adventurer to a racer, learned to train harder and smarter, and ran the Iditarod twenty-one more times."

"That's impressive," Dad said.

Wow! Dr. Adkins was a big shot in the mushing world. I was impressed too.

"Did you ever win?" Dad asked.

"There are four factors to winning a dog race. The first is genetics. The second is nutrition. The third is training or conditioning. The fourth is luck, and I've never had much luck. Mostly with weather—seventy-one below and whiteouts for miles, fifty-mile-an-hour winds and blown-over trails, getting lost, delayed or stranded—and this was thirty to forty years ago before the good cold-weather gear we have now.

"In one race, I was hit by a middle-ear infection and was too dizzy to stand up on the runners and couldn't finish. One time I broke my hand in the Dalzell Gorge. Then in 1991, I finally had a team I thought could win. I got to the Ophir checkpoint in first place, then had to break trail after a huge blizzard snowed it in. When your dogs are breaking trail through deep snow, you're obviously going slower and working harder than the teams behind you. When we got to the end of the Yukon River, my team got a virus, and I had to drop five dogs at the next checkpoint."

As Dr. Adkins talked, I listened, spellbound. It sounded terrible, grueling, dangerous—awesome!

"Bad luck all around," he said. "But it doesn't matter. The pull of distance racing is the unexpected. That, and the test of the limits of human and animal endurance," he continued. "You forget the frostbite, and you forget the heartaches, and you just remember the good parts. If I died tomorrow, I'd have had a full life just running the Iditarod . . . It's the thrill, the danger, the joy. Running dogs gets in the blood and changes a man . . . Makes him better somehow. And once you start . . . well, you can never stop running dogs of your own free will . . . Consider yourself warned," was the last thing I heard before the magic of the moment drowned out their voices completely.

The moon had risen, spilling bucketsful of molten light over the forest. Dad and Dr. Adkins flicked off their headlamps. My eyes and ears stretched wide to collect every detail. I didn't want to miss a thing.

The only sounds were the whisper of the runners gliding through the snow beneath me, the rhythmic patter of the dogs' feet, and the musical clinks of their necklines. The black and white beauty of the wintery, moonlit forest seemed surreal.

The dogs loped along with gaits as graceful as a dancer's, their tongues hanging loosely out the sides of their mouths, their breath smoking the air. Those closest to the sled kicked up snow into my face as they ran. The wind lashed at my cheeks. Once in a while, the sled would hit a divot in the trail, and I'd bounce and let out another spontaneous whoop. Occasionally a dog would dip its head and take a bite of snow as it ran. A few of them even pooped mid-stride in funny, choreographed, spraddle-legged hops while keeping pace with the team. The stench would slap me in the face as we zoomed by. I loved every bit of it.

Watching the dogs run, doing what they clearly loved to do, I experienced a pure happiness unlike anything I'd ever felt. The spirit of the huskies called to me, and I knew then that I would never—could never—get enough of this. It was better than my best dream. It was magical. I *had* to have a team of my own.

The moon climbed until it was a bellybutton on the great big dome of the sky. The night grew darker revealing stars the color of ice. I lifted my face to gaze at the scrap of Milky Way visible through the treetops. Instead of feeling small and insignificant, I felt like the focal point of the whole universe. If I could stretch time like taffy, this would be the moment.

I snuggled in deeper and watched the stars wander across infinity. Up here on King's Hill, they seemed to hang so low that I could reach up and pluck them like fruit. Every so often, Dad would lay his hand on my head, his fingers molding to the shape of my skull through my parka. A church was no more peaceful and holy than this. In fact, I was pretty sure this was exactly what heaven was like.

The dogs ate up the miles effortlessly. We made a big, sweeping loop through the forest without talk or stops. I wished for the hundredth time the ride would never end, that these dogs could pull me clear to the ends of the earth, to somewhere other than real life.

Too soon I caught the glint of the moon off the metal of the truck through the trees. I let out a shuddery breath and went boneless in the bag. I figured we'd been gone a couple of hours. I didn't know how something could feel both played out in slow motion and over in hyper speed. Yet somehow this did.

The dogs trotted up alongside the truck, tongues slavering off the heat from their run. "Easy," Dr. Adkins murmured. They stopped in unison and immediately began stretching and shaking out their coats. They all seemed to be smiling and acting utterly satisfied. Some of them turned their heads upside down, flipped over onto their backs, and shimmied around in the snow to cool off.

Now that I was no longer moving, I noticed I was a human ice cube. I crawled clumsily out of the bag, stomped some feeling back into my stiff legs, then went over to pitch in with whatever came next.

When I neared the dogs, I saw the most incredible thing: their breath had turned to hoarfrost around their mouths and clumped white in their eyelashes and brows. Some even had icicles hanging from their muzzles. I ached with cold and was shivering uncontrollably, but the dogs appeared perfectly content—gleeful even.

"Sled dogs do their best running when it's real cold," Dr. Adkins said coming up beside me. He was carrying another 5-gallon bucket. "Ten above zero to ten below is their sweet spot. Any temperature above thirty degrees is uncomfortable for them, especially when it's sunny out and they're running more than a handful of miles. That's why we went at night."

Yep! Superheroes!

Dr. Adkins held the bucket out to me. "Here. Give the dogs a snack. They've earned it."

I went down the line, handing out frozen salmon steaks. Some of the dogs bolted theirs down in one big bite. Others ate like princesses, holding the steak between their paws, peeling off the thin ribbon of metallic skin, then nibbling a bit at a time. All of them reveled in the rubs and scratches I gave them while Dad and Dr. Adkins took each dog out of harness and boosted it back into the truck.

"So, what did you think of your first dogsled ride?" Dr. Adkins asked as he came by with an armful of harnesses. His teeth flashed at me in the moonlight.

I was on my knees in the snow with my hands all over a gray dog called Catfish. I glanced up at Dr. Adkins, fumbling for something big and meaningful enough to describe what I was feeling. I loved words, was really good at them, but I suddenly found the English language totally lacking. "Um . . . awesome," I said lamely. I'd used that word millions of times, but now it seemed frail and toothless up against what this man had just given me.

I shot Dr. Adkins my best smile to strengthen my pathetic response. Without sounding like a total dork, I didn't know how to tell him that my life had just changed forever, that the kid who'd climbed in the sled was not the same kid who'd climbed back out, or that right now, surrounded by these happy, canine superheroes, and with visions of the Iditarod dancing in my head, I was the most alive I'd ever been.

Twenty minutes later me and Dad were pulling out of the parking lot, headed for home and the mundane. "What took us so long to discover this?" Dad said more to himself than to me. His voice held the same wonder I was buzzing on. "It's got everything I love," he continued dreamily. "Adventure, the outdoors, animals, challenge—all wrapped up in one sport." He glanced at me. "Don't know about you, but I'm hooked."

I stared back at him with a grin I couldn't wipe off if I tried.

Chapter 7

"Nobody pick Spencer," Nico said in a stage whisper. "He can't even wipe his own butt without missing the bullseye."

The titters that spread in ripples through my PE class turned my face into an instant inferno. I looked down at the gym floor, wishing I could crawl inside myself and disappear.

"Okay, everyone!" Mrs. Chester called out as she emerged from the storage closet with her arms full of balls. "Line up on the red line."

Kids peeled away from me until I was standing all alone.

"Let's go, Spencer!" Mrs. Chester barked.

"I have a stomachache," I mumbled to my feet.

"Then go sit against the wall," she said as she swept by me.

Head down, I skulked to the shelter of the cold cinder blocks. Then I sat with elbows on bent knees and chin in cupped hands while my classmates chucked balls at each other and darted around the gym. Their squeals and the squeak of rubber soles against the floor was the background music to my gloom. I felt like a contagious disease. Why couldn't I just be like everyone else?

Loneliness had taught me there was always someone who understood. Too bad those someones were mostly dead, or fictional and in a book. I heaved a heavy sigh. Since I hadn't figured out how to disappear in the flesh yet, and I couldn't disappear into a story right then, I did the next best thing: I disappeared inside my head.

My head was a place filled with endless magic. Mom had seen the stars in our eyes when we'd come home from our first dogsled ride with Dr. Adkins last Saturday. So, with her blessing, Dad had been calling and emailing everyone advertising dogs for sale online. If this horrible school day would hurry up and get over with, we could hit the road. There were a couple of dogs up in Kalispell waiting to be mine. My heart jumped. It was really happening! I was getting a team of my own!

Something smacked me in the face. I yelped. I'd been too lost in my imaginings to see the ball coming at me. Pinwheels of light burst in my head as the ball bounced to the floor and rolled away. My face felt like I'd been stung by a bee. Tears pricked my eyes. I blinked the pain off, then glanced over to find Nico smirking at me.

"Loser," he mouthed before sauntering back to the game.

My hands balled into fists. *Not anymore,* I thought. *I'm gonna be a musher! I'm gonna race sled dogs! I'm gonna do something so awesome—so special—you're gonna worship the ground I walk on!* I sent a withering glare at Nico's back. *Beat that, Mosquito barf!*

Then the doubts swooped in and started circling my plans like vultures. *What if you can't do it, gimp? You have that stupid skinny leg. If you can't make an easy tackle, what makes you think you can drive a sled dog team?*

I squared my jaw and rubbed my throbbing face. Maybe I couldn't do it; maybe I could. No matter what, I had to try, and one thing was sure: I was going to give the trying everything in me. I wanted to prove Nico wrong worse than anything.

The next day we came home from Kalispell with Goblin, a big, muddy-looking dog born on Halloween, and a gray and white female named Charlie. Dogs! In my backyard! Funny how my doubts were suddenly bare specks in the back of my mind.

More dogs trickled in over the next few weeks. It was all super exciting. A musher traveling through Montana after running races in Canada dropped off three dogs: Silver—a freakishly skittish dog with a metallic-gray coat, Fitty Cent—a yellow and black goofball, and Izzy—a coffee-colored Anubis (picture the Egyptian god of the afterlife). Then a hobby musher from Michigan agreed to meet us half-way in North Dakota with a couple of dogs. We drove twelve blissful, junk food-filled hours for Patch—a shaggy black and white dog, and Jude—an old racing veteran with a graying muzzle and tons of valuable experience as a lead dog.

In between weekend trips to collect dogs, we built dog boxes, painted them red and arranged them in neat rows behind the barn. We poured over websites with mushing gear, made lists, ordered stuff, read mushing books, and bought a secondhand sled from Dr. Adkins. For the first time in my life, I got up in the morning with something to look forward to. Mom was happy because I was happy, and I was happy because I was busy turning my *can'ts* into *cans* and my *dreams* into *plans*. Basically, I didn't long for the earth to crack open and swallow me whole anymore—even when Nico gave me a shove in the hallway or tripped me out on the playground.

The last dogs we bought that spring were Trip and Haulin. Haulin had one blue eye and one gold eye. And get this! Trip, she was born with only three toes on her right front foot! Now she was my kind of athlete! Dog by dog, my hologram had become a tangible thing, and by early March we finally had a team.

Sort of.

I reached in and pulled Fitty Cent out of a compartment in our home-made dog trailer we'd towed up to King's Hill. The moment Fitty's feet hit the ground, he jerked out of my grip with one upward wrench of his head, nearly ripping my arm from its socket. Next thing I knew, I was on my backside in the snow, and Fitty was doing a neener-neener dance between the dogs chained up along the bottom of the trailer while they lunged and barked scolds at him. I scrambled to my feet. Before I could snag his chain, he bolted for the trees.

Dad took off after him, shambling through the deep snow. They played a little game of cat and mouse while the rest of the dogs barked their heads off, and I shuffled my feet feeling as useless as the G in lasagna. Dad finally got Fitty's chain pinned down with his big snow boot and tackled him. Then he marched back toward the truck with Fitty trotting politely beside him. I swear that dog was grinning from ear to ear.

At around seventy pounds, I was your average-sized almost eleven-year-old (except for my skinny leg, of course, which looked more like your average six-year old's), but some of our dogs weighed nearly as much as me. My spaghetti arms were clearly no match for these enor-mously strong super jocks. I shoved my hands in my pockets and pulled my chin into the neck of my coat. Our very first run with our very own team, and I was good for nothing. I felt miserable. How was I supposed to stick it to Nico, when I couldn't even hang on to a dog?

"Hey, bud!" Dad called. "I need you to tell me where to hook up each dog on the line."

"Okay!" I called, dashing over. While Dad arranged the gangline out in front of the sled, I fished out the diagram we'd made the night before and clumsily unfolded it with my gloved fingers. "Hook Jude in first at lead so she can hold the line out straight."

Dad gave me a thumbs-up and a swift, leaping smile. All the mushers we'd talked to during our travels to get dogs had told us to start with four dogs, if we expected to live. But after discussing it, we'd concluded that there was no possible way four could pull us both, so Dad had harnessed them all.

He clomped over and grabbed Jude by the collar. She popped up on her hind legs and kangaroo-hopped alongside him all the way to the gangline. It looked hilarious. In fact, all the dogs did that funny kangaroo-hop thing when he brought them over, and each new dog he put on the line affected the others until, by the time the seventh was clipped in, the noise was deafening, and the atmosphere had the sense of a ticking time bomb. My heart began to jackhammer in my chest.

The dogs' hysteria seemed to be affecting Dad too. By the time he put Haulin and Goblin at wheel—wheel dogs are your biggest, strongest dogs you place right in front of the sled to pull it out and around corners or trees—Dad was going back and forth from the trailer to the sled at a dead run.

I dove into the sled bag and zipped myself in. My body felt electric.

The sled rocked as Dad stepped on the runners. "Ready, Spence?" he called in a voice pitched with excitement.

"Ready!"

He nudged my back with his knee. "You say it."

I stretched my neck out past the zipper and yelled at the top of my lungs, "Hike, hike!"

Dad pulled the quick release, and the dogs took off like they were on fire. I felt Dad tilt and the sled wobble with his effort to right himself. "Oh crap!" he yelled as we tore out of the lot. "We should have started with four!"

I don't think the sled hit the ground more than twice before we reached the tree line. I grabbed the sides of the sled and held on for dear life. Holy cow, these dogs were strong! Despite all the questions we'd asked and the advice we'd been given, we hadn't had a clue how powerful sled dogs truly are. Even from down in the bag, I could feel how impossible nine-dogs-worth-of-energy was to control and how hard Dad was working just to stay on the sled, and that first big bend in the trail was coming up fast. My breath bottled up in my throat.

"Drag mat!" I yelled.

But Dad was already fumbling behind me. The sudden resistance of the heavy piece of rubber dragging snow was a thing of beauty, slowing the team just in time. When we hit the turn, they cut to the inside corner. I reflexively hunched my shoulders and ducked my head as we nearly hit a tree.

The sled tipped up on one runner, doing its best to buck Dad off. His feet pinwheeled in the air, but he somehow managed to hang on while letting loose a few words I'd never mention to Mom. I started laughing like a maniac.

By some miracle, we made it around the turn unscathed and began a straight uphill climb. Things were going good. Our patchwork team of dogs seemed to know what to do. They weren't synchronized and polished like Dr. Adkin's team, but they were all facing forward, pulling on their tuglines, and running in the same direction. And so far, we hadn't eaten any snow.

As they worked to pull us up the hill, the dogs slowed way down. With their breaths puffing out behind them and their harnesses straining against their shoulders, they looked like a bunch of miniature steam engines, and they'd all begun to grow frosted beards.

Now that my stomach had climbed out of my throat and settled back into its regular spot, I could focus my attention on my surroundings. In the daylight, the dreamlike vibe of the forest was gone, but it was no less magical. Endless miles of evergreens drooped under the weight of piles of heavy snow. The air sparkled with cold, and the reflection of the sun off the snow dazzled my eyes so that I had to squint to see. Here in the backcountry, the perfection of the winter wonderland was unspoiled by humans, and with a dome of cloudless sky arching above us, it was as if we were traveling through a snow globe just waiting for a good shake.

A trumpeting call drew my gaze to the sky. A small flock of birds was soaring through the perfect gumball blue. "Look," I said, freeing my arm from the sled bag to point. With their massive wingspans, long necks, and long, dark legs trailing behind, they looked like a bunch of flying pterodactyls.

"Sandhill cranes," Dad said in a bare whisper as if anything more would shatter the world like glass. "They're migrating from their winter grounds in Texas back to the Arctic." He reached down and cupped my head. While we watched the birds fly over, I was hit with a water balloon of happiness.

When we crested the hill, the snow machine trail we were following dropped off steeply on the other side. We instantly picked up speed. "Fifteen miles an hour," Dad called out as he read his handheld GPS device. "Eighteen miles an hour . . . Twenty-one!"

We swooped down the hillside, my face cutting through the wind. My smile was so wide, my lips froze to my teeth, and the thought broke through my exhilaration, *Who needs to run when you can fly!*

The trail was icy and slick here, and the sled started bumping all over, rattling me around in the bag. All of a sudden, the sled came to a dead stop so hard and so fast, my head nearly snapped off my neck.

Dad came sailing over the handlebar, over me, over the entire sled and plowed face-first into the wheel dogs' butts. For a heart-stopping moment, it was an awful kaleidoscope of human and dog parts until he came to rest in a heap between the wheel dogs and the front of the sled.

I gaped at Dad's limp form, paralyzed with panic. The dogs stared over their shoulders in bewilderment too. The next few seconds were some of my worst ever. Finally, Dad flopped over onto his back with a groan. "What happened?" The words were sloppy on his lips.

Time started up again. Sound came back into the world. My breath left my lungs in a rush. I twisted around to look behind us. I zeroed in on the stray tether trailing out behind the sled and tracked it to the culprit. "A snow hook's stuck in a log!" I blurted. Snow hooks are like heavy metal anchors with prongs you throw off the back and stomp into the snow to keep an excited team at a stop. I whipped back around to look down at dad. "It must've bounced off the handlebar."

The dogs were starting to whine and make tentative tugs on their lines. Dad's chest began to shake with silent laughter. "Dr. Adkins made it look so easy," he wheezed. He shook his head back and forth, making a little trough in the snow. "Oh Spence, we've got a lot to learn."

This sad fact was confirmed the following Saturday when we gave our team its second go. The weather was pushing forty degrees, and the sun was out, so the snow was too sloppy to give any serious traction for slowing or stopping the sled with the foot brake—a bar with two metal claws attached to it, which dig into the snow to bring the sled to a stop. But it was the best we were going to get in late March, and it would probably be our last chance to run our team that season, and the urge was just too strong to resist. So, we suited up, loaded the dogs, and drove back up to King's Hill fueled by a manic desire to run our team.

It wouldn't prove to be our brightest move.

When the harnesses came out, the dogs went wild, stoking our fire and squelching any of our lingering doubts. As far as I could tell, any moment the dogs are attached to the sled is the best moment of their lives.

Dad hooked up all nine dogs again (yes, we had a death wish, and yes, my dad *is* slightly insane) and within a couple of miles, they'd settled into their run. We had no real control of the team yet, but we were feeling pretty smug in a "pride comes before a fall" kind of way.

I was leaning back in the comfort of the sled bag picking out the cool little details in the backcountry—rabbit tracks over here, a tiny black-capped chickadee over there—when, about three miles in, we came to a sharp turn in the trail. With the snow being so melty, there was no control, no braking, no hold-back to slow the dogs even a little. We hit that turn at warp speed. The dogs whizzed around it like bullets. They made the curve, and the sled started to as well, but in the heat of the moment, Dad forgot to lean into the turn.

He's a big guy with a high center of gravity, and the sled careened onto its side, dumping me out of the bag. I rolled a couple of times before coming to rest sunny-side up against a downed log while Dad hung onto the tipped-over sled, dragging on his face through the snow.

Our dogs—they didn't stop, they didn't slow, they didn't even break stride. Off they went in a state of pure glee, completely ignoring the train wreck going on behind them. After fifty yards of plowing snow with his forehead and belly-slapping the ruts in the trail, Dad broke the first rule of mushing: No matter how long you are dragged, no matter how much it hurts, as long as you have life in your cold, white-knuckled hands, *don't let go of the sled!*

Dad let go.

You'd think a team would at least stop for their downed driver— "No man left behind," and all that. It doesn't. Sled dogs are genetically wired to run. Once they are harnessed and on the move, it's "See ya later, alligator." A sled dog is single-minded in its pursuit of the horizon. It wants only to run and to pull and to see what's over the next hill and will only stop for the occasional meal and warm bed. When they are in the zone, we simply don't exist for them.

Our beloved dogs—they left us in the dust.

Dad popped up like a Bop Bag and set off after them, hollering and windshield-wiping his arms above his head as he ran. The louder he yelled, the faster they seemed to go. He pulled off his mitts and flung them aside. His hands began fumbling at his front. He threw off his parka. It landed on a baby Christmas tree. Twenty yards later he shucked off his black beanie and let it fly. It landed in another scrawny fir, startling a pair of finches that burst from the boughs in a little explosion of snow. More running and more fumbling ensued. Then his blue jacket came off and flapped down into the middle of the trail like a wounded bird, while I watched it all, bent over in half, holding my stomach and laughing so hard I nearly peed my pants.

By now, some of the back dogs had started going faster than the front dogs, and when they were about a quarter mile away, the team got into such a massive tangle, they came to an awkward standstill. I knew luck had kicked in and saved us. Now Dad could catch them, and once he straightened them out, we wouldn't have to make a long walk of shame all the way back to the truck without a team.

From where I stood, the tangle of dogs looked like a giant tarantula, skittering a few feet this way and that. I realized with a sudden pang of fear that they were getting agitated. When Charlie got into an aggressive stance, hackles raised, the laughter dried up in my mouth. Dad put on a burst of speed and threw himself between the dogs just in time to keep snarling Charlie from taking a bite out of Patch.

While Dad untangled the lines and got the dogs turned around, I wandered up the trail, picking up the gear he'd tossed along the way. It wasn't long before we were streaking back toward the truck, our gangline of dogs throwing up wings of snow alongside them as they ran.

As I lounged in the sled bag watching our dogs do their awesome thing, a rerun of Dad's strip chase played through my head, and I snickered into my armpit. "I thought you'd be naked by the time you caught the team!"

Dad kneed me in the spine. "A lot of help you were."

"The world is not your garbage dump," I said imperiously. "Don't you know litter is killing our wildlife. Eleven and a half *billion* dollars is spent every year to clean up people's trash. Most *idiots* don't stop to think how their littering affects the whole country. Someone had to stay behind to save the animals and keep America beautiful. You should thank me for cleaning up your mess."

"Ha, ha, funny guy." Dad bonked me on the head with a fist. "You know, they say you're not a musher until your team has run off and left you."

I wrenched my neck around so that I could catch his eye. "Guess we're true mushers now."

"Not very good ones, I'm afraid. We can't seem to make it back to the truck in one piece."

I melted back against the handlebar, feeling utterly content. "But even when things go bad," I sighed. "I'm still having a blast."

Dad chuckled. "Me too, Spence . . . Me too. Just remind me to pack a big bottle of Advil from now on."

A few mornings later we woke up to five inches of snow at the house. When Dad got home from work that night, he hooked Jude and Trip to the sled and attached a lead rope to the short neckline that stretched between their collars to connect them. Then I stood with legs wide apart, each boot balanced on a runner, gripping the handlebar tightly, while he led the dogs around the backyard as fast as he could run in the snow.

He'd juke to the right, and I'd topple off. Then I'd brush off the snow and climb back on. He'd juke to the left, and I'd fall off, stagger to my feet, and climb back on. I got so that I could keep ahold of the sled when I went down, and Dad would drag me around on my face (a little too gleefully, I might add). Mom watched it all from the kitchen window with an amused look on her face, and every now and then we'd send her a wave and a smile.

We did this every night until the darkness drove us indoors, and every day until I could stay on the sled no matter what Dad and the dogs threw at me. I ate so much snow while finding my center of gravity, Dad ribbed me about bringing along some paper cones and flavored syrups to make my training more bearable.

Truth is, that wild, wonderful time in my backyard with my Dad and our dogs, it was the happiest of my life.

Chapter 8

Our goal was to have enough dogs for both me and Dad to run a team. So, the week after school ended in June (good riddance, fifth grade, don't let the door hit your rear end on the way out), we drove all the way to British Columbia, which is practically to the North Pole, to pick up another load of dogs.

I knew Earl was special the moment I saw him. When we walked with Mr. Warren toward his dog yard, the dogs went crazy, barking and jumping and twisting on their chains. Except for Earl. He stood there calmly, regarding us through intelligent, soulful eyes.

Earl was a big, barrel-chested dog, built more like a fullback than a tailback, and his coat was an interlocking puzzle of brown, black, and white pieces and as fluffy as a teddy bear's. Not only did he physically look different than any sled dog I'd ever seen, being so thick and all, he had this freaky human-like vibe about him too.

"Earl's a Swingley dog. A five-time Iditarod finisher," Mr. Warren said as we neared Earl's box. "I bought him from Doug after he retired from racing a few years back."

At that, my gaze shot up to Mr. Warren's bearded face. A Swingley dog! No Way! I'd read all about Doug Swingley. He was one of the greatest mushers of all time—if not *the* greatest. He competed in the Iditarod every year from 1992 to 2002 and won it an incredible four times! The fact that he was from Lincoln, Montana, which is practically in our backyard, and the only musher in the lower 48 states to ever win the Iditarod made him even more awesome. Doug Swingley was my mushing hero, and to think we'd have one of his sled dog celebrities in our kennel thrilled me to the core.

"Earl's a dog that will teach you how to mush," Mr. Warren said to Dad. "He's real old, but he's seen it all, so he can get you through anything."

"*Anything*, as in . . . " Dad prodded.

Mr. Warren tapped a finger against the side of his nose. "Oh, a raging blizzard on the Bering Sea . . . or a real long race by using brute strength to literally pull a tired team out of the last checkpoint . . . or you know, an ugly divorce . . . stuff like that."

Dad's deep laugh scraped the air.

"Earl's bombproof," Mr. Warren added, then tipped his head my way. "Plus, he's gentle as Jesus for your boy here."

I reached down to scratch Earl between the ears. He raised his head to look at me. His gaze latched onto mine and held, and something powerful zinged between us. I dropped to my knees and wrapped my arms around his shaggy neck. *This dog will be important to you,* my gut whispered to my heart. *He is your Gandalf, your Yoda, your Dumbledore.* I squeezed him tight, loving him instantly, and he licked my face in return—just one big swipe of his tongue from chin to brow.

After we loaded Earl up into our trailer, along with three more dogs, Mr. Warren jerked an elbow toward a dog box at the edge of the yard. "I've got this little female over here who's no use to me. She's too small to put much strength on the line, but she's got a big heart and will be a great team mascot. I'll throw her in for free if you'll take her."

Dad scratched his jaw, and I could almost see the wheels turning in his head: another mouth to feed, another box to build, a waste of space, *Mom.*

"Her name's Mojo," Mr. Warren said, almost as an afterthought.

My hand froze on the door handle of the truck, and my head snapped up.

Mojo.

Since Dr. Adkins had told me that I had some "crazy, powerful mojo" all those months before, "mojo" (which means magic), had ousted "discombobulate" (to throw into confusion) as my new favorite word. I'd lived for three months on that bit of praise. Something akin to a lightning bolt streaked from scalp to sole. This dog was meant to be mine. Mojo was my talisman. I just knew it! I *had* to have her! I looked at Dad and begged with my eyes.

"Sure. Why not," he finally said with the shrug of a shoulder, and I felt a smile hijack my face.

Mojo was black and tan with a white belly and legs, but her triangular ears and long-pointed muzzle gave her the look of a fox. When I bounded toward her, she skulked inside her box. I frog-squatted in front of the opening and peered in. She was huddled up against the far corner. I clearly had my work cut out for me with this one. I'd need all the mojo I possessed to earn her love and trust. *Mojo for Mojo,* I thought and snickered to myself at my cleverness.

When we tried to lead her to the truck, Mojo tucked her tail and locked her elbows. Dad had to drag her all the way across the yard.

"Can we put her up front so she can get used to us?" I asked when he got her to the trailer.

"Great idea," Dad said. "Open the door."

I did, and Dad heaved her in.

For the next several hours, Mojo cowered on the floorboard while I read. Once in a while, I'd reach down and give her a pat and murmur her name, enjoying the teeter-totter of the syllables in my mouth. Halfway home, Mojo slinked up onto the seat beside me and put her chin on my leg. I was so discombobulated from the exhilaration flooding my system, I had to reread the same page ten times at least.

We rode snuggled up together the rest of the way, and by the time we rolled into our backyard, Mojo had decided that I would be her human forever. I didn't know it then, but the day would come when Mojo's love and devotion and old Earl's wisdom and skill would get me through the greatest test of my life. But first, I had to learn to drive a team.

Hurry, winter. Step on the gas!

Chapter 9

After we came home from British Columbia with five more dogs, Mom made an official decree that the Bruggeman family was at its dog limit. *Boo and hiss!* So, you can imagine our agony when, in September, Dad found an advertisement on a mushing web page that read: For Sale—Last of the Swingley dogs directly from Swingley.

Hack off our limbs and dunk us in lemon juice!

To make matters worse, my sixth-grade year at Sacagawea Middle School was about to begin. Can we all just agree that nothing good happens in middle school?

For me, the "nothing good" started within seconds of climbing onto the bus on the first day of school. Nerves jangling, I hitched my backpack strap higher on my shoulder and scanned for an empty seat. Sighting one near the back a few seats in front of where Cory and some of the cool kids were sitting, I headed for it.

I was almost to my target when I stumbled against a pair of legs sticking out into the aisle. "Sorry," I mumbled, darting a look at the face belonging to the legs. It was blocked by a retro *Voltron—Defender of the Universe* comic book. The comic came down just enough to reveal a pair of eyes the color of dog crap. Familiar eyes. Eyes that sent my heart on a Splash Mountain plunge into the pit of my stomach.

"Hey, it's the handicap," the Mosquito said cheerfully, tossing the comic aside. He flashed me his trademark annoying smirk.

My chin hit my chest. "I'm not handicapped," I muttered.

"Gimp, then."

"Leave me alone, Nico. I just want to get to my seat." I tried to step over his legs, but he raised them, propping red Converse sneakers on the bench seat across from him and blocking me.

I saw red.

Yeah, the color of those sneakers, but I saw the anger red too. I'd wanted red Converse sneakers more than anything, but the stupid lift I had to wear on my skinny leg side wouldn't fit in such a thin shoe. My lift wouldn't fit inside 99% of the shoes on the planet actually. Trust me, I'd gone all Cinderella's-ugly-stepsister on salespeople in five different stores with the trying. Short of cutting off the bottom of my foot, I was stuck wearing these same boring black and white sneakers, in the same boring style, in the same boring brand I'd worn last year—just in a bigger size. The urge to roundhouse kick the smug smile right off the Mosquito's face was a strong one. "Let me pass, Nico," I hissed between clenched teeth.

Nico crossed his arms over his chest, jutted out his chin, and beefed up his smirk.

"Get your shoes off my seat!" demanded a yellow-haired girl wearing glittery blue stuff over her eyes. She started whacking at Nico's feet with a glittery pink binder. "That's disgusting."

"Gimp here has to pay the toll first," Nico said, pointing at me with his chin. Before I could react, he'd grabbed my backpack and yanked it off, wrenching my arm in the process. A hot spike of pain shot from my elbow to my shoulder.

"Give that back!" I snapped, lunging for my backpack. But Nico already had it opened and my lunch bag out.

"These'll do," he said, holding up my single serving pack of Pringles (Original flavored). His triumphant grin lit up my amygdala like a supernova.

My skin felt cinched too tight around my ribs. My breath started coming out in short, fast bursts while I just stood there, my balled-up fists hanging limply at my sides.

Nico peeled back the foil and shoved half the Pringles stack into his mouth. "BBQ is my fav," he said as he chewed, spraying flecks. "Remember that for next time," he added, interjecting an obscenity. The name he called me set my ears on fire. He'd apparently added the M for Mature expansion pack to his vocabulary over the summer.

Glitter Girl sent him a withering look across the aisle. "Your mom would get out the soap if she heard you talk like that?"

"I don't have a mom, so I can talk any way I want to," Nico shot back in an ugly *neener-neener* voice.

"Well, you can't use that word in *my* face," Glitter Girl sniffed.

Turning his back to her, Nico stuffed my lunch bag back into my backpack. "Here ya go," he said, repeating the obscenity to my reflection in the window. Then he swung the backpack into my chest with enough force to knock loose a grunt. "Happy now?" he said to Glitter Girl with a lips-only sneer.

I hugged my backpack to my chest as Glitter Girl laser-beamed Nico with her eyes. "Does anyone even like you?" she asked. Nico made a rude noise. "Everyone that matters, fish face."

"That's tropical fish face to you, Neanderthal," Glitter Girl said with a syrupy smile and dismissed him with a flip of her hair.

Nico harrumphed and went back to his comic book while I threw a quick glance around the bus. Some kids were busy chatting. Others had their faces glued to phones. A few meerkat heads had popped up over seat backs to watch. Feeling less than zero, I dropped my gaze to my dorky shoes and high-tailed it to the empty seat. I dove in and scooted over against the window.

My head fell against the glass with a thunk. A bus ride with Nico five times a week for the next 25.7 weeks, given your standard 180-day school year, suddenly loomed before me like the fiery pits of hell. My stomach started aching something fierce. At least in school I had a chance to duck down a hallway or dissolve into a crowd or skulk in the bathroom. No escaping or evading to be had in a bus. I squeezed my eyes shut to block out the world. I'd give anything to sleep like a modern-day Rip Van Winkle until the last day of eighth grade—even my fist-sized prehistoric shark tooth.

When a burst of happy laughter ricocheted around behind me, I shut down my ears, so I could only hear one thing: the inside of my head. With the warm rumble of the bus beneath me, I went on an adventure with Mojo and Earl and the rest of the gang in my mind. When we turned into a circular BUSES ONLY driveway, I pulled out my schedule the school had sent us in the mail. It showed my six periods, teachers' names, and classroom numbers. I looked at it dully and read, "Homeroom 8:05–8:17, Room #212."

Head down, I filed off the bus then moved along with a big bunch of kids, circling the main building and funneling into the four sets of double doors. I swam through the crowd to the stairwell and climbed up to the second floor, then walked around until I located room #212. The orange sign on the door said Mrs. Kopetski.

I opened the door and went in. Mrs. Kopetski, a woman with glasses and spiky, white Ursula the Sea Witch hair, gave me a cheerful hello and told me to find an empty desk. I found one near the back and slumped into it.

A flick to the back of my head made me jump and bang my knee-cap under the desk. A body collapsed into the seat next to mine. "Hey, gimp. Looks like we share homeroom."

At the sound of that voice, my heart took another Splash Mountain dive. I gripped the edges of my desk and stared numbly ahead as my new middle school reality sunk in: The Mosquito's mission in life was to make mine miserable.

I swear my mom's omniscience (the state of knowing *every stinking thing*) is surpassed only by God's—and that's just barely. A few weeks into my crappy new, Mosquito-infested school year, I was sitting down to a tall stack of Oreos and a glass of cold milk when she ambushed me in the kitchen. "Kids are mean for lots of reasons," she said without any warmup as she pulled a saucepan from the cupboard.

Every part of me went perfectly still.

"Sometimes they bully because they have an unhappy home life," she said, moving toward the stove. "Or it might be because they feel bad about themselves for some reason."

The clank of the pan against the metal grate of the burner gonged painfully against my eardrums.

"Or maybe it's because they don't have any talent or skill to impress their peers, so they poke fun at someone else to get cheap laughs, and it makes them feel important or powerful."

"I know that," I muttered to my Oreo tower.

Chase strolled into the kitchen carrying his big green football duffel and wearing a sweaty cut-off T-shirt which revealed that dark column of hair below his bellybutton. "Want me to take care of the little knuckle-dragger for you?"

"No," I growled. I wanted everyone to mind their own beeswax—that's what I wanted! I wanted to do my emotional eating in peace like grown-ups did. But apparently alone time with my comfort food of choice was too much to ask for in this family. *Grrrrr.*

"This is a private conversation, Chase," Mom scolded with a tilt of her head toward the door. "Go shower before we all pass out."

"Fine," he grumbled.

Mom shrugged a shoulder. "Nico could be jealous of your big brain," she went on. Before I could dodge it, she swooped in and stamped a kiss on my forehead. Grossing out, I dragged my shirtsleeve across the wet spot to eviscerate it.

"When I volunteered to help with reading in your class a few years ago, I could see that learning is hard for him."

Waa waa, cue the tiny violins.

"You might try killing him with kindness," Mom said in that annoying, birdsongy voice.

Sheesh, I didn't want to kill the guy. I only wanted to pee in his Wheaties . . . hawk loogies in his tacos. Either/Or. The pictures my mind invented to go with those sweet thoughts brought a tiny, private smile until the sound of the garage door opening chased it away.

"Hey, hon," Mom called over her shoulder as Dad walked in. I suddenly felt like a beetle pinned alive to a bug board.

When Chase poked his head back into the kitchen, I wanted to treat myself to a basement scream. "Nico's the type of kid that pulls the wings off bees for fun," he said. Gripping the doorframe above him with both hands, he hung into the room orangutan-style. Noxious fumes poured from the patches of long, wiry hairs sprouting from his armpits. "He'll be a serial killer when he grows up. You wait."

"Chase," Mom warned. "Shower. Now."

He gave her a cheeky smirk before disappearing again.

I shot a glance at Dad out the corner of my eye as I took a big, nervous gulp of milk. I wished I could disapparate with a crack like a whip and apparate instantly out of thin air in my bedroom à la *Harry Potter.*

On his way past to drop his briefcase at the foot of the stairs, Dad bent near my ear and mumbled out the side of his mouth, "I happen to think the little punk's compensating for something the size of a Tic Tac."

Geysers of milk shot out my nose.

"I heard that," Mom's muffled voice came from the pantry.

"Me too," Chase called from the hallway. "And it was awesome!"

Dad gave me a wicked grin, and I was instantly content about my non-magical state of being.

Chapter 10

School may have stunk, but every day I had fourteen good friends waiting for me when I got home. Just the sight of my dogs made something warm and liquid seep through my body. I'd feed them, and pet them, and scoop their poop while they wagged their tails and jumped around me all vying for my attention and acting like I was the greatest thing that had happened to the world since AC/DC (the alternating and direct current electrical systems which enabled modern-day power thanks to Thomas Edison and Nicola Tesla, not the rock band, although *Back in Black* is a blow-your-face-off awesome song). An hour with my dogs always filled the dark and lonely places inside me. They didn't care what I could or couldn't do. They just wanted to love and be loved. Why couldn't people be more like dogs?

Mom had a strict "no dogs in the house" policy. Don't tell, but sometimes at night, I'd sneak Mojo in through my bedroom window. She'd curl up beside me on the bed, and we'd sleep like a clam in its shell until I'd sneak her back out at dawn. I barely even cared that she'd hop down in the middle of the night and pee on my carpet every single time. I took to keeping a roll of ultra-absorbent paper towels, a spray bottle of carpet cleaner and an old scrub brush under my bed.

Then there was the singing. Hazer would usually start it. Sometime after dinner, just as the setting sun was beginning to stain the sky pink, he'd hop up onto his box all noble-looking, arch back his head and loose a string of long, mournful howls into the sky. The rest of the dogs would come out of their boxes and join in. They'd sing and sing—their haunting chorus cooler than any music I'd ever heard. It always gave me a hair-raising tingle at the back of my neck. Funny how my dogs possessed the magic to distract me from the gloom in my life.

When the evenings finally grew cooler, things got even better. We'd learned that mushers strength-trained their dogs in the early fall, before snow, with wheeled vehicles a team could pull from a gangline hooked to the front.

Dad bought a new Polaris ranger, which is a big, enclosed utility ATV with a steering wheel. Now we could run our team on the labyrinth of trails we'd mowed that summer in the prairie around our house. It wasn't nearly as fun as running a team in the snow, but it was great to be able to work with our dogs again and to be diverted for a few hours from the parts of life that stunk—until the night our training run stunk worse than everything else put together.

We were cruising along at about nine miles an hour, headed toward an old, abandoned farmstead about a half mile away. All fourteen dogs were hooked to the ranger with Jude and Earl in lead. The dogs were dragging the ranger with so much power Dad had to stand on the brake just to maintain a little control. The motor wasn't even running. The headlights were on low—just enough so we could watch them run and make sure everything was working out all right. And everything was.

The sun had just set, and the stars were beginning to wink out. The dogs were all perfect. Everything was great. A working dog burns over 10,000 calories a day, so we planned to let them run for an hour, then snack and water them on the trail and let them run another hour.

There was absolutely nothing that could go wrong that we couldn't handle (thought no sane person ever).

I was relaxing back in my seat, busy conjuring a sweet Iditarod fantasy when a bunch of stuff happened in a matter of seconds. Jude lunged forward, let out a yelp and leaped to the side of the trail. Earl dragged her back over, but Jude was shaking her head violently and staggering around, so the dogs in back started piling up behind her. Then the front half of the team went crazy.

I jackknifed forward in my seat, looking wildly out the windshield. "What's happening?"

In answer, Dad hissed a bad word and hit the high beams on the ranger. There was so much confusion up front I couldn't make sense of anything going on. Then I caught my first putrid whiff and screwed up my face in disgust.

"Earl's seen a million skunks and won't fall for it," Dad bit out as he jerked his foot off the brake. "Here you go, boy. You've got all the power now. Hurry them past the little bugger."

Earl threw his powerful shoulders into his harness, and the ranger leaped forward. The team instantly picked up speed, and Earl swung them out around the skunk.

Poor Jude was senseless with misery. She was hacking and shaking her head and blinking like crazy while stumbling along beside Earl who virtually pulled the whole curious team past the skunk.

With the trouble behind us, the dogs began to settle down, and I settled back into another sweet race fantasy. They were just falling back into their rhythm when Hazer hung a hard right, and Dad hissed another PG-13 word. I saw the tail-end of a skunk melt into the darkness beyond the headlights.

Hazer went after it with Odie close at his heels and Izzy another half beat behind. Earl tried to hold them, but it was like trying to hold a train. Earl skidded sideways raking the dirt and grass with his claws, and suddenly the ranger was bouncing out through the tall grass with Hazer in hot pursuit.

Hazer was hooked somewhere in the middle of the gangline, and now the team looked like an arrow of geese with Hazer at point. Dad was riding the brake again and trying to steer the ranger, but he might as well have been driving a bumper car at the state fair for all the control we had. We were at the mercy of a cute, furry animal and a dog hankering for the taste of fresh skunk. Then Hazer let out a yelp.

"Dun, dun, dun," I sang, "another one bites the dust."

If Dad's eyes could have thrown knives, I would have been dead. "It's all fun and games until we have to get out and put the dogs away," he bit out.

My eyes shot wide, and my mouth clamped shut.

While Hazer was hacking and shaking his head and wallowing in Jude's same misery, the skunk dove into the wood stacked up against the abandoned farmhouse. With skunk off the menu, Earl was able to skirt the team past the house and swing them back toward the trail, while we watched from the safety of the cab.

"I swear Earl's half human," Dad said with a shake of the head. "He's worth his weight in gold, that one. Too bad he's not a younger fellow."

I had a sudden mental image of Batman shuffling in after a grueling night saving Gotham City from an evil villain, removing his dentures and dropping them into a glass of Polident before crawling into bed. I was giving this a private, little chuckle when skunk number three scrambled across our path.

Dad threw up his hands. "You've got to be kidding me! What is this, a stinking skunk convention!"

Earl and Jude veered sharply to the left in an attempt to avoid it, toppling me against Dad.

"Skunks are crepuscular animals," I said as I righted myself.

Dad crooked an eyebrow at me as he sawed at the wheel in vain.

"Crepuscular means they are active at dusk," I said in a rush, my hand seeking a grip on the handle above the door. "Skunks are also solitary animals. So, these are most likely a mother and her young which were born in the spring and will stay with her until they are ready to mate at about one year of age."

"Remind us to run at noon from now on," Dad snapped.

By now, the dogs who'd gotten the worst of the blasts had wizened up to the fact that the black and white flag waving in the air meant *bad news,* not *dinner.* So, most followed Earl meekly at a brisk trot, giving the skunk a wide berth.

I was just getting to the part in my description about how mother skunks are known to forage for their kits during the day, so there really is no safe time to run, when Fitty lunged at the skunk and caught it by the shoulder. He was trying to swallow it whole when Trip made a grab for it. Fitty growled low in his throat.

Dad flung the door open and was halfway out when Fitty swung the skunk away from Trip, and suddenly its dangerous business end was aimed at the wheel dogs. Dad scrambled to pull himself back in, but before he could get the door closed, the skunk let loose.

Poor Haulin and Goblin. At wheel, they were hooked so close to the ranger, they had too short a line to get out of the way, and the skunk blasted them right in their faces. The whole team erupted into chaos.

I let out a howl of my own and yanked the neck of my jacket up over my mouth and nose as evil fumes poured in through the open door. Fitty gave the skunk another hard shake before letting go. You'd think the skunk's firepower was all used up. Nope. It sprayed the rest of its hefty ammo across the front of the ranger.

My eyes burned and began to water. My throat rolled in silent gags. It was the torment of torments, the nastiest of nasties. I wanted to curl up right then and there and be done with this whole cruel business of living, or at least find a boring indoor hobby that would never put me near a skunk's butt again—chess or speed stacking, maybe? The stench was so potent I didn't think that if I did live through this particular torture, I'd ever be able to smell anything but skunk for the *rest of my life.*

Now, Dad pulled the door shut. He broke off a fit of coughing to look over at me. His eyes were red and watering too. "How many kits does a skunk usually have?" His words were muffled by the arm barred across his mouth and nose.

"Four to six," I wheezed.

Dad made a horrified face.

"On average," I added, and we broke into a mixture of laughter, coughs, and gags.

Dad swiped the wetness from his cheeks with his sleeve. "I think we've had enough skunk for one night. Let's get the heck out of here before hazmat shows up to dispose of us."

The ridiculousness of men in biohazard suits swarming the abandoned farmstead sent me into another spasm of laughter coughs. "I'll take hazmat over Mom any day," I choked out.

Dad made another horrified face.

In the end, Earl decided for us. He took the shortest route back to the dog yard, cutting our training run in half. We reeked so bad I'm sure a cloud of green fumes hovered over us as we made our pitiful way home. By the time we unharnessed the dogs and put them up, we were drenched in stink.

Those skunks sure didn't do us any favors with Mom. She turned us away at the door. We weren't allowed inside the house until we were naked as naked mole rat babies and our clothes were dumped in the garbage bin beside the garage. The dog yard smelled like skunk for at least a month. I didn't even begin to dare sneak Mojo in at night.

And that stunk worst of all.

Chapter 11

Running our dogs in the acreage around the house soothed the sting of Mom's dog ban a little, but Doug Swingley's advertisement still glowed inside our heads in neon capitals. The prospect of all his wonder-dogs being sold off to other mushers was an agonizing one. *You snooze, you lose* had taken on a whole new meaning.

In October, Mom went away for a girl's weekend, so us boys spent a few boring days washing and mending harnesses, cleaning the barn, and watching MythBusters reruns.

Yeah right.

After Mom drove away, we nearly broke bones and assorted pieces of household furniture in our mad dash to get to the computer. Before she was even halfway down the driveway, Dad had an email shot off to Doug Swingley. A few minutes later, a message pinged in Dad's inbox with five measly words: I'm here. Come on over.

It only takes five words to change your life.

Lincoln, Montana, with a single blink-and-you'll-miss-it main drag, is 88 miles by car from Great Falls. Just over an hour later, we turned off the highway onto an old logging road. After a few bumpy miles, we pulled up to a rustic log cabin tucked amid towering ponderosa pines not ten miles from the Continental Divide nearly 6,000 feet above sea level.

"Wow," Dad said, climbing out of the truck. He had a reverent look on his face as he made a sweeping scan of the rugged surroundings. "Millions of acres of national forest land right out his front door. Doug has all the training ground he needs without ever having to haul his dogs anywhere." He turned to me with a boyish smile and gleam in his eye. "Now *this* is get-yourself-lost country. My favorite kind. Nobody else for miles. Think we can convince Mom to move?"

I gave him my best are-you-crazy look.

"Nah, me neither. But a man can always dream." He tutted and made a pained face as we crunched across the gravel toward the cabin. "Right in the middle of prime northern Rockies' elk and moose country too."

I knew from reading Iditarod books that Doug Swingley was sixty, but the man who strode out to meet us didn't look like an old man at all. He was compact and athletic with a sharp-cut nose and skin stretched taut over the bones of his face. The only thing even remotely old about Doug Swingley was a mouthful of gnarly teeth, which he revealed when he grinned down at me. "I'm Doug," he said, holding out a hand to me.

When I took his hand, I was gripped with a fierce bout of shyness. "Spencer," I said in something embarrassingly close to a high-pitched, girly whisper before my voice locked up for good.

It was clear from the get-go that Doug didn't suffer from the same affliction. He was a man who was confident in his awesomeness and liked to talk about himself—*a lot*. He sat with Dad at the kitchen table telling story after story while I wandered around the living room ogling all his cool race stuff and hanging onto his every word.

"I was trying to navigate the Dalzell Gorge 250 miles into my 10th Iditarod," he was saying as I reached for a framed photo of him appearing on *The Today Show* in New York City. "It's treacherous country, and my goggles were fogging up. So, I took them off to see better, and my corneas froze."

I whipped my head around to gawk at him, my hand suspended in mid-air.

He nodded at me as he went on, "I came into the next checkpoint blind in one eye and half blind in the other, and it wasn't getting any better. I talked to a doctor by satellite phone, and he said he wanted to see me right away, that the pressure in my eyes could cause permanent blindness. So, I scratched from the race and flew to Anchorage. It was a real bad deal." He shrugged. "But I wanted my eyesight more than I wanted that race."

"That's quite a story," Dad said, eyebrows soaring.

"Yeah, it is . . . Distance racing's not for the faint of heart. The best mushers not only expect to suffer—to take a beating—but they revel in it too. It feeds their will to win."

My head rocked back. Say what? Revel in suffering? Why would someone allow themselves pain and thrive on it too? I needed to think on that some more when I had a long stretch of alone time.

"A few miles into my 1999 Iditarod," Doug said, tearing me from my thoughts, "we took a 90-degree corner. I went down with the sled, and when I hit the ice, a battery pack in my pocket drove into my chest." He leaned back in his chair and laced his hands atop his head. "I ran 1,000 miles with two broken ribs and still won the sucker."

Dad went all bug-eyed. "You're kidding! How'd you manage that?"

"I was hungry for a new Dodge Ram truck. And I'm always dangerous when I'm hungry. I'd already won three of them, but I sold two of them to buy an airplane, and my last one was falling apart. No way would I actually *buy* one," he scoffed. "*That*, and a lot of Advil."

Dad snuck a look at me, and we shared a knowing smirk.

"I also race the fastest sled dogs alive," Doug added as I moved on to study a framed Outside magazine article hanging on the log wall. It ranked Swingley No. 14 among its "25 most extraordinary adventurers, outdoor athletes, and explorers"—five spots above Tour de France champion Lance Armstrong. *Wow!*

"In my third Iditarod, back in 1995," he went on, sounding very pleased with himself, "I posted the first sub-ten-day time and completely changed the game. Through twenty years of breeding, I developed an incredibly athletic and resilient line of sled dogs that have pulled me across more than a few finish lines." He pointed his coffee mug my way. "But if you want to know the real secret to winning—it's dedication and hard work done 365 days a year. If you can master yourself, you can master dog sledding."

As Doug looked intently at me from across the room, I had a sudden, almost painful, hope that this wouldn't be the last I saw of him. I wanted him to pour out all his wisdom and knowledge into us to the very last drop. I could listen to him—learn from him—all day long.

Doug took a slug of coffee. "It's good to see a young Montanan excited about the sport," he said on a swallow. "Few kids these days have what it takes to run sled dogs—grit, work ethic, mental toughness, guts, a desire for anything not attached to a brain-sucking screen. And, it's been a long time since someone in the lower 48 has taken the Iditarod away from the Alaskans. Not since me in 2001, in fact." He barked a laugh and smacked his mug down on the lacquered table. "And they hate it!"

He sprang up from the table and took a ball cap from a peg beside the back door. "Did you know I'm the only musher in the lower 48 ever to win the Iditarod?" he said as he strode over to where I stood looking at a photo of him mushing six dogs down New York's Madison Avenue.

I pulled my lip between my teeth and bobbled my head up and down, rendered temporarily mute again by his nearness and his sudden raptor-like attention on my face.

He held the ball cap out to me. Underneath all the dirt and sweat it was white with *Iditarod 2005* and a howling dog embroidered across the brim in bold blue letters. "I'm counting on you to get one of these for yourself someday." I caught another glimpse of bad teeth as his lips tipped up. "But until then, you can borrow mine."

I gaped at the ball cap, frozen with disbelief. Holy cow! Doug Swingley was offering me a piece of his win. It was as if he had plucked a string that ran straight down my center. I was thrumming from head to toe.

I was already dog smitten. I loved what little mushing we'd done on King's Hill and in our backyard. But after meeting Doug and hearing his stories, I knew the small stuff wasn't going to be enough. I wanted to be good at something super-duper hard—no, I wanted to be great at it. Like Doug, I wanted to *master* the sport—to master myself. Was I a kid with grit? Did I have the passion and perseverance that separated the greats from the ordinary? *Nah, you're a loser*, sneered a voice inside my head that sounded a lot like Nico's, and my gaze fell to my ugly shoes and stuck there.

"Spencer sure has a way with dogs," Dad said.

I glanced up to find him studying me through narrowed eyes. He flashed me a big grin, though his forehead was wrinkled up with concern.

"Do you now?" Doug said. "If you have a sixth sense with sled dogs, you're already way ahead of the pack. Most of what you need to learn about mushing, only the dogs can teach you. Gain their trust, give them your love—*earn* the run, and they'll pull you to the ends of the earth . . . or to Nome." He chuckled. "Which is basically the same thing."

When I didn't reach out to take the ball cap, Doug pulled it onto my head and tugged it down low on my brow. Heat swept up the back of my neck and scorched my face. I felt like an undeserving fraud. A burning need to confess my wimp status, to admit the truth to this icon loosened my tongue. "I, I . . . er . . . have a sk . . . skinny leg," I rasped out. "I'm not a very good athlete."

"That's good!" Doug's words came out like a little explosion.

My eyes snapped to his.

He nodded sagely down at me. "In my experience, the one who has to work harder almost always gets further ahead in the long run. It's grit more than talent that makes a winner out of someone. You've just got to want it bad enough."

I let that soak in for a second. Could Doug really be right? I'd only ever thought of my skinny leg as a *dis*advantage. I had some serious thinking to do.

"So, when you're eighteen, I'm counting on you to show those Alaskans what's what," Doug said with a swat to the brim of the ball cap. "Until then, I'll tell your dad about some smaller races you can run to get your feet wet." He turned back to Dad. "In fact, Montana's Race to the Sky starts right here in Lincoln. It's one of the most beautiful races in the world, but also one of the most challenging with all these high mountains to climb. There's a 350-mile Iditarod qualifying route for the diehards, plus a 100-mile race as well."

One hundred miles. *Gulp.* It seemed an impossible length measured against my eleven measly years. While I chewed at a hangnail, I played a game of verbal tug-of-war with the evil fiend who lived inside my head.

Evil fiend: *You could never do a hundred miles; you can't even make an easy tackle, gimp.*

Me: *Doug says being an underdog's a good thing.*

Evil fiend: *This race is super tough, idiot.*

Me: *But so am I—so bring it on.*

Evil fiend: *Hang on while I change my underwear. I just laughed so hard I peed them.*

Me: *I'm not afraid of hard things.*

Evil fiend: *I just rolled my eyes so hard I saw my brain. You can't even stand up to a little puke like Nico.*

Me: *But . . . but . . .*

Evil fiend: *Let me know when you're done wussing out on him. Then we'll talk.*

"Let's go out and look at dogs," I heard Doug say.

At this, I lifted my head and reentered the world. Underdogs and Swingley dogs—the day just kept getting better and better! Despite the rival voices still battling away in my mind, a smile broke out on my face as I strutted toward the dog yard. I was wearing Doug Swingley's Iditarod hat. *Heck yeah!*

A bitter wind with the taste of looming snow swept down from the mountaintops, searching out the openings in my jacket and sending a big shiver through me. I tugged my zipper to my chin. Gray clouds had moved in, dimming the sky with a hint of mystery and magic. Before, above, and all around me spread a shadowed forest of thickly set trees in various stages of growth and rot. What had seemed so appealing when we'd stepped out of the truck just hours before suddenly seemed formidable.

On the drive up, Dad had told me about this psycho named Ted Kaczynski, dubbed the "Unabomber" by the FBI. Kaczynski was a genius who retreated to these very woods to live off the grid away from everybody and everything. He hated technology and believed it was ruining the world. He built himself a small cabin without electricity or running water and spent his time hunting rabbits, growing vegetables, reading, scheming, and building bombs. As a protest against human progress, he mailed a bunch of them to universities and businesses, killing three people and injuring 23 more. Twenty years! That's about how long it took the FBI to find him up here.

As I took in my wilderness surroundings with Dad's creepy story playing through my head, my smile faded away. *Needle, meet Haystack*, I thought, and I shivered again; but this time it wasn't from the cold.

When the dogs saw us coming, they raised their muzzles and bawled gleefully, then began tearing around in circles on the ends of their chains. Me and Dad had agreed that if we only brought one dog home, Mom probably wouldn't be the wiser, but any more than that and she'd definitely know. She'd been such a good sport already; we didn't want to push our luck.

Doug took us down the line of the few dogs he had left, telling us about each one. A tall dog with a brown back and tan chest caught Dad's eye, but Doug directed us over to a light brown and cream dog with a face like a chocolate and vanilla swirl ice cream cone. "This is Harley."

Harley's bright eyes were shining right at me, and his tail was whipping back and forth hard enough to rattle his butt off his body.

When I got within striking distance, he started jumping all over me, trying to lick off every inch of bare skin he could find.

"Harley's only eighteen months," Doug said. "He's my youngest dog, but he's also the happiest dog that's ever existed." He grinned down at me and Harley who were tumbling around together in the mud. "Every team needs a happy dog to keep the stoke high when the going gets tough. A dog like that is indispensable."

Dad pulled me up by the scruff of my jacket. "Tell me about that one." He motioned to the tall, brown and tan dog.

"That's Patriot. He's an older dog, real experienced . . . has run every race there is to run, including the Iditarod. He's a solid bet, a great asset to any team."

When I reached out to pet Patriot, Harley bawled with jealousy, begging me to come back. Dad tipped up the brim of my ball cap, so he could see into my face. "The choice is yours, Spence."

But there really wasn't any decision at all. I bounded back over to Harley and unclipped him from his chain. "Come on, happy dog. You're coming home with us."

Little did I know how indispensable Harley's particular super-power would one day prove to be.

Chapter 12

Humans have superpowers too. This is going to sound corny, but I've decided that the greatest superpower of all is kindness. Go ahead, give it a good chuckle if you want to.

Now hear me out.

The Wednesday after we brought Harley home, I threw down my pencil and stomped into Mom's office. "Where's Dad?"

Mom glanced up from her computer. "He's at a mandatory CPR recertification course for work tonight. Why? What do you need?"

"Help with math," I grumbled. "I'm trying to graph a parabola so that I know where to cut the shoebox you gave me to make my solar hotdog cooker for my science project. But I keep messing up when I try to convert y equals ax squared into standard form."

"What's a parabola?

I rolled *duh* eyes. "It's a U-shaped curve lined with something reflective to collect the sun's rays and reflect it to a central point."

Mom looked at me blankly. She was good for help during a poetry unit, but with math, she was as useless as rubber lips on a woodpecker.

I gave her a hound dog's look of patient suffering. "Picture a shoebox cut into a mini skateboard half-pipe and covered with tinfoil."

"What's a half-pipe?" I made a disgusted sound.

"I'm kidding!" she teased. Then her eyes fluttered closed. "I am visualizing a little Tony Hawk performing a stale-fish grab in the air with a little twist and tweak for style points." She cracked one eye open. "Carry on."

"A hotdog lying on the vertex—or bottom—of the half-pipe will only collect 5 watts of energy, so it won't get very hot," I explained. "But there's this mathematical point a few inches from the vertex at the axis of symmetry where all the light passes through. It's called the *focus* and gets hot enough there to cook a hotdog. That's where the wooden skewer has to be suspended. I need Dad to help me do the calculations. This math is way out of my pay grade, and I *really* want to make this project for school. It's going to be epic! When will he be home?"

"I don't expect him before nine."

Blowing out a breath through my lips, I locked my hands behind my head. "It's due by Friday. If I don't get my solar cooker done before Dad leaves for his bird hunt tomorrow, I'll be stuck making a stupid baking soda and vinegar volcano."

"The horror," Mom mocked, a hand flying to her mouth.

"Mom," I said, stretching out the tiny word into a three-syllabled protest. "This is *serious*. Can I please stay up past my bedtime? It's an emergency."

"We can't have you taking a baking soda and vinegar volcano to school now, can we?"

"Not unless we want to be responsible for the apocalypse."

"I guess I'll have to be content with a pumpkin for a son. The destruction of the world would be a very big burden to bear."

Time crawled, Dad *finally* got home at 9:19 p.m., and when the bus pulled up to school the following morning, I zombie-walked down the aisle bearing a marvel of solar engineering. Our masterpiece had taken us until midnight (an hour that's totally overrated BTW). But it was worth it. My science project was going to command the respect and envy of all privileged to lay eyes upon it.

One second I was stepping off the bus, and the next, a stumble sent me pitching face-first toward the sidewalk. My body had a short wrestling match with gravity before I went *splat* on the cement. The impact launched my hotdog cooker into the air and into a puddle a few feet away. As I lay sprawled in a forest of moving legs, the sound of crunching cardboard brought my head up sharp—just in time to catch the flash of a red Converse sneaker.

"Hey! I saw that!" shouted an angry voice above me. An unfamiliar voice. A girl's voice? Someone frog-squatted beside me. The touch of a hand on my shoulder made me flinch. "Are you okay?"

"I'm fine," I muttered to the knee in my face, wishing I could melt into the sidewalk and cease to exist.

"What a jerk! That guy totally tripped you!"

I shrugged off the pain and pushed up on all fours. Fighting the shameful urge to cry, I crawled over and fished my crushed science project from the slush.

"Ohhh . . . Is that a parabolic solar reflector?"

At the wonder in the voice I glanced up to find a pair of dazzled eyes the color of dark chocolate pointed at the soggy cardboard. Her cheeks were so round and full they looked like sacks of brown sugar hanging from sharp cheekbones and glowed as if she had a red light on inside her.

I fingered the broken skewer. "It was a minute ago," I said bitterly, tipping my face to the sky to drain all the tears back inside before one made a run for it.

The girl swiped a fist under a nose that slanted straight down her face like an arrow. Her expression was thunderous. "This is awful!" she bit out, then shot such a violent look over her shoulder, her long, black hair whipped me across the cheek. "That jerk can't be allowed to get away with something so mean. You could've gotten hurt! I'm going to tell a teacher."

I shoved back onto my heels. "Wait! No!" But she was already up and shouldering her way toward the double doors.

Before she disappeared in the crowd, a rolled-up something sticking out from the waistband at the back of her jeans caught my eye. Only a T and an R with a section of a robotic arm was visible on the tube, but by the familiar sword-shape of the T, I knew instantly that it was a retro *Voltron—Defender of the Universe* comic book.

I had a fleeting impulse to chase her down, but let's face it, me chasing anything but a beached starfish is a joke. So, I blew out a breath, collected my stuff, and climbed shakily to my feet.

Bubble-wrapped in misery, I shuffled toward the double doors. On the way into the school, I tossed my dripping piece of junk—formerly known as my Epic Science Project—into the trash barrel and sank down into my seat in homeroom just as the bell rang.

"Class."

At the sound of Mrs. Kopetski's voice, I pointed my glower at the front of the room. At the sight of my own personal Voltron standing beside the teacher, my curiosity shoved my dark mood aside.

"We have a new student," Mrs. Kopetski announced as I sat up straighter in my seat. "I'd like to introduce Josephine Runs Through."

A snort sounded beside me. "That's ironic," Nico whisper-hissed. "Nothing's gonna run through that. It's built like a brick wall, but ten times uglier."

That earned him a couple of snickers, and not the candy bar kind either. If I was a cat, my back would have arched, and I would have been hissing. That guy had cancer of the personality.

From this vertical position, I could grasp the full scope of the new girl's size. Josephine Runs Through was taller even than Mrs. Kopetski.

I shot Nico a dirty look.

"Joey," the new girl added with a smile.

I knew the moment she spotted me. When our eyes caught and her smile exploded on her face, light pooled in my chest so bright I almost laughed with the feel of it. Hers was the smile of a friend who plays with you in forts you made together out of old tires and plywood, a friend who swaps secrets and silly stories with you while you're sprawled across your bed together when it's rainy outside. I couldn't help but smile back.

"Joey comes to us from the town of Browning on the Blackfeet Indian Reservation," Mrs. Kopetski said. "Maybe some of you have driven through there on your way to Glacier National Park."

Most of us nodded.

"All of you please make her feel welcome."

With the sense that the world had tilted a degree or two, I watched Joey go to her desk while we all stood for the Pledge of Allegiance. The crackle of the intercom interrupted the "with justice for all" part. "Nicholas Mustard," a disembodied voice called into the room. "Please come to the office."

We all sat down in our seats, except for a scowling Nico. As he stalked out of the classroom, Joey sneaked a look over her shoulder and gave me a tiny smirk—and life in that moment seemed easier than breathing.

Joey wasn't in any more of my morning classes, and I couldn't spot her in the cafeteria during lunch, so I migrated to the second loneliest place in the whole known universe—the cinder block wall in the outside commons. I stood in the sharp-cut rhombus of shadow beside the school watching Cory and a bunch of the athletes toss around a Nerf football, my frozen hands stuffed into my jean's pockets, black beanie pulled down low over my ears.

Being alone was a feeling so vast it echoed, especially since their shouts and laughter seemed to make my silence even louder. I hadn't played team sports since last year's football fiasco. I was never destined to be a defensive end; I knew that now. I was done trying to be something I wasn't meant to be. For me, my dogs were a hundred times better than football. I'd take snowy backcountry to chalked grass any day. But, boy, those guys' togetherness was sure squatting like a sumo wrestler on my chest.

"Over here!" Cory shouted, waving a hand. All the guys seemed to orbit around his gravitational pull. He was so cool he could give the sun a brain freeze. When Nico threw the football to him, Cory sprang straight up in the air, snatched it one-handed, then ran the length of the practice field so fast smoke practically came off his shoes.

When Max threw the ball, it went long and disappeared out of sight past the edge of the school not far from where I was standing. "I got it!" Nico called, barreling past me. A few seconds after he'd vanished around the side of the school, this air sewage dribbled into my ears: "Why don't you go back to the rez where you belong, snitch."

I suddenly felt like my insides had been pulled out, stomped on, and put back into me. I shrank back against the wall.

"Nobody wants you here," Nico snarled. "Now give me the stinkin' ball."

It was as if some cosmic thumb hit the pause button on the world. Everything seemed to stop: the noise, the movement, my heart, all of it. I couldn't even seem to breathe.

And then a football sailed into view. It spiraled through the air in a perfect arc over the commons area, across the width of the practice field, and landed in a green construction dumpster on the other side of the fence.

"Whoa!" I heard Cory exclaim from the courtyard.

Nico made an ugly sound. "A boy with long hair. I knew it. You're too big and ugly to be a girl. You even have a boy name."

Heat flooded my face. My tongue was a dried-up fat piece of meat sitting in my mouth. Someone came charging around the corner. It was Joey. The sight of her face made me want to give Nico paper cuts—lots and lots of paper cuts. Her eyes were hard, lips tight. But when she spotted me, her inside light flickered back on.

"Hey, there you are!" she said, breaking into a smile. "I was looking for you."

She was?

I unstuck myself from the cinder blocks and met her halfway. "I . . . um . . . " I kicked a rock. Shifted my feet. Tried again. "I heard what Nico said. I really think there's something wrong with that guy. He needs a personality transplant."

Joey's eyes slid away from mine, and she hugged her ratty, old boy's coat tighter around her middle. She'd gone sad again, and somehow that made me sad too.

I mustered a crooked smile. "Nico was probably dropped on his head as a baby," I ventured. "I don't know . . . Someone could've left him at the fire station when he was born. For sure he eats vipers for breakfast."

Her giggle lit sparklers in my chest. When she looked down at me again, I was so relieved to see the shine back in her eyes.

"Maybe he was raised by a troop of howler monkeys," she said, covering her snicker with a hand. "He could be a troll trapped inside a human body."

I scoffed. "I wouldn't be surprised if he sleeps in a drawer in the morgue."

She tipped her head to where Nico was hovering beside a concrete table full of girls. "I bet he steals blankets from babies for fun."

"He picks his nose and eats it. I've seen him. I doubt he's even litter-box trained."

By now we were both caught in a tsunami of giggles, and all the oxygen had flowed back into the world as if someone had turned on the valve.

"Let's vaporize him with our minds," Joey suggested.

In perfect synchronization, we narrowed our eyes on the back of Nico's head, and sure enough, he reached back and scratched the place our gazes were burning into his scalp before toddling away. We burst into another fit of laughter.

"He's going somewhere to suck his thumb in private," I said, which made us laugh even harder.

"Or cry into his pet kitten," Joey added.

"I bet he has a bed with eleven teddy bears on it," I choked out.

We hooted. It felt *awesome*.

"What's your name?" she asked when our snickers finally trailed off.

"Spencer."

"Your parabolic solar reflector was really good, Spencer. You're gonna make another one, right?"

Joey's question sucked some of the happy gas right back out of me. Biting my bottom lip, I shook my head. "The math is super complicated. I need my dad to help me convert y equals ax squared into standard form, and he's gone until tomorrow. That's when our projects are due."

Joey scrunched up her nose. "$4p$ times y minus k equals x minus h squared," she quickly rattled off. "Where p is the vertical distance of the focus from the parabola's vertex." She shrugged. "Piece of cake."

I felt my jaw swing open like one of those creepy Christmas nutcracker thingies.

"I can help if you want." She said it like a question with a little lift at the end.

"Okay," I sputtered. "Let's go call your mom and see if you can come to my house after school."

"I live with my grandma," she said and started twisting a piece of her hair. "My mom's in a movie right now, so she's gone."

"In a movie?" I parroted.

"Yeah."

"That's cool."

Joey nodded while her fingertip turned purple with the twirling. "Universal is making a motion picture about Sitting Bull in South Dakota and Hollywood. My mom went to an open casting call she saw advertised on Facebook and got a main part, so she's going to be on location for a long, long time," she said in a rush. "Aluminum foil isn't a very effective reflector because it crinkles so much. Let's use the inside of a bag of chips on the parabola this time. It's way smoother so it'll reflect better."

"Um . . . Okay," I said as we walked side by side toward the office. Even though I was reeling a bit from subject-change whiplash, life seemed to be easier than breathing in that moment too.

Chapter 13

Hang on tight!" I called over the racket to Joey. She stood stiffly behind me on the runners with her hands next to mine on the handlebar. The four dogs I'd hooked up were putting on a great show for her—screaming and jumping and hitting the end of their lines like total maniacs.

"They have so much excitement in their eyes," Joey yelled near my ear.

"Running is their way of having fun!" I shouted back through my grin as I yanked the rope holding my new sled to our hitching post. "Hike, hike!"

The team shot forward, their instant silence making Joey's sudden squeal of laughter especially loud near my ear. Her arms went tight against mine as we rocketed out of the dog yard.

Since that awful-turned-awesome parabola day a few weeks ago, Joey came over all the time after school. We hung out and did homework together, then she'd help me "do the dogs" (mushers speak for feeding them and scooping their poop). I didn't think it could get much better than that until a storm last night gifted me with six inches of fresh snow in my backyard. Now I got to show off for my friend.

Joey threw back her head and let out a loud, "Aaaaaaaah," to the sky. "This is so *awesome!*" she bellowed as the dogs flew over the snow-covered prairie.

I shot her a grin over my shoulder. Her sparkling eyes were every brown shade of excited as we swooshed along the river glazed pink by the setting sun. The wind whipped against our hair, and ice crystals grazed our faces. I let out a shuddery breath. I had a friend with me on the back of my sled while my dogs ran through fresh snow with all their might, their tongues flapping, spit flying in all directions. I was dreaming with my eyes wide open.

"Your dogs are so fast!" Joey gushed. "You're so lucky you get to race!"

My stomach gave a sudden, hard twist. *Race.*

After our visit with Doug Swingley a couple of months ago, Dad and I had set our sights on a small race in West Yellowstone called the Rodeo Run. The Rodeo Run included a four dog/six-mile junior race for me and an eight dog/twenty-two-mile adult race for Dad. I wanted to run the famous Race to the Sky up in Lincoln someday. It shone like a bright star in my head ever since Doug had hung it there. I was working toward it in my mind and in my ability. The thought of traveling one hundred miles on the back of a sled, in a wilderness full of wild animals, at night, in the winter, all alone, still freaked me out a bit (okay, *a lot*), but six miles in the bright light of day sounded like a blast. Mostly.

"I know I'm lucky," I said. "I'm super pumped for the Rodeo Run next week. I just hope I don't wipe out and lose my team."

"You won't," Joey bubbled. "You've been training a lot. I'm sure you're ready."

"I hope so . . . "

Since the mountaintops had turned white, me and Dad were spending every weekend at King's Hill on our sleds. After weeks of boring training runs with the ranger on the trails around our house this fall, our dogs were strong, bursting with energy, and excited for snow. I'd left the King's Hill parking lot on my face, my stomach, my rear end. I'd dragged by the arms for a mile, two miles, ten. I'd lost my team five times, twenty times, a bazillion while the world became a big blur and I became a big, frozen bruise. Dad would scoop me up onto his runners as he zoomed past, and we'd loop back around to the truck to find my dogs snoozing underneath the trailer (the traitors).

But with each wreck and tumble, I'd gotten better. I'd gained confidence. I'd toughened up. My muscles had gotten stronger too. I could harness my own dogs and hook them on the gangline without losing an arm or being mowed over. During my first solo snow runs, I was tight and rigid on the sled—afraid of falling off and losing my team. Now I stood easily on the runners and held the handlebar loosely.

"Loosen up," I said over my shoulder. "You're too stiff." I felt Joey's knees bend and her hips relax against my back. "That's better," I said. "Feel this . . . " I rocked my hips from side to side, and the sled creaked and gave with my movement. "See how flexible the frame is. Riding is more of moving as one with the sled rather than trying to control it. What I imagine surfing is like."

"How about we go to Hawaii after your race so we can compare. I like warm best."

"Good plan," I snorted. "I'll start working on my mom." We were nearing a bend in the trail. "Haw!" I shouted to my dogs. When Jude and Trip hung a hard left, my body made an automatic shift. "Lean in!" I called to Joey. She made a quick shift of her weight, and we glided around the turn. I grinned to myself. During the past weeks of training, the sled had become an extension of my body, just as I'd become an extension of my dogs. A week until the Rodeo Run, and I felt like a real musher.

Almost.

When we headed for the final turn into the dog yard twenty minutes later, I could see Chase, silhouetted by the sinking sun, moving between the dog boxes and slopping food into the bowls. The dogs still in the yard were all yapping their heads off, bouncing around, excited for dinner. My brother lifted the scoop at us in greeting as we hit the bend in the trail.

At the sight of the dinner bucket, my dogs put on a burst of speed. My knees dipped and body naturally leaned into the turn. Joey, standing as straight as a post behind me, let go of me to wave back.

The sled tipped up on one runner.

"Lean!" I yelped.

Joey let out a loud squeak as her arms went around my chest like a vice. In a flash, we were airborne, and with Joey clinging to my back, baby monkey-style, there was nothing I could do about it.

We crash-landed in a deep pile of soft snow. While we flailed around in a tangle of arms and legs, the team beelined it for the dog yard pulling the sled on its side. We were laughing too hard to sort ourselves out, and when our laughter trailed off at last, one of Joey's arms was flung across my stomach and one of my legs was hooked over her knee.

I huffed and threw my hands in the air. "I feel like I can't trust you anymore." I shook my head at her and huffed again.

"Sorry," she giggled behind her glove.

"No, you're not," I scoffed.

"Okay, I'm not. That was fun." When her eyes twinkled at me, liquid happiness flowed through my veins.

For a minute we just lay there side by side gazing up at the spectacular sky in perfect contentment, our frosty breaths mingling in the air and the cold from the snow seeping into our bones. Then Joey pulled something from her coat pocket and dangled it above my face.

"What's that?" I reached up to finger the smooth gray stone hanging from a leather cord.

"A river rock from the Two Medicine River up by Browning," she said, then flipped it around so I could see the black engraving on the other side. "The bear paw right here, it's a good luck omen. This used to hang from my mom's mirror in her truck."

When I rolled my head to look at her, the snow singed the bare skin of my face. "It must be good luck! She got that big movie part, right!"

I was confused when Joey's eyes darted away from mine. I watched her throat work as she swallowed. "My momma used to say it was because she got me for her girl," she murmured. All the carbonation had gone out of her voice.

I suddenly felt scooped out like a pumpkin, and I wasn't sure why.

Joey puffed her red cheeks full of air and blew it all out. Then she wrapped the leather cord around the stone and pressed it into my palm. "Anyway, this will help you for your race," she said as she climbed to her feet. "You should wear it. With all the crashing you do, you need all the help you can get." The little smirk she gave me put my insides *almost* back to rights.

"Very funny, Amelia Earhart," I said dryly.

"Come on," she ordered, waggling her fingers at me. "Get up out of the snow."

"What do you have against snow?"

"Besides the fact it's cold and wet and dripping down the back of my neck?"

I grinned up at her. "Well, you'd better make friends with it."

"Why's that?" she asked, wrinkling her nose.

I gathered a handful of the white fluff and chucked it at her. "So you can come to the Rodeo Run with me next week," I said as the little snowball exploded against her shoulder. "That's why."

The smile that broke across her face was like a sunbeam through dark clouds.

The night before the Rodeo Run, all the mushers paraded down West Yellowstone's main street with their rigs and dog trailers all decked out in Christmas lights. I felt a bit like a rock star as I hung out our truck's window grinning and waving at all the locals and a few tourists who'd crowded along the boardwalks to see the mushers. Joey hung out the other side, waving just as much.

I felt even more like a rock star the following day when fans wandered from rig to rig meeting the mushers and their dogs before the races. I loved introducing our dogs and answering questions about dog sledding while Chase tied my sled off to the bumper of the truck, sorted my gangline, and harnessed my team.

I know, I know, I'd lost the ghost pepper challenge, but Chase had still come as my dog handler, which is basically like the pit crew at a car race. When we'd started running dogs, Dad had offered my brother a team of his own, but Chase had declined, saying that he had football and that I needed something to make me stand out and feel important too. And now he was over there scooping the steaming turds around the dog trailer the instant they hit the ground while I chatted with our fans. He was content to do all the grunt work without any of the limelight. Have I mentioned I have the best brother ever?

When the first of the racers brought out their harnesses, their dogs started barking. Barking dogs generate more barking dogs, and soon a hundred and fifty excited huskies were making a ruckus that could doubtless be heard from the moon. The energy was contagious—carried to the people, the dog handlers, the mushers—especially to me. I was buzzing like a live wire.

We'd decided that I'd use Jude, Patch, Trip and Mojo for the Rodeo Run because Jude was a good leader, Mojo would only pull for me, and Patch and Trip were super fast. The trucks and trailers created a long tunnel down to the start gate which was at one end of a neatly groomed airstrip. It took two minutes per team to get them in the chute, counted down and gone. Adults went first, then juniors. As dogs were hooked up, their barks turned into high-pitched screams that demanded hurrying, so once the teams started going out, everything picked up speed. In no time, the whole place was whipped into a frenzy.

Mom helped me and Dad tie on our orange bibs over our parkas. I had drawn the last number, so me and my dogs—harnessed and crazy to go—had to watch all the other teams pass on their way through the tunnel of trucks to the start gate. By the time I got my five-minute call, my dogs were going bonkers, and inside I was too.

Dad had gone out about an hour before. So, it was up to me and Joey and Chase to get my team to the start. We hooked my dogs on the gangline, then I stepped on the runners and stiffly gripped the handlebar while Chase clipped a short lead to the neckline that stretched between my leaders' collars. He led us down to the start gate while Mom jogged alongside us, her camera slapping against her parka, and Joey jogged along with us on the other side. In their excitement, my dogs nearly trampled Chase as he threaded them into the chute. I bent down and set a snowhook while my dogs lunged and screamed and bared their teeth at the trail. It was crazy—somewhere between the truck and the start gate, my nice dogs had morphed into unrecognizable, snarling beasts.

Excited spectators lined both sides of orange construction fence that ran along the first fifty yards of the trail. Music pumped from loudspeakers, sending little shivers of power through me. Now I definitely felt like a rock star, standing center stage in an arena packed with screaming fans. The thrill of it fizzed through my veins.

Chase and Joey were having a heck of a time holding my team out straight while we waited for the clock to tick down. The next minute felt like ten. Wings were flapping so hard in my stomach, I was having a hard time not throwing up. When my dogs were to the point of near hysteria, a woman with a clipboard, noted the number on my bib and grinned. "You ready?" she yelled near my ear.

My heart started kabooming in my chest. Through my layers of clothes, I fingered the bear paw hanging around my neck then shot Clipboard Lady a wobbly smile. I was excited but scared at the same time. I looked down the trail over the heads of my four berserk dogs. I could see the team that had just gone out before me streaking across the distant tree line—the blue sled and pink coat of the driver a bright smear on the wintry landscape—and was bombarded with thoughts of everything that could go wrong: I could fall off, lose my team, take a wrong turn, a dog could get hurt—or worst of all, *I could lose the race.*

Before I had time to completely freak out, a man stepped beside me, lifted a megaphone to his lips and shouted, "Ten!"

The spectators joined in the countdown, their collective voices pulsing through me like a drumbeat.

"Nine!"

"Eight!"

This was it. I was going to go out the chute hanging like an imbecile on the back of the sled.

"Seven!"

"Six!"

My breath came out in short bursts. I zeroed in on Mom who was kneeling in the snow out past Chase, her camera aimed at us.

"Five!"

"Four!"

I let out a big breath.

"Three!"

With one gloved hand death-gripping the handlebar, I reached down and yanked out my snowhook with the other.

"Two!"

Chase let go of the leaders and dove out of the way.

"One!"

My dogs were off so fast, I was almost jerked off the sled. I felt the jar all the way up into my shoulder sockets, but I held on tight. I heard the crowd at my back cheering me on. Two hundred yards of flat, groomed airstrip stretched out in front of us before the trail disappeared into the trees and the unknown. My dogs ran wide open, their tongues flying, ears laid back, tails down. The cold wind lashed my cheeks and stung my eyes. It was the most incredible feeling in the world.

We reached the trees in no time flat, and the airstrip narrowed into a hard-packed snow-machine track. Just inside the forest, we came upon our first sharp bend in the trail. I flipped down the drag mat and dug my heels into the snow on the insides of the runners, but my dogs offset the resistance by putting on a sudden burst of power.

They flew through the snow like bats out of hell, pulling me wildly behind them. They cut to the inside corner where the snow was all mash-potatoey. At the peak of the turn, the outside runner sank down and caught, flipping the sled on its side. Suddenly my feet were above my head, and I struck the hard-packed snow with the point of my shoulder in a bone-rattling blow. Then I began to drag.

I skidded recklessly down the trail. But I didn't let go. Pain poured power into me. I struggled, and I fought until I finally muscled my sled upright. I fumbled my knees onto the runners, then balanced myself on my haunches one foot at a time and stood in tricky stages, my dogs never breaking stride.

Chest heaving, I brushed the snow from my face with a violent sweep of my mitt and shook the packed snow from my clothes. I was rigid with panic, and my heart was trying to break out of its cage. I knew I had to take charge of both my muscles and my pulse if I was going to make it across the finish line with my team. *Relax, breathe, concentrate, Slow Down! You can do this,* a voice inside me urged. I forced my body to go all loosey-goosey like I'd practiced on our runs at King's Hill.

A sudden gust of wind corkscrewed powdery snow across the trail and blasted it into my eyes. But I barely noticed, I was so focused on listening to the sled's song. Wispy threads of sound, music really—the hiss of the runners, the gentle creaks of the sled joints, the whuffle of the dogs' rhythmic pants, and the jingle of tug clips against collar rings—trembled on the brittle air and spun me in a web of calm. My breaths slackened, and my heartbeat slowed, and inside half a mile I'd found the familiar harmony.

I was one with the sled, taking the curves and ruts smoothly, gaining confidence with each passing tree. When the next hairpin turn came up, I led the sled out to the opposite side of the trail with little shifts of my weight so that I'd have a wider turning radius. We sailed around the bend.

The next time my runner sank into deep snow, I hopped off, moved the sled a few steps to the right then hopped back on, all at my bumbling run. Everything—everything with the dogs, with the sled, with my skinny leg, with my life, everything was great. I could do this! Nothing that felt this right could possibly go wrong. It just couldn't.

A couple of miles in, we were starting an upward climb when I caught a flash of pink through the trees. Pink Coat Girl! My heart started pumping fast again. But it was the good fast. I let loose a soft whistle that started on a high note and dropped to a low. Snow flicked up from the dogs' feet as they picked up speed. My first smile of the race split my face. We were going to catch her!

Trip had a horrible sense of humor. She chose that moment to stop dead in the trail and squat to pee. One instant my dogs were making some serious tracks, and the next they were accordioned up behind Trip, and their lines were a pile of spaghetti in the snow.

I fired a loud, "Hike, hike!" at the dogs to get them going again, hoping they could sort themselves out. Jude lunged at my command, pulling them forward, but my team was all tangled up. I growled through clenched teeth. Four catawampus dogs weren't going anywhere fast. Even worse was the risk of injury when necks or legs were tied up in lines and a team was on the move, and I had maybe eight seconds before Patch chewed through the line caught around her ankle or tripped in the chaos and started to drag.

I tossed out my snowhooks, jumped off, and stomped them in deep. Then I rushed over and started unclipping lines while all the lost seconds ticked down in my head and tied my guts up in knots. It took an hour to sort out my dogs and wrestle them back into place. Okay, not really. But it sure felt like it.

In probably less than a minute, we were on our way again, zipping along through a real-life Christmas card. Sunlight broke through the smoke-colored clouds, turning the snow to glitter. The sparkle matched my mood. I was surprised to feel happiness bubbling in my chest. I'd salvaged a fall. I'd untangled my dogs by myself. I hadn't lost my team. I could handle whatever the dogs or the trail threw at me. Best of all, I could also see Pink Coat Girl about halfway to the top of the hill—and they were moving like a sloth.

Something like lightning flashed through my veins. "Run, run!" I hollered to my dogs. It instantly felt as if they shifted gears. With a little hop, I switched my skinny leg from the left runner to the right, then started pedaling alongside the sled with my good leg. This took some of the workload off the dogs, making us go even faster. We charged up the side of the hill.

The slope grew steeper and steeper. The dogs started straining with effort, and we slowed way down. I leaped off the runner and started to push. My breath tore from my lungs, and I could feel sweat trickling down the little divot in my back chilling me from the inside out, but my body reveled in the exertion, and soon we were right on her tail.

With a final heave, the sled crested the hill, and I hopped back on the runners, eager to make my move. "Trail," I called out between gasps (which is the signal that a musher wants to pass). Pink Coat Girl followed the musher's rule of etiquette by aiming her sled to the side of the trail and slowing her team with the foot brake.

"On by! On by!" I yelled to my dogs to verbally push them past hers. I felt a little bit sorry as we left her in the dust (not to mention the snow we sprayed in her dogs' faces as we zoomed by). But by the time we overtook a second team slowed by a dog stumbling along with a front leg caught over its neckline, any hint of remorse had been devoured by my hunger to win. As we blew past them on the downhill sweep, my face longed to break into a smile, but I held it back—almost.

The trail spit us out through a break in the trees back onto the airstrip, and the red banner bowed by the wind across the finish line, as small as a horseshoe in the distance, came into full view. Some mushers wear ski goggles, but when I'm looking through plastic lenses, I feel separated from the world. Plus, goggles fog up so quick when my body's working hard, and I like to see things clearly, so I don't usually wear them.

I blinked away the stinging, icy film from my eyes and narrowed them at a myriapodous (having a ton of legs) blur about a hundred yards ahead of us. At the sight of another dog team skittering toward the finish line, I was blindsided by an ugly memory of my infamous missed tackle, and all my muscles locked up tight. "Not this time," I hissed under my breath after a private council of war. Me alone might be a joke, but me plus four canine superheroes were proving a force to be reckoned with. "Go home!" I yelled to my dogs.

"Go home" is the card up a musher's sleeve. It means a warm meal and bed are close at hand, and when you use it, tired dogs will dig down deep for a final burst of power to get you through the last hard bit of a race. Dogs don't have the same sense of distance as humans do, so "close at hand" has a loose interpretation. On a distance race, you might use it to get your dogs through the last ten brutal miles. On a sprint race, like this one, you'd pull it out for a wicked-fast home stretch. But you only ever use it when you truly mean it, so your dogs will always trust you.

My dogs floored it. The arctic wind pushed back my hood and stung my bare neck. I didn't care. I watched my dogs' backs flatten and extend, their ears pin back, and their pink tongues swing from the sides of their mouths like long strips of Hubba Bubba Bubble Gum Tape. Every tugline was as tight as a guitar string, each dog fueled by the joy of a run. My dogs were giving their whole hearts for me—especially little Mojo who had to run doubly fast to keep pace. As we closed the distance, the love I felt for them put an ache in my throat that didn't shame me at all.

My dogs' long, floating lopes ate up the last stretch of the trail. I felt as if carried on air. "Go! Go! Go!" I chanted to my team through a grin of pure delight while the faint cheers of the crowd grew louder and louder.

Soon the red banner loomed before us, and the cheers drowned out the pump of my blood in my ears. With her bright red hair and yellow parka, Mom was easy to spot, crouched in the snow just beyond the finish line, her camera poised in front of her face. And just beyond Mom, I could see Chase and Joey ready to catch my team the instant we crossed the finish line and lead us back to the truck.

I relished the weight of a hundred sets of magnetized eyeballs on me. I felt taller and stronger and wiser than I'd been a mere hour before. As we streaked along the orange construction fence, my subconscious superimposed the faces of my Grid Kid teammates—especially Nico's and Cory's onto those of fans in the crowd, and I was filled with a rare and wild exhilaration.

We'd closed in enough on the other team that I could make out the Sorel brand stamped on the heels of the boy's snow boots. Another ten seconds, and we'd have him. I hurled another round of *go's* over my dogs' heads like little lightning bolts, and we flew.

But we didn't have another ten seconds—or another hundred yards in the trail. If we would have, we'd have passed them; but there wasn't, and we didn't. Sorel Boots flashed across the finish line with us crossing a few skimpy seconds behind. The crowd roared. My face burst into a smile.

We'd smoked them anyway.

Since the five Junior racers had started at two-minute intervals, it wasn't who crossed the finish line first that determined the winner, but rather who'd finished the race in the fastest time—and Sorel Boots had started the race way before me. It sure would have been fun to pass him though, especially in front of a crowd.

Actually, I smoked everyone.

When the official time sheet was finally posted, and I saw *Spencer Bruggeman* in the top spot of the Junior's column, the sixteen black and white letters of my name seemed to leap off the page and spin in strange patterns around my face. First place! For the first time in my life, I was a winner! No one would have to be gentle with me today or try to cheer me up with spicy Mexican food. The intense feeling of well-being and happiness that lit me up from the inside out was so unfamiliar, it felt as if I was reading the results through someone else's eyes. And now that I'd experienced it, I knew I'd be chasing this euphoria for the rest of my life.

Dad, on the other hand, didn't do so well. When I read his name listed fourteenth out of nineteen, I was aware in the most secret place inside me that I was glad about his lousy standing. Thing is: Dad thrives on challenge. He can never sit back and not let something he wants become the best it can possibly be. Mom says this is both his greatest strength and his Achilles heel—two sides of the same coin. Dad would never in a million years be content with fourteenth place. He never settles for being an amateur at anything, and by the hard set of his jaw and the narrowing of his eyes as he scanned the results, I could practically hear his inner voice snarl, "Game on!"

It was a good thing too. If not for Dad's poor showing at the Rodeo Run, me and my team never would have been prepared for what lay ahead.

Chapter 14

I know you."

At the sound of that voice, my heart gave a heavy pump, and the dog stew I was setting in front of Hazer sloshed out of the metal bowl and onto my hand. I was still basking in the glow of my hours-old win, and it suddenly got even brighter.

I slung the greasy chunks from my glove into the snowbank and braved a look over my shoulder. All around me, our dogs were scarfing down their post-race grub—except for Earl, whose upturned head was plastered against Doug Swingley's thigh, his eyes rolled back in ecstasy.

"Earl was a phenomenal dog in his day," Doug said, scratching Earl behind the ears. "Probably the smartest dog I ever had . . .   But like most of my dogs, he's getting old."

Earl made a low hum of pleasure in his throat while I was stricken with another miserable bout of shyness. I bit my lower lip and started fiddling with the zipper pull on my coat, nervously alive to the presence of this man who seemed to fill up too much space. I wished

Chase and Joey hadn't just wandered over to the concession stand for hot chocolate. I needed a buffer.

Doug lifted his laser eyes to mine. "Good race, Spencer."

My face went burning hot. I hadn't known *the* Doug Swingley was at the race. I felt both flustered and enormously pleased.

"You know," Doug went on in that confident way of his, "the rule is, once you've won a Junior race, you have to compete with the adults."

I rooted around in my head for a clever reply, itching to wow him with my wit and intelligence. Instead, I simply gawked at him like the village idiot while the dog bowls clanked together at our feet with the force of a dozen eager tongues. My breath steamed and vanished in the air three times, four times before Dad finally rounded the front of the truck, rescuing me from my pathetic self.

Doug thrust out a hand to Dad as I let go a shaky breath. "It looks like you need a few better dogs!"

Dad flashed a grin. "It looks like you need a few better teeth!"

My eyebrows shot up. I ducked my head and bit my lower lip to conquer the quiver that had sprung to the corners of my mouth.

Doug barked a laugh. "Well, it looks like we can help each other out then," he said as they came together in a vigorous handshake.

When they broke apart, Dad said with a gleam in his eye, "I'd like you to come meet my wife." As he led Doug Mom's way, Dad glanced over his shoulders and, waggling his eyebrows at me, gave me a wily grin.

Mom didn't stand a chance.

It's Monday morning. I walk into school. Everyone stops to stare at me. The slap of my sneakers against the checkerboard tile is the only sound in the hallway. Someone starts to clap. The sharp cracks of sound echo through the corridors. Others join in, teachers too, and the clapping follows me as I strut toward my classroom. Students pour out of open doorways to see

what all the fuss is about. Soon the whole school is clapping—clapping and smiling at me. Someone begins to chant my name; soon the whole school is chanting it. The noise is so loud, it drowns out the ringing of the bell. Some of the kids, including Cory and Nico, hold out hands for me to high-five or fists for me to bump as I pass on my way to homeroom. I smile and wave to everyone. I am King of Sacagawea Middle School.

I breathed hot air onto the truck's window, instantly turning my daydream into a circle of frost. *Besides Joey, they probably won't ever know*, I thought wistfully as I watched the frozen world whiz by outside on our way home from the Rodeo Run. I was like Peter Parker, minus the cool web shooters and Spidey senses: Academically gifted—check. Shy—check. Science nerd, bullied, harboring a secret identity—check, check, check. To them, I'd always be the Gimp. A *loser*.

With a fingernail, I scratched a #1 into the icy, white film on the window and smiled a little to myself. Too many good things had come out of West Yellowstone for me to pout about my schoolmates being oblivious to my amazing sled dogs and my own special superpowers.

For starters, after seeing me and Dad race and meeting Doug, Mom had lifted her dog ban. The reflection in the window gave me back a devilish grin. We'd also left West Yellowstone with an open invitation from Doug to run dogs out of his place in Lincoln any time. I curled my fingers into the fur at Mojo's neck, and she sighed and snuggled in closer. Life couldn't get much better than it was right now with my friend asleep in the seat beside me, my best dog snuggled against my leg, and the first win of my life under my belt.

Okay, who was I kidding. Life would be *way* better if the kids at school had seen me race, or at the bare minimum, knew about my dogs.

But now I was just being greedy.

"What's that weird noise?" Joey asked when we went inside the barn to get a hammer for Mom to hang a picture a few days after the Rodeo Run.

"No clue," I said, flipping on the light. "It sounds like electricity through a wire. We'd better check it out."

We followed the sound to a little brown scrap wedged between the concrete floor and the wall. "No way," Joey breathed, sinking to her knees beside it.

Me, though—one glimpse of those pointy black ears, knobby knees jutting above a furry, cinnamon-colored body, clawed feet, and leathery black wings pulled in tight and I couldn't get away fast enough.

"Ohhh, he's so beautiful," Joey gushed, putting her hand on her heart. "Look at his sharp, little teeth. I *love* him."

My body made a violent shake as I screwed up my face in disgust. I *hated* bats. "It's very loud," I called from where I stood plastered against the wall on the opposite side of the room.

"He sounds like he's shooting sparks," she marveled, reaching out a hand. "One more reason to love him."

"Don't touch it!" I shrieked. "Rabies!"

"Calm down," she said, grabbing a rag from Dad's work bench. "The 'silver-haired bat'—*Lasionycteris noctivagans*—is responsible for almost all human rabies infections. This is a 'little brown bat'—*Myotis lucifugus*. Plus, it's winter, silly." She gently scooped the noisy bat into the rag, then sat crisscross applesauce on the cold cement with it cradled in her lap. "Why aren't you hibernating, little sweetie?" she crooned.

Little sweetie? Ugh. "I bet my stupid cat got it from the rafters in the attic," I said from across the room. "I saw bats fly out from here at night last summer."

"Did that big bully sneak up on you while you were sleeping?" she baby-talked, dark head bent over the bat. Then she shifted it in her lap. "Oh no, look . . . I think he's hurt."

"I'm sure it is. My cat likes to play with his food, and that's definitely not a happy sound it's making."

When she tucked the bat in close to her chest and started rocking it back and forth, my lip curled, and I shuddered again. That thing creeped me the heck out!

"One summer day thousands of years ago," Joey began in a lullaby voice, "Napi the trickster, spread his robe on a rock to rest because he was hot and tired. He told the rock to keep the robe in exchange for letting him rest there. Suddenly the wind began to whistle, and rain started to fall. Napi got cold and asked the rock to return his robe, but the rock said, 'no.' Napi got mad and just took it. As he walked away, he heard a loud noise. He looked over his shoulder and found that the rock was rolling after him."

Joey's story and the rhythm of her voice possessed the power to peel me from the wall. As she talked, my footsteps slowly closed the space between us. By the time I found myself hovering over her shoulder, the bat's metallic screech had wound down to a thin trickle leaving me strangely hollow.

"Napi ran for his life," Joey went on. Were those tears in her voice? "The deer, the bison and the pronghorn were Napi's friends, and they tried to stop the rock by running in front of it. But the rock just rolled right over them. So, Napi called on the bats for help. They burst from their cave and dove at the rock, colliding with it. One of them finally hit the rock just right, and it broke into pieces. Napi was saved."

The bat was completely silent now, lying limply in her hands. "That's why . . . " Joey sniffled. "That's why you have a squashed little face." Her voice trailed off.

A silence grew until it became an odd, heavy thing. Joey had gone so still, she seemed chiseled in stone. "Um, I think it's dead," I finally blurted, needing the noise. "Let's throw it outside."

Joey was still bent over the bat, but I didn't miss the tear that slid down her cheek.

I shoved my hands into my pockets. "It's just a bat, Joey."

"My mom . . . my momma used to tell that legend to me when I was little," Joey said in a choked voice.

"It's a really neat story. I liked it a lot."

Joey's tears started falling fast. They were dripping off her face, polka-dotting the rag in her lap. The air in the barn seemed to thicken. It pressed in on me from all sides until it was hard to breath.

"My momma's not in a movie." Joey said it so low, I barely caught it.

Suddenly, I felt all shivery cold. "She's not?" I wobbled out.

Her long, black hair swished against her back with the shake of her head.

"Where is she?" I breathed. My heart had started to thud.

She hunched her shoulders even more. "Jail," she murmured.

"Jail?" I echoed dumbly, hoping the air had somehow bent a friendly word, like *shale,* into an ugly shape before it slipped into my ears.

When Joey bobbed her head up and down, I tried to swallow but choked on my own throat.

"For selling meth," she finished dully.

The awful truth came at me in great, bloody chunks. *Jail. Drugs.* Out back, Hazer began to sing. One by one, the others joined in, their mournful howls filtering faintly into the barn. I licked my lips. Shuffled my feet. Fumbled for something to say. "Gosh, Joe. I'm really sorry," I finally managed, knowing my words were lamer than wet fireworks. I couldn't imagine a life without a mom in it. "That's so sad." My voice sounded so shallow, so utterly not me.

She nodded again, then looked up. Tears trembled on her spiked lashes. Her cheeks were wet, eyes big and glassy, and the saddest I'd ever seen. If I'd ever felt worse, I didn't know when.

"At least I have you," she whispered.

Warmth gushed through me. I never knew you could be both happy and sad at the same time until that moment.

"And Mojo," I added, ripping off a blue, shop paper towel. I handed it to her. "She likes you more than she likes me these days. The traitor."

Wiping her face with the towel, Joey snorted a watery little laugh.

I stuck my hands back into my pockets, unsure of what to do now, yet desperate to do something. I wanted to see that sparkle come back in her eyes more than I'd ever wanted anything. "Do you wanna go in and have some Oreos?" I finally asked.

"We need to bury him first," she whispered, holding out the dead bat.

"The ground is frozen," I whispered back.

"The Blackfeet used to wrap their dead in a robe then bury them on a platform up in a tree."

My eyes instantly went to work scanning the barn. They snagged on a box of matches on a shelf. I darted over, grabbed the matchbox and dumped the matches into an empty can. "How about this?" I asked eagerly, holding out the inside part.

She swiped at her drippy nose and nodded.

I found a thin piece of leather in Dad's box of fly-tying supplies. After Joey wrapped the bat in it, I tied it all up with a couple pieces of bailing twine. Then she reverently placed the little bundle into the matchbox, and we took it outside.

The sky hung low enough to touch and was a solid, gunmetal gray. All the color had leached from the world to the black and white of the Great Falls Tribune. With Joey looking on, I climbed a naked tree in the backyard and lashed the makeshift coffin to a branch. When I dropped back down on the ground beside her, she gave me a tiny, guarded smile.

I smiled shyly back. For the first time ever, I was officially someone's secret keeper. As we crunched across the frozen earth toward the house and Oreos, I stuck out my tongue and caught a colossal snowflake. The bat had died, Joey's mom was in jail, and it had started to snow, yet it somehow felt a little like springtime in my heart.

Maybe that's what grown-ups meant by "bittersweet."

Chapter 15

Doug must have glimpsed our teams through the trees because he was standing on his porch holding a steaming cup of coffee and watching as me and Dad came back in from our longest training run ever. It was the Saturday after the Rodeo Run, and we were knee-deep in the bitterest days of winter. Eight hours in the cold had sapped me to the bone, and the run we'd just done had about finished me off. For the first time since becoming a musher, I was discouraged. Even worse was this odd, little knot of panic that had formed behind my sternum.

We'd just discovered that there was a huge difference between running a short sprint race for fun and running a forty-mile endurance stretch through mountains practically as tall as Everest. In our idiocy, when we'd started mushing, we'd assumed that if we simply collected enough dogs (and any ole dogs at that), we could throw them together and it would all work out somehow, that we could conquer anything—any mountain, any distance, any race. But today our teams had performed more like three-ringed circuses than well-oiled machines. I'd left the Rodeo Run with a sense of greatness, and now my Ego Tower was starting to crumble.

As I brought my six dogs to a stop behind Dad's, Doug pointed his coffee mug at Charlie and called out, "You need to switch that dog to the other side of the line."

Charlie flipped over onto her back and began shimmying around in the snow, feet waving in the air, seeming to thumb her nose at us in her bliss. I blinked some feeling back into my frozen eyelids and gave her a sour look. Charlie was on my team today, and her tugline had been slack for most of the run. The lazy piece of baggage had barely pulled at all.

"And that one there," Doug said, tipping his head toward Auke who had this ridiculous quirk of running sideways like a crab when she pulled, "her gait will straighten out if you run her on the left, and she'll be much more efficient."

Dad stood on his runners with a blank look on his wind-chapped face while steam pigtailed up from Doug's coffee and our dogs shook the snow from their coats and rolled around to cool off.

Doug took a sip from his cup. "Dogs are left or right-handed, same as people. They run better on one side of the line or the other."

Part of me stepped back to examine this little news flash while the rest of me watched Dad's expression change. Suddenly he was gazing at Doug as if he were the Dalai Lama himself.

"Some dogs are ambidextrous," Doug added with a shrug. "They run equally well on either side of the line. You just got to figure out which is which."

Dad stepped off his runners with a purposeful stride. Now he was grinning like the Cheshire Cat. "How about we buy you a steak as soon as we get our dogs put up," he called over his shoulder while he started unclipping tuglines.

A little while later I sat with Dad across the table from Doug at Bootlegger Bar and Restaurant. My hands and feet were in agony with the slow return of warmth. The artificial heat in the restaurant magnified the smell of fry oil giving it substance and weight I could lick from my lips and blink from my eyes, and the classic rock streaming from small speakers above the bar seemed to blare after long hours in the silent, snowy woods.

Doug cut a bite from his ribeye. "I wasn't a wizard at mushing, I was a constant observer of dogs," he said as he chewed. "Sure, I raised exceptionally gifted athletes, but I learned through twenty years of trial and error that there's a certain art and science to organizing a winning team. It's not just a 'slapdash hook up random dogs and barrel to the finish line' approach that gets you the win . . . or even to the end of a long race." He reached for his glass. "You've got to know your dogs, watch them as if you are an NFL scout and take notes . . . figure out their strengths and weakness then use them to your best advantage. You wouldn't put a tight end on the defensive line."

The ice clinked as he took a gulp of his Coke. "Take Earl, for instance. He's incredibly smart, an exceptional leader, but he's old and slow. *And*, he's smart enough to know he can set the team to whatever pace he wants to go and that you're not experienced enough to know otherwise. Next run, put Harley up with Earl in lead, and the youngster will get the old man stepping out a little faster."

Dad was so intent on what Doug was saying, his steak sat forgotten on the plate, the fat congealing to a white, unappetizing skin on top. He didn't even notice when I swiped the little plastic cup of bacon bits from beside his baked potato and dumped them into my bowl of clam chowder.

"Right now, you have a bunch of dogs," Doug said, waggling his greasy fork at us. Then he flashed the movie star smile Dad had given him in exchange for two dogs, Patriot and a blonde female named Tenille. "And what you boys need is a team!"

Imagine having Michael Phelps toss out breaststroke tips from the pool deck as you swim, or Tom Brady give you pointers on throwing a football in your own backyard. That's how it was for us. Dad would sit with Doug at his kitchen table picking his brain for an hour or two before a run, pumping him for information—when to use booties (snug-fitting, nylon socks designed to protect paws and toe pads from rough trails), how to feed correctly, how often to rest them—while I perched on Doug's couch sipping hot chocolate, thumbing through his mushing books, and absorbing every spoken word. Then there were the scoops of mental ice cream Doug would serve up to us after we'd come in from a long Saturday training run, frustrated and beat.

"Use shorter necklines so it's harder for your dogs to get a leg caught over them."

"Slow your dogs on the downhill; you're asking for a shoulder injury when you let them fly like that."

And this . . .

"It's not enough to give your dogs some food and let them rest at a stop. Every aspect of the dog needs to be considered. Muscles, coats, pee, feet. A team is only as good as its feet. Feet need to be examined at every stop; the toes spread to look up inside the web of the foot for signs of irritation. Every toe. Every foot. Every dog. Every time you stop. Your dogs are your everything. You need to take care of them. Hands on dogs, eyes on dogs, all the time."

Mostly, this . . .

"The best way to learn about running dogs is to run dogs, so get to it."

We devoured every bit of Doug's advice, ran our dogs fifty miles each weekend, and got better.

"Before you can truly be competitive in distance racing, you need to beat yourself," Doug announced over bacon and eggs one Saturday morning.

Dad paused with a piece of bacon halfway to his mouth, the shadow of a question in the tilt of his head.

"Camping runs," Doug explained as he mopped up rogue egg yolk with his toast. "Your dogs are in decent enough condition. It's time to start doing camping runs." His eyes ping-ponged between me and Dad. "One overnight camping trip is more valuable than a thousand miles of trail in the day. It's how you learn most about your dogs." His gaze stopped on my face. I felt the object of his unnerving scrutiny. Then he smiled clear up to his eyes and said, "And more importantly, yourself."

The master had spoken.

So, when the final bell rang the following Friday, Dad was parked out in front of the school with our loaded rig and attracting all sorts of curious stares. It wasn't every day one saw a truck pulling a red plywood honeycomb on wheels full of dogs peering out from metal grates and topped with two colorful sleds plus a bale of yellow straw. I must admit there was a swagger in my step and a smirk on my face as I zig-zagged between kids on my way to the truck.

"Hey, Big and Ugly! I know why you're called 'Runs Through.'"

The air sewage sliced through the noise and bludgeoned me from behind. My smile shattered. Jerking to a stop, I shot a glance over my shoulder scanning for Joey's dark head towering above the crowd. I spotted Nico first. He was standing on the sidewalk with a few other guys. Air-squatting, he poked his tongue between his lips and blew a loud squirt sound. "That's why you stink so bad, Indian," he called to Joey as she shot past. They all brayed with laughter.

My sudden blast of anger could've powered a small town. I longed to reach into Nico's mouth and yank his tongue out. Just then, he looked over, and our eyes met. I wished I could telepathically cause him excruciating pain, but when he gave me a smirk, I dropped my head.

Joey jogged up beside me. "Come on," she said breathlessly, grabbing my arm. "I want to say hi to the dogs before you go." Then she tugged me along like a pig on a rope toward the trailer, and *I let her.*

She went from box to box touching noses poked through metal grates and murmuring sweetly to each dog while I stood off to the side, hands shoved in pockets, hat pulled down low on my brow. *You're such a wuss,* the evil fiend scoffed in my ear. *A human invertebrate. She trusted you with her darkest secret, and you can't even stand up for her! Worst friend ever.* All the excitement, the pride I'd felt minutes before, had fled right out of me. Nothing can stand up to shame. It's the Genghis Khan of emotions.

"Have fun!" Joey chirped as I climbed into the truck. "And be safe, okay!"

"I will," I mumbled, unable to look my best friend in the face.

Once me and Dad were on the road, I leaned my head against the truck window and pretended to sleep. Nico's air sewage sat in my stomach like a dirty diaper all the way up to Lincoln while Khan's metal fingers kept a chokehold on my throat. I was relieved when we pulled into Doug's place and I had to get to work right away because now there wasn't any more time to think about all my defects and to stew about my gutless state of being.

Dad tied off our sleds to the truck grille. Then I started packing my sled. After I had all my gear loaded—alcohol cooker and fuel, dog bowls, sleeping bag, dog food, people food, snowshoes, ax, extra dog booties, dog coats, and first aid supplies—I didn't think there was any way my dogs could pull it.

While we worked, the sun left pink smears down the sky, and when it slipped behind the mountains, it was suddenly cold enough to "pee and lean on it," as Doug would say. But I was too busy to worry about what it meant about the night ahead. Good thing too. Because if I'd have known how snotty Mother Nature was going to treat us, I'd have high-tailed it straight back to the truck.

We worked fast in the fading light to harness the dogs and Velcro booties around their ankles. Once we'd bootied them all, we started hooking them to the sled. First, I hooked Earl in the lead. He leaned into his tugline, holding the gangline tight behind him while I put Harley next to him, Trip and Patriot at wheel and Mojo and Tenille in between, each dog adding a frantic decibel to the barking.

Hookups are always wild. The dogs are so stoked to run, their mouths foam, their eyes sparkle, the air vibrates with an intensity that lifts the hair on my neck and gets my blood pumping. While our dogs hit the ends of their tugs and screamed to go, I arranged the band of my headlamp over my skull cap so that the light was centered on my forehead and pulled up my parka hood with its massive fur ruff. Then

I stepped on the runners, and with a hard yank to the brake line, we were off.

It felt strange and a little scary heading into this get-yourself-lost country as darkness was falling. But the dogs didn't mind. They charged into the woods with wild abandon, excited by the run and juiced by the frigid cold. We headed north and west, up into the mountains, and as the trail steepened and the snow grew more powdery, the dogs slowed and settled in for the long haul over Huckleberry Pass.

The last traces of light seeped from the sky and a moon, so bright it had an artificial look, rose, casting menacing shadows that seemed alive. But even in these eerie woods that had once harbored the most dangerous serial bomber in U.S. history, with the back of my dad just visible in the furthest reach of my beam and six other beating hearts close by, I felt safe and daring, and the luckiest kid in the world.

Hours passed, dark and silent but for the dogs' whuffling breaths and the hiss of the runners beneath me—soothing sounds that lulled me toward sleep. At some point, I started to teeter. My eyelids snapped open, and I steadied myself. Heart racing, I took five deep breaths, then put in my earbuds and cranked up some tunes.

The wind kicked up, and the cold became a menace. It came at me from everywhere—icy blasts hitting my face, barging in from any microscopic opening, any seam, any pinhole in my arsenal of winter clothing. It bullied me and badgered me, never leaving me alone for a second until the cold had penetrated clear to my bone marrow, and I couldn't concentrate on anything else but how miserable I was. The dogs though, they were as happy as could be—their bodies perfectly engineered for these conditions.

We were nearing the top of the pass when Dad brought his team to a stop in the middle of the trail. I groaned inwardly. I was desperate to get to our camp in a spot out of the wind and dive inside my arctic sleeping bag. I kicked in my snowhooks and pulled out my earbuds. "What is it," I yelled, the wind whipping away my words.

Dad aimed the cone of his beam at a line of deep punctures in the snow. The grapefruit-sized black holes zig-zagged across the trail and disappeared into the woods behind us. "Moose tracks," he called over his shoulder. "Silver stepped in one and injured his wrist. He's limping. We've got to bag him."

Dogs in harness hate to be thwarted mid-run. We'd learned from experience not to underestimate our dogs' ability to rip the sled out of our grasp or a snowhook from the ground and tear down the trail without us. So, while our dogs went ape, Dad worked fast to tie off our sleds to big trees and unhook Silver from the gangline.

He was bringing Silver over to the sled when I noticed Trip biting and pulling at Tenille's tugline in her wild craze to keep running. With an angry shout, I sprang from my runners. Before I could reach her, two ragged ends of tugline dangled limply in the snow. My eyes wide with panic, I looked up at Dad, blinding him with my beam.

"Fix it," he barked as he lifted Silver into his sled bag.

I pulled off my mitts with my teeth and pinned them under my armpit. With our dogs still gunning to run, I rummaged through my sled bag for a new tugline then dashed over to exchange it with the ruined one. At this subzero temperature, frostbite could set in within minutes, so every small task we had to do with our mitts off became a risk. I grabbed the clip on Tenille's harness. In the orange glow of my headlamp, I fumbled to open the snap with fingers clumsy with cold and shaky with nerves. Before I could get the clip undone, Tenille lunged, and it flew out of my hands.

Growling through clenched teeth, I went for the end attached to the towline. But the sled was rocking so hard with the dogs' attempts to jerk it free from its anchor, I might as well have been trying to milk a snake for as much luck as I was having to get the snap open. I threw my mitts to the ground in a fit of frustration.

I felt Dad looming over me. In seconds, Tenille was back on the line and the severed tug was stowed away. Dad picked up my mitts, handed them to me and bonked me playfully on the head before jogging back to his sled.

A few minutes later, Patch quit pulling. Not long after that, she started stumbling to keep up with the team. So, we had to stop again to bag her before she got hurt. With the extra weight of a fifty-pound dog in each jam-packed sled bag plus a couple more stops to sort out tangles and rearrange dogs on the line, the two hours it should have taken us to travel the last fifteen miles took us nearly four. It was long after midnight when we reached our fifty-mile goal and found a flat spot in the trail out of the wind to make camp.

I was no stranger to hard work or the cold, but in my nearly twelve years of living, I'd never experienced anything like this. I was so stiff and frozen and beat, I could hardly stay on the sled. It was hours past my bedtime. The cold was a knife that sliced right through me, agonizing me from the inside out. It had singed my face. Even my teeth ached with it. I could no longer feel my fingers and toes. My skinny leg had bad circulation on a warm day, and now it screamed with an agony that made me long for a hacksaw and a wooden peg.

Worst of all, after hours battling darkness and cold, my brain had quit firing on all cylinders. Everything, both mentally and physically, is ten times harder in the cold. Everything, both mentally and physically, is ten times harder when you're tired. Right then I was one hundred times more miserable than I'd ever been in my life. I'd had no clue how brutal a long night-run would be.

I eased my team to a stop behind Dad's. While he began moving between his dogs, I stood on my brake locked in a pain trance, staring blankly into the void of darkness, a hand pressed to the small of my screaming back. Instead of reveling in my suffering, as Doug claimed the best mushers do, I wanted home with a sudden fierceness that brought heat to my eyes and an ache to my throat. And we were only halfway done—less than, actually, if you counted our rest. My head sagged forward on my neck. It was all I could do not to collapse on the ground and give way to the darkness and cold and exhaustion and simply quit.

While I wallowed in my misery, the evil fiend whispered in my ear, *Maybe you're just not cut out for this.* A giant pit seemed to open in my stomach. Maybe I wasn't. I squeezed my eyelids shut to keep the tears from leaking out, and my eyelashes instantly froze together. The world seemed to go in a slow spin around me. I tightened my grip on the handlebar as I swayed on my feet.

It was the sound of silence that brought my head up sharp. My headlamp flashed down the length of my team. Instead of barking and lunging to keep running like they'd done every other time we'd stopped, my dogs were standing still, ears drooping, tails tucked. Steam was rising from their hot torsos. Mojo twisted her head around to stare at me, a look of pure trust on her foxy face, and I suddenly understood—if I asked her to keep going, even though she needed food and rest, she would joyfully die in harness for me.

The bond that had developed between me and our dogs was truly amazing. Every single day, every day of the year, I gave them care—warm meat, massages, foot ointment and booties, vaccinations, doctoring, protection, and most importantly, love. And they gave me everything they were or could be in return. As my eyes connected with Mojo's, I felt the tug of that bond right below my heart.

Back there somewhere, back in the real world, I had a home, and a mom, and a brother, Joey, another life. But here, now, was everything I needed—the sled, food, my dad, sixteen good friends—all that I'd become. With all of this, I was whole. With my dogs, I wasn't a nobody.

Would I give up dog sledding because it was hard, because it hurt, because I was tired and cold? I dashed away my icy tears with a hard sweep of my glove. No way! Everything I wanted to see, to feel, to do, to *be* was *not* at home, but right here in nature with my dogs. I owed them so much.

They needed meat. Feet checked. Pats and hugs. I set my jaw then stumbled off the runners on legs too stiff to bend. *Starting tonight,* I silently vowed as I shuffled toward Dad, *home is wherever I am with my dogs.*

I could barely put one foot in front of the other. My wobbly body still felt like I was in motion like a sailor too long at sea. When the cone of my beam swept Dad's face, I could see that his eyes were hollowed by weariness, the blades of his cheekbones blanched white with frost nip. I cleared the lump from my throat as I came up beside him. "Dad, what should I do first?"

He bundled a rope into the crook of his arm then laid a hand on my shoulder, something he did often. That hand on my shoulder always spoke to a part of me words could never reach. Whenever I felt insignificant or not good enough or discouraged, that hand told me otherwise. He gave my shoulder a gentle squeeze. "Get some snow, son."

While Dad tied the sleds to trees and anchored the teams out straight with snow hooks, I moved like a walking zombie to dig out the food bags, fire up the alcohol cookers and put buckets of snow on to melt. We left the dogs in harness, and while we waited for the water to boil, we went down the line pulling off booties, unclipping tuglines and velcroing on dog coats (fleece liners with windstopper nylon shells).

As we moved from dog to dog, we flexed wrists and rotated shoulders to check for injuries and examined 4 toes per foot x 4 feet per dog x 16 dogs - 1 toe on Trip's front right foot = 255 toes for cuts and splits. The math came together slowly in my numb brain, my fine motor skills fuzzy in the murderous cold. But we were driven by worry—worry that in our ignorance and with our lack of experience we'd cause damage to our dogs by mistake. So, we gave over a big chunk of our sleep time to studying toes and rubbing pink ointment into feet—all by the light of our headlamps.

Dad dropped bricks of frozen meat for the dogs into the boiling water. Mom had made us some homemade beef stew and froze individual servings in double layers of Ziploc freezer bags. I love Mom's beef stew. Dad dropped these sealed packets on top of the dogs' meat. I was *starving*, and when warm meat smells began wafting from the cooker, the wolf in my stomach started to growl.

I went over to pull out our dinners from the steaming water. When my beam flashed down into the bucket, a little strangled gaspy groan came from my throat. "No, no, no, no, Noooo!" I moaned at the sight that met my eyes. Big holes had melted in the Ziplocs, and all our stew was leaking out and sinking down into the dogs' meat.

Their "meat" is a conglomeration of whole chickens and salmon heads and liver and leftover beef fat scraps from the butcher, wild game and the occasional fresh roadkill—basically whatever cheap, high fat/high protein stuff we can get our hands on. Then we grind it all up together on a course setting and freeze it into blocks. It's totally gross. The dogs love it.

At the sight of Mom's carrots and potatoes swimming around with a chicken toe, an eyeball, and big, white globs of fat, my face twisted in disgust and I battled the urge to throw back my head and howl. "Dad . . ." I called out tonelessly when I could trust myself to speak. "We're having Pop-Tarts for dinner."

I stirred the steaming bucket with a long-handled ladle, poured the sludge over kibble and set sixteen steaming bowls in the snow. Tails wagging, our dogs dug in with relish while we tore into a box of frosted blue raspberry Pop-Tarts with rainbow sprinkles on top. It was the first time in my life I felt hostile toward the scrumptious little breakfast pastries. We couldn't even wash them down with Gatorade—it had frozen solid in the bottles.

After dinner, as Doug had instructed, we broke open the bale and gave each dog their own cake of straw. The dogs raked the straw around and fluffed it, then laid down and shuffled it around some more until they'd made perfect beds for themselves. I was amazed at how quickly they transformed from fierce running machines into quiet little bed warmers. Shortly there were small streams of steam rising from their noses which they'd tucked beneath their tails.

While our dogs slept contentedly, we cleaned up the gear and packed it all away. I unclipped Mojo's neckline. Then finally . . . *fi-nal-ly*, nearly two hours after we'd stopped to make camp, I spread my -40-degree Arctic expedition, waterproof, wind-proof, 800-fill down sleeping bag on top of my sled. When I took my parka off, the cold got a really good shot at me, and I broke all sorts of speed records getting inside my bag. Mojo hopped up on the foot of the sled and curled up on top of my frozen feet.

In the budding warmth of my bag, I pulled tight the drawcord around my face until I was peering out a donut-sized sphincter. I made a jaw-cracking yawn followed by a gusty sigh that floated up out of my body like a ghost. Then with a prickly sting so terrible it was funny, the feeling began to return to my fingers and toes.

It was that clearest, coldest, quietest time of night I'd never actually been awake to experience but had only ever read about in books. From my infinitesimal spot in the universe, I stared up at the stars. They were extraordinarily bright this close to heaven, and the sheer number of them boggled my mind. It looked as if they'd been smeared across the sky with a cosmic butter knife.

As I gazed up at the stars, I felt oddly exhilarated. I had mushed my team through some of the wildest backcountry on earth in cold like I'd never even imagined with only my headlamp to guide me. I'd brought me and my dogs safely to a campsite, and doctored, fed, and bedded them down. I'd pushed myself to my absolute limit, and had not given up, even though I'd wanted to. Was this what Doug had meant about beating yourself? One thing was for sure: I could do hard things. I pulled in a deep, satisfied, breath through my nose, and my nostrils froze shut.

Big and Ugly . . . Big and Ugly. Now that my body was still, Nico's air sewage wafted back in, bringing that sick feeling with it. *Ugh.* I never wanted to feel these squirming maggots in my belly again. I was Joey's secret keeper. She deserved better from me. *Well, if you can do something this hard*, whispered a friendly inner voice, *surely you can manage a little puke like that.*

I stiffened inside my bag. *Could I?* While my eyelids drooped closed, I turned the possibility over and over in my mind until it slowly faded away.

Then the growling started.

Chapter 16

G o back to bed, Hazer!" Dad called out from his sled bag.
I rolled onto my side and peered hazily through the little
ventilation hole in my sleeping bag. By starlight, I saw Goblin, who
was bedded down beside Hazer, poke his head up out of the straw.
Hazer climbed to his feet and made another warning growl at him
low in his throat.

Dad sat up and flicked on his headlamp. "I mean it, Hazer!" he
barked. "Go to sleep!"

Hazer's lips peeled back, and he snarled at Goblin, his slick gums
and sharp canines glinting in the glare of Dad's beam. Goblin stood
and faced Hazer. His hackles rose, and he growled a warning back.

I hunched my shoulders and ducked my chin. Hazer dove at
Goblin in a spray of straw and snow. In an instant, he had him by the
throat and began to shake him like a rag. It was all so horrible I could
hardly look.

Dad shot out of his bag, his beam making a jagged slash through
the sky before blitzing across the trees and landing on the snarling
mass of fur. He scrambled through the snow in his wool socks and

base layer, grabbed Hazer by the hind legs and swung him hard into a snowbank.

Dogs were designed by nature to run in packs with a clearly defined order of authority from the top dog on down. They need a strong, powerful leader to unite them, to give protection and to provide food. So, within a group of dogs, there is a constant, instinctual struggle for dominance. Little arguments erupt among our dogs all the time over food, sleeping territory (as in Hazer versus Goblin), a female in heat, or a ton of other things only known to canines. Unless you have a whole bunch of dogs like we do, the regular pet owner never sees this innate need to lead or be led and to know one's place in the pack. But it's there in every dog, buried under thousands of years of evolution. All dogs want to know who's the boss, and as Doug had told Dad over the kitchen table just the week before, "A musher must be the alpha of his team."

Human power struggles aren't so different than dogs. The idea struck me as good one, so I shoved it away to analyze in a moment less stressful than this one.

Dad stuck his knee on Hazer's neck. "No!" he shouted into his face while Hazer cowered beneath him in the hard disc of light. "No! No! No!" There was no anger in Dad's discipline of the dog, only an imposing display of authority.

Some of the dogs lifted their heads from their nests. The rest came to their feet. The veterans, like Jude and Earl, slept on without so much as pricking an ear while I watched wide-eyed from the shelter of my bag, my lungs full of air I couldn't expel.

When Hazer licked his lips (the sign that he'd given in to Dad's dominance), Dad pulled him up by the collar. Then he unclipped his neckline, tied him to a tree, and scrambled back into his bag.

Now I was wound too tight to sleep, so I turned to the sky for comfort. While the breath leaked out of me, I searched for Canis Major (the Big Dog), my favorite constellation. By the time I'd mentally connected the blue-white stars to form his body, my heart had settled back down, and my eyelids were at half-mast. Then I saw nothing at all.

At the sound of more growling, my eyelids flew open again. Canis Major hadn't even moved. I buried my face in my arms and groaned.

"Knock it off, Auke!" Dad's sleeping bag muffled his shout.

A louder, stronger, meaner growl rumbled from Auke's throat. Dad sat up with a jerk and flicked on his headlamp. I sat up too, bundled like a mummy with only my face exposed. Patch was standing, remaking her bed, the quiet rustle of straw the sound of a thousand rushing wings in the still night. Auke raised her hackles and growled some more. Patch stopped fluffing her straw, puffed up, and growled back. I sucked in a sharp breath. Dad flailed inside his bag.

Auke flew at Patch. Patch flew at Auke with equal rage. Suddenly they were a snarling, slashing, tearing tangle of teeth and fur and claws. It was explosive and mean and awful to see. Huddled in my bag, I gripped my throat and swallowed around the pressure of my fingers.

When male dogs have a nasty fight, they are usually buddies again a few minutes later. But when two female dogs (called bitches) have it out for each other, it's all-out war for the *Rest. Of. Their. Lives*—like some girls you probably know at school.

Dad kicked free of his bag. In three great bounds, he had Auke by the scruff. He yanked her off Patch, who was dripping blood from a tear in her ear, unclipped her neckline, and tied her to a tree.

Breathing heavily, I slumped back down and grabbed my head, elbows around my ears and willed the world away.

"I wish you'd quit making so much noise so I could get some sleep around here," Dad muttered as he high stepped it past me on his way back to his bag. I let out a snort, and it felt really good. He gave my sled a little shove so that it wobbled, shaking a bit of spirit back into me. My numb cheeks stretched into a grin for the first time in hours. I suddenly remembered how glad I was to be here even though there were so many things to fight against. Then I lay there listening to the soft rustles of Dad settling back in his bag until I dropped off into nothingness.

It was the physical sensation of Mojo's low growl vibrating through my feet and up my legs that woke me the third time. I came awake instantly and completely. Mojo leaped down and stood beside the sled, a continuous menacing growl rumbling from her throat. I fumbled with the drawcord on my sleeping bag to get an arm out then put my hand on the X of Mojo's harness where it crossed on her back. Her muscles were locked in readiness, hackles raised.

I looked over the sled and found all the dogs on their feet—rigid black silhouettes in the starlight with noses pointed in the same direction and hackles raised too. Some were whining, some were growling, but they were all on high alert. The baby hairs on the back of my neck stood on end. Something was out there hidden in the shadows.

"What is it?" I whispered so low my lips barely formed the words.

Dad flicked on his headlamp and aimed the beam in the direction the dogs were looking. Then I saw it—deep in the trees, not a stone's throw from our sleds, two disembodied orbs caught the light and glowed back at us from the dark. My body shivered right down to my bones. The dogs' whining increased, and their necklines made cheerful jingles as they began to nervously pace and dance around.

"Cat," Dad whispered back, and the eyes vanished in the space of a blink.

I shrank back against the handlebar, mouth gone dry. My heart felt like it was beating too fast for me to breathe. This was no harmless, little kitty cat skulking around our camp, but an 8-foot-long, 200-pound predator on the prowl.

I started inching down the handlebar, my gaze fixed on the black void where the eyes had just been. *The mountain lion (puma, cougar, jaguar, ghost cat, plus thirty-five other names) hunts alone from dusk to dawn, stalking silently and taking its prey—deer, elk, the random pet, or jogger—from behind.*

I froze when my bag crackled. The moon was up, so the snow caught the light and filled the woods with pale images and shadows that seemed to move, playing mean tricks on my eyes. *A mountain lion sinks its talon-like claws into flesh to hold its prey while its jaw muscles deliver a powerful strike to the neck, breaking it instantly.*

I could feel the hard tick of my pulse in my throat. I risked another few inches down the handlebar. *A mountain lion can leap 16 vertical feet in the air and 45 feet in one horizontal bound.*

The joints in my sled creaked. I went rigid again. *Or was it 40 feet? . . . No, definitely 45.*

Somewhere close by a twig snapped. In one fluid motion, I slid all the way down on my back, burrowed deep in my bag and jerked the drawcord tight. *And, they can sprint as fast as a car.*

I balled up in the sanctuary of my bag, panting softly into the crook of my arm, and pretended I was invisible. *In the rare event of an attack, fight back.* This line from one of my animal fact books bored into my head and began its nefarious work, and with my butt hanging off the side of the sled, my imagination ran away with me to a place I did not want to go.

"Here kitty, kitty, kitty." Dad's soft singsong nosed into my bag through my ventilation hole the diameter of a straw.

I edged my tongue around my lips then tried to swallow but couldn't.

"Here kitty, kitty, kitty," he sing-songed again.

I wrestled a hand out of my bag and flapped it around until it connected with one of my snow boots. I chucked it in Dad's direction and felt satisfaction when he made a loud grunt.

The dogs settled back down, but it took me a long time to ride that particular adrenaline wave to shore. As I lay there wide-eyed visualizing in Technicolor the account of a mountain lion snatching a six-year-old California boy during a family hike and dragging him through the brush (the kid's parents fought off the lion, saving him—but still!), clouds moved in, blotting out a few stars at a time. Soon the darkness was absolute. Thick and heavy, it sucked me under like quicksand, filling my mouth and nose and eyes. A few minutes later, flakes of snow—not the big, fluffy kind, but small and mean—started pelting my sleeping bag and face like handfuls of rice, the hard crystals poising for a second on my skin before melting and dribbling down my neck.

That's when I gave up on sleep for good.

Chapter 17

It wasn't long before the sun crept over the horizon spilling a hazy gray light through the trees and chasing away all the shadowy places to hide. Dad was already up seeing to the dogs. While I groaned my way out of my bag, he was detonating little swear bombs left and right. I emerged from my warm cocoon to find that Fitty, Izzy, and Harley had all chewed through their harnesses in the night.

"They're useless," Dad spat. As if on cue, Fitty nudged up against him, tail wagging, wearing a big toothy grin, the mangled ends of his harness straps dangling from his shoulders.

I swung my legs off the side of the sled, and the cold rediscovered me instantly. The morning was so crisp and clear, if I flicked it, I swear the world would've shattered. "We have more harnesses, right?" I asked nervously through chattering teeth as I shrugged into my parka.

Fitty playfully swatted Dad's leg with a paw. "Not with us. It didn't even cross my mind to pack extras."

I ground my fists into sore eyes, then glanced far off toward where Lincoln lay some fifty miles over the mountains to the east. "What do we do?"

"There's nothing we *can* do." Dad scrubbed a hand over his whiskered jaw. "They'll just have to run without harnesses."

"But that's three less dogs to put strength on the line! We'll never get home!"

"Four, actually . . . Silver won't put any weight on his leg. He's still sore from stepping in the moose track."

My eyes shot to Dad's bloodshot ones. As we shared a worried look, I felt a strange, desperate urge to laugh.

"Put on your big boy underwear," Dad said as he knelt to wrap Silver's ankle. "We're in for a long day."

Were we ever.

Dad's lips were set in a rigid line as we massaged each dog's muscles to work out the stiffness the cold brings, fed and bootied them, ate the last of the Pop Tarts, and broke camp. The humans may have been stony-faced and dragging tail, but the dogs, after only five hours of rest, they were full of spunk and raring to go. Once we started clipping tuglines to harnesses, they went ballistic, their barks and yelps ringing through the trees. If we could bottle and sell a sled dog's powers of recovery to humans, we'd be kazillionaires. Their resilience blows my mind.

It took us nearly two hours to get ready to leave. Finally, Dad zipped Silver into his sled bag, then we lined out our dogs, jerked our hooks and started back toward Doug's place.

After the dogs' initial burst of power and they'd settled into their run, the going was frustratingly slow. I scowled against the wind tears in my eyes.

Dad twisted around to look over his shoulder. "Only forty-eight more miles!" he called back to me with a grin. It earned him a small one in return. My dad was indestructible. Someday I would be too, I hoped.

The sun inched its way up the sky as we wound our way through the trees. It had quit snowing before dawn, and now there wasn't a single cloud in a sky so blue it was hard to imagine the malevolent black of the night before. There wasn't a breath of wind, and the sun was deliciously warm where it hit my face.

One second I was staring dully at the tugs, and the next I was falling straight off the back of my sled. I hit the ground so hard it knocked the breath out of my lungs. While I lay in the snow struggling for air like a fish in an upturned bowl, my team ran off and left me.

Of course, they did—the little jerks.

Dad caught my AWOL dogs as they swept by him riderless and fancy-free. If you were wondering why my dad always runs ahead of me, now you know. He held both our teams until my lungs resumed the crucial business of breathing, and I caught up to them, clutching my side and gasping for air.

The sun wreaked havoc on our dogs too. As we worked our way back up Huckleberry Pass, they dipped down and snapped up snow as they ran to keep themselves hydrated. We had to make lots of stops in shady spots to rest them and snack them on frozen salmon steaks. We'd expected to be back at Doug's gorging on double bacon cheeseburgers around noon, but lunchtime came and went under some random trees at about mile twenty-stinking-five with me and Dad passing peanuts and frozen jerky back and forth while our dogs panted in the shade and rolled around in the snow.

An hour more down the trail, which included a ton of steep parts where I had to pedal or get off and push, Dad brought his team to another stop.

"What is it now?" I moaned as I whoa-ed my team up behind his and threw out a snow hook.

"Haulin's decided he's done for the day," Dad said over his shoulder. "He laid down and is letting the team drag him."

I squeezed my temples to push away the exhaustion. It had seeped in between every cell of my body so that I shook and felt nauseous with it. Lying down and letting the team drag *me* didn't seem like such a bad idea. I had a powerful urge to complain to my dad, to whine about my misery. I bit my lip on the tumble of words then gave my cheeks a few hard slaps with bare hands before helping him load our biggest, heaviest dog into my sled bag.

By mid-afternoon, my crooked hips and back from having a gimp leg were wrecked from the jolting of the runners. I was completely fried from the lack of sleep. I couldn't think in straight lines. I was functioning on fully automatic, focused completely inward so I could simply make it through. That's why I didn't see the downed log jutting into the trail. I clipped it with my runner. My sled tipped, flinging me into the snow.

For an instant I was stunned, pain ringing down through my whole body like a terrible bell. Then I started to laugh. I writhed on the ground, arms wrapped around my middle, convulsing with laughter, unable to stop. I had snow caked on my face and packed in my nostrils. I didn't even care. I'd been on this little joyride for nearly twenty-four hours. I'd traveled through Tired and way past Exhaustion and had finally arrived in that faraway kingdom called Hysteria where the air is made of helium, and everything is funny, and your IQ instantly halves. It sure is a strange place to be.

After I'd laughed myself dry, I lay there in the middle of the trail, legs spread, arms flung wide above my head, unable to the muster the strength to get up. A shadow fell over me. I squinted up to find Dad's silhouette dangling an industrial-sized bag of Jelly Bellies over my face. "It's time to break out the big guns." He toed me in the ribs with a boot.

I scrambled to my feet, scraping my wet eyes with mittened knuckles. "Where you been hiding those?" I exclaimed. There isn't much Jelly Bellies can't handle.

Dad poured them into the pouch hanging from my handlebar until it bulged and sagged. Powered by a steady stream of sugar, I accomplished the last ten miles of the run.

The setting sun was painting the snow in pastels when we barreled triumphantly into Doug's yard, a virtual avalanche of churning legs and paws covered in bright neon booties. "Whooooa," I called out in a calm yet confident voice, commanding my team to stop.

Yeah, right. *Scoff.*

But it sure made an awesome mental picture, didn't it?

Doug was waiting for us on his porch, coffee mug in hand when we straggled back into his yard. Unfortunately, the picture we made didn't inspire much awe.

Okay, none.

Our dogs flopped onto the ground, their ears drooping forward, pink tongues working like pistons. I felt like I'd just gone twelve rounds in the ring with a boxer—and lost. It was all I could do to keep from pitching face-first off my sled into the snow.

"If you guys were gone much longer, I was going to send out Search and Rescue," Doug called out.

When Dad twisted around to set his snow hook, I saw the muscles in his jaw clench. Then Fitty, who'd chewed through his neckline a few miles back and was running loose because the snow was too soft down here to hold a snowhook, bounded out of the woods and up the steps. He plunked down at Doug's feet and grinned up at him while trembling with joy. My sled bag crackled dully with Haulin's struggle to climb out.

Doug looked down at us from the porch, smiling as big as I'd ever seen him. "It appears your first camping run went exactly like I hoped it would."

I saw Dad's jaw tense again before I scowled down at my boots.

"Why don't you come in and warm up by the fire and have a bite to eat," Doug said cheerfully.

All of me hurt. My arms were ready to drop off. Once the sun had started going down, it had gotten super cold again. My bones were petrified with it. I was aware in some back room of my mind that this overnight camping run was the most important thing I'd ever done, that the kid who'd just come out of those woods was way different than the wimpy kid who'd gone in the night before. Tomorrow a sense of accomplishment would probably kick in, but right now I was mentally and physically wrung out. I wanted nothing but sleep, a medically-induced coma, or death—I wasn't picky.

Dad strode over to his leaders. "We're tired," he said as he unclipped Jude from the line. "We're going to load up and drive home. We'll talk later."

"No need," Doug chuckled with delight. "I can see with my eyes all there is to talk about."

Dad grabbed Jude by the collar and kangaroo-hopped her toward the trailer while I reached for the zipper on my sled bag to get Haulin out. "We saw a cat," I said to Doug, too tired to remember to be shy.

"Bet that got your blood pumping."

I nodded.

Doug propped a foot on the log railing. "Cats aren't a threat to your team. It's moose you have to worry about."

I stopped mid-zip and turned to look up at him as that little eight-cylindered fact clicked into place on the massive Lego fortress of them I'd been building in my mind my whole life.

"They see your team of huskies as a pack of wolves," Doug added. "They'll attack it and kick the dickens out of your dogs, especially if it has a calf."

Wolves are a moose's main predator, I thought as a memory of last night's, grapefruit-sized moose tracks sprang full blown in my mind. My insides crawled with ice. Then Haulin burst out of the bag, and all worries about cats and moose and wolves were forgotten as I scrambled to chase him down and wrangle him into the trailer.

When we pulled away from Doug's a half an hour later, I curled up on the seat beside Dad. The brush of his calloused fingers wrapping around the bare nape of my neck sent tiny, warm shivers all through me. "I'm proud of you, son," he said quietly as we rumbled down the road toward home. "You're one tough kid."

His words floated in the air between us like nine little iridescent bubbles. I didn't stir for fear they'd burst and fell asleep against his leg as content as any boy had ever been.

Chapter 18

Doug was right, of course. I learned a lot about myself during that miserable camping run, and once I'd rejoined the land of the living later that weekend, a sense of accomplishment kicked in—and with a vengeance too. Yeah, our overnight camping run had been a total disaster, but I'd come home with this new I-can-do-hard-things swagger in my step, and gosh, it felt good!

It felt so good in fact, it gave me the sense that I could take on the world. Well, maybe not the *whole* world, but Nico, at least. His ugly words to Joey had been festering inside me since Friday, and this awful maggoty feeling had to go. I was ready to do something about him once and for all.

For the rest of the weekend, my brain was on a Nico spin cycle— I couldn't even concentrate on a book—and as I washed the spicy, firecracker meatball sauce from the dinner dishes Sunday night, I stumbled on a plan.

Monday morning, for the first time ever, I sat in the bench seat across from my nemesis *on purpose*. As the bus lurched forward, my fingers dipped into the neck of my "I Lost an Electron! Are you

Positive?" T-shirt to touch the bear-paw stone that hung there. Then I unzipped my backpack, set the open end toward him, and waited nervously for Nico to take the bait I'd stuck in at the top.

"I'll take those," he said, lunging across the aisle.

Bingo.

Before I'd even squawked out a fake protest, the Mosquito had half the mini pack of BBQ Pringles shoved into his mouth. "You're a good guy to have around, you know that, gimp," he said cheerfully, spraying reddish-brown flecks.

"You're not," I growled under my breath, gaze riveted on his face as he chewed. *Wait for it . . . Wait for it . . .*

A few little hiccups popped out of Nico. Then his whole body went statue still as a befuddled expression took over his face. When his eyes widened to the maximum diameter, and he flushed the color of a cooked lobster, I dragged my hands over my face to wipe away the naughty smile that had sprung to the corners of my mouth.

Nico started squirming around in his seat. "It's hot," he wheezed, hand flapping in front of his mouth. "It's hot! It's hot! It's hot!"

His lips rounded in a shallow pant. Then I watched with deep satisfaction as sweat sprouted out on his brow and body juices began to drip from every orifice in his face.

"I'm dying!" he shrieked, clutching at his throat, aka "the sewer pipe."

Heads popped up over seat backs. Necks craned to see—including Cory's.

"No, you're not," I scoffed. "Not even close." In an effort of supreme willpower, I'd restrained myself. I'd blown barely any Bud's Wicked Tickle Ghost Pepper Powder into the BBQ Pringles pack through a tiny slit in the foil with a juice box straw. I wanted to give Nico a tickle, but not a *wicked* one—just enough to immobilize him while I said what I needed to say.

Nico cut his bugged-out eyes to me. "I'm gonna kill you!" he roared.

"Yeah," I said calmly. "You probably will, but not until you hear me out."

He was panting like a racehorse now, and when he made no move to clear the stringy snot yo-yoing off his chin, I knew his body was in full freak-out mode and that he'd lost the power of speech. So, I swung my feet into the aisle, braced my hands on my knees and leveled him with a look. "You're a real jerk, you know that," I began, flexing the new muscles I'd grown on the inside that weekend and loving the feel of them.

Locked in a pain trance, Nico only whimpered.

"I've had about enough of you harassing Joey," I ground out. "She's my friend, and I want you to lay off her." At the thought of Joey, I felt my jaw harden, and my neck chords pull tight. My mom always said that I was an open book, so I swatted Nico's arm to make him look at me. I needed him to see the genuine hurt written on my face, so he'd know that I wasn't being mean just for the sake of being mean.

He slanted me a watery glare.

I fished a red and white carton of milk from my backpack. "I have zero tolerance for any more of your bull crap," I said between clenched teeth, waggling the avenging dairy product in front of him. "Do you understand how mean that is to make fun of someone for something they can't change? How much that hurts?" I felt my body go rigid from my toes up. "You don't do that. You don't attack someone in a fight that isn't fair!"

"Yeah, dude," someone piped up from the back of the bus, "Spencer's right. It's not cool."

Holy cow. In fact, it was the *Holiest* of all cows, the *Mother of All Bovines*—that was Cory's voice! My pulse rocketed at the sound of it. The coolest guy in school had just totally backed me up! That sent an extra shot of nitroglycerin into my already fiery mood. "If you mess with Joey again," I snarled at Nico, "I'm gonna rub my dirty underwear on your head, spit in your mouth while you're sleeping, and put sand in your crack. Got it?"

Still whimpering, Nico bobbed his head.

"Good," I said, opening the carton. "Glad we have an understanding." When I thrust it at him, he brought it to his mouth so desperately milk sloshed up his nose and ran down his chin.

By now, most of the kids on the bus hovered at an appropriate blast radius and were watching Nico glug. A few snickers flitted around the bus. I'm not gonna lie, if I could've collected them all like butterflies to display in a glass case on my wall, I totally would have. The sun had even sneaked over the mountains to peek in through Nico's window, causing his slick, red face to shimmer with gold. Can you blame it?

Breathing heavily, Nico flung the empty carton aside. Then anger tapped me on the shoulder again, and I anchored Nico with another hard look. "About Joey's name," I growled. "She's called 'Runs Through' because her great-great-grandfather was a total ninja at stealing horses during war party raids against the Crow. Beat that, *Mustard*." I said his name with relish (the wicked, gleeful kind—not the gag-a-maggot pickle kind in a jar in the back of your fridge).

More snickers flitted around the bus. Nostrils flaring, Nico swiped the stringy snot and milk from his mouth with the back of a trembling hand.

"Now about you and me," I hurried on as the bus turned up the street to the school. "We've got approximately six and a half more years to share hall space. You have two choices." I held up my index finger. "You can pretend like I don't exist—don't look at me, don't talk to me, don't enter my airspace. Or . . . " I put up another finger just in case he didn't know what came after one. "We can be friends." I shrugged. "It's that simple. Take your pick. But if I were you, I'd choose the second."

Nico worked his jaw.

I produced a tube of yogurt and held it just out of his reach. "You gonna quit being ugly?" I asked, eyes narrowed. "Choose carefully." I tipped my head from side to side. "You've got a whole lot of witnesses."

"Including me," Cory called, "And I'm pretty sure you want me to catch your passes."

Snuffling up his snot, Nico nodded then lunged and snatched the tube out of my hand. He ripped it open. With one hard squeeze, he shot the pink goo into his mouth, moaning as it slid down his flaming pipes.

The bus let out a loud screech as it slowed. When it rocked to a stop on a loud exhale, my heart scrabbled in my chest. It was time to make myself scarce. I grabbed my backpack and jumped to my feet. "Clean yourself up, dude," I said, tossing a tiny pack of Kleenex into Nico's lap. "You look terrible." Then I booked it up the aisle.

Nico was under siege—he just didn't know it yet.

The next morning, I marched up the bus aisle toward Nico, rolling my lips between my teeth and fingering the bear paw hanging under my "Decimals Have A Point" T-shirt. When our eyes locked and held, my stomach made a flip-flop. *Look brave, feel brave*, I chanted in my head. I didn't want to die today, but by the "dead meat" look on his face, I knew it was a real possibility.

I sank down next to Nico in his bench seat, and we entered into an old-fashioned staring contest. "I oughta squash you like a bug," he growled as our eyes battled it out.

I pulled out a full-sized canister of Pringles from my backpack. "Yeah, you probably should," I said, hoping that last sentence wasn't going to go down in history in the category Famous Last Words. "But then who'd help you with your homework?"

His eyes widened, and his eyebrows shot up before he looked down between his knees, all tense and vibrating suddenly like a rabbit pinned under a bush.

I popped the top and held the open end out to him. "Cheddar Cheese," I said. "So you won't think I sabotaged them too."

Nico sent me a glare out the corner of his eye.

"Plus, I like cheddar best," I plowed on since I hadn't died yet. "When you get to the broken pieces at the bottom of the can, they somehow get even better. I like shaking the can until it's a drinkable dust of dehydrated potatoes and cheese."

Nico just kept on scowling at his shoes.

"Ever wonder why they always have Cheddar Cheese Pringles on the airplane?" I tried.

"Never been on a plane," he muttered.

My heart gave an uncomfortable squeeze. "Originally, I thought it was because Cheddar Cheese was ranked #1 in a blind taste test of 16 Pringles flavors. But I've decided it's because if a plane goes down, rescuers can see their neon orange color from two miles away."

Nico looked up at me. I was prepared for his world-of-hurt face. Instead he gave a little eye roll/snort combo that popped the balloon crowding my lungs.

"Here," I said, tapping the canister on his leg, "take some. It's an olive branch."

His look turned incredulous. "No, it's not, *idiot*. It's a stinkin' can of chips."

"Yeah, it is," I agreed in a rush. "In both Greek mythology and Christian theology, the olive branch symbolizes peace. When you extend someone an 'olive branch,' it means you are making an offer of reconciliation."

A deep V appeared between the brown eyes he suddenly narrowed on me. At first, I thought the V signaled "Violence Imminent" and braced myself, but then he asked in a low voice, "What does 'reconciliation' mean?"

"It's like making up," I said on a sharp exhale. "In ancient Greek and Roman times, people would offer real olive branches to their enemies when they were tired of war and ready to call a truce. Today we give Pringles and offers of homework help, maybe a *can* of olives—stuff like that—instead of a literal olive branch."

Nico huffed. "You are such a weirdo."

"Tell me something I don't know."

Nico slid a single chip from the can, then poked his tongue into his cheek and thought for a second. "You can light a fart on fire."

My body instantly felt like I was plugged into the mains. I wanted so bad to tell him that yes! lighting a fart on fire is known as "pyroflatulence" or "flatus ignition" and that if the gas in your colon is mostly hydrogen, you'll get an orange flame, while a high methane content will turn the flame blue, but you have to eat a ton of cruciferous veg-etables such as broccoli and cabbage to make methane, and that fart gas has no oxygen and therefore is unbreathable air, so if you saved up all your farts for a year in a scuba tank and then made someone breathe it, they would die. But my brain sent up a warning flare just in time, so I held it back and said instead, "Cool."

Yay me!

For the next several days, Nico circled me like a wary dog. So, maybe we weren't to the slashing of palms and mingling of blood point in our relationship, but he'd quit being ugly, so . . . progress. Funny thing was though, Nico's zero treatment wasn't enough for me. I felt like I was stuck at a checkpoint during a long race. Crazy, but I wanted more where Nico was concerned.

Me and Joey went to Nico's basketball game Thursday after school and cheered extra loud for him when he swished the ball from the three-point line. I swear he glanced at us out the corner of his eye as he jogged past.

The following morning, I dropped another full-size canister of Pringles into his lap and sat down beside him on the bus. When he saw the Loud Fiery Chili Lime label, he gave an amused little eye roll/snort combo. *Wonders never cease*, as my mom would say—the Mosquito had a sense of humor in there after all. *Phew*. My choice of Pringles flavor had been a gamble. But my instincts had paid off.

When we got off the bus together fifteen minutes later, empty Pringles can in hand, Joey bounded up beside us as planned, and we flanked Nico on our way to the big double doors. "Check out my new *Voltron—Defender of the Universe* comic book I got for my birthday!" she said excitedly, pulling it from her bag.

Nico lit up like a neon sign. "No way!" he breathed. "Is that a Holofoil edition?"

"Yes!" Joey gushed. "2003! First issue!" She held it out to him. "Want to borrow it? You can give it back after school."

His gaze flew to hers. He just stared for a few seconds chewing air. It was the first time I'd ever seen Nico speechless.

"Serious?" he finally gurgled out.

"Serious," Joey shot back with her 100-watt grin, and my heart filled up so dang full right then it was a wonder it didn't explode.

A handful more Pringle bus rides later and Nico the Mosquito was sitting at my kitchen table surrounded by Oreo crumbs, mechanical pencils, and textbooks. Yes, you read that correctly, and yes, a zombie apocalypse is imminent. After me and Joey double-teamed him on his homework, we all put on coveralls and muck boots then went merrily out to do the dogs all 3-Muskateerish—as if we'd stepped into some crazy alternate universe.

In the barn, I handed Nico the poop rake and long-handled pan and hooked a five-gallon bucket on his arm. As we walked toward the dog yard, me and Joey shared a silent, toothy guffaw behind his back. We'd neglected to explain the full magnitude of what awaited him on the other side of the barn. Basically, the poor guy had no idea how many gigantic, frozen Tootsie Rolls he was in for. *Snicker, snicker.*

When we rounded the barn, and the dogs went ballistic at the sight of us, Nico reared back, mouth falling open. "I knew you were weird, Boogerman, but sheesh!" Whistling low, he made a slow shake of his head. "The crazy cat lady's got nothing on this! You must really love dogs."

Chapter 19

My buddy Nico was right, I did love dogs—especially *my* dogs. But once me and Dad had done a few long camping runs that demanded more from them, something became obvious: people had unloaded their wash-out and problem dogs on us. Old dogs, young dogs, small dogs, tired dogs, slow dogs, lazy dogs, dogs that made mischief, dogs that made war, dogs with defects, dogs that gave up, dogs that were all heart but no talent and others that were all talent but no heart—we'd gotten them all, the dogs nobody else wanted. The scraps. We hadn't expected that mushers would sell us their best dogs, but they were more than happy to pass off their worst. We'd even gotten the last picks at Doug's.

When we started mushing, we barely knew a thing about it. With a little experience under our belts, we now understood that all sled dogs are not created equal. The best distance dogs are not only super athletic but have hearts of a champion and incredible mental strength too. In a world bursting with dogs, dogs of this caliber are super rare— like Cory rare. And not only did we not have a star in our kennel, we had a bunch of rejects.

So, our sled dogs weren't perfect specimens. Neither was I, in case you'd forgotten. I was a team reject too. Me and my dogs, we were all *less than* in our own way—flawed. Truth is, I wouldn't have had it any other way. It seemed fitting somehow—all of us misfits *and* doing the best we could with what we had to achieve something amazing together. That amazing thing, of course, was to run the Race to the Sky. Now that we'd learned the basics of mushing and dog care, all our training was geared toward this titanic goal.

That's how me and Dad found ourselves white-knuckling it through this dicey stretch of McCabe Creek Trail on our last training run of my sixth-grade year. We'd decided to run a fifty-mile portion of the official Race to the Sky route that weekend, so we could learn it, and McCabe Creek Trail is six grueling miles in the first quarter of those fifty. It starts in a creek bottom on a forest service road that closes for the winter and follows the creek to a towering summit.

For the past hour or so, we'd been making a slow climb up switch-backs. I was driving my team a short distance behind Dad's like usual, and we had nearly reached the top. Up here the road was cut into the side of the mountain and had a steep drop-off at the edge. As if this wasn't scary enough, a few days before, a big storm had dumped a ton of new snow here, and the wind had blown it across the road in big, diagonal drifts which sloped toward the edge. Then a short warm-up followed by bitter cold snap had put a sheet of ice over everything.

It was the most hazardous bit of trail we'd ever been on. My dogs were clawing their best to stay on the road, and I had to stand on the inside runner and pull the sled over at an angle to keep it from sliding down the mountain. I was rigid with nerves, breathing shallowly, putting all my faith on Earl to get us safely through. And he was so good at it, going by feel as he picked his way along the safest path. Slow and patient, his bulky form tugged out in front of us like a beacon. Always, but especially today, I was so glad he was mine.

We were pussyfooting it along, the sled runners hiss-scritching on the ice, when a churning white vortex of wind swept down the mountain with a fury and hit Dad from the side like a bulldozer. The blast was quick and violent, pushing his sled sideways toward the drop-off. I shrieked his name, but the gust tore it away.

One second he was there; the next he was gone, vanished in a poof of white. My dogs chugged along, unfazed by the disaster unfolding ahead, while I watched, paralyzed by horror, as Dad's dogs were dragged by momentum in pairs over the edge after him. My scream echoed down the mountainside. By the time it ricocheted back, Dad's leaders, Jude and Silver, had gone off the side, leaving only the white static of an old TV where his team and sled had been an instant before.

I threw out a snowhook. It hit the ice and bounced with a chink. I jumped off the runners and yanked my sled over to the side of the trail at a run, the snowhook skittering along behind me. It caught the edge of the trail, bit in, and jerked the sled to a stop. With one hand gripping the handlebar and my heart in my mouth, I leaned out over the edge and looked down.

About thirty yards below and twice that distance in front of us, Dad's sled was stopped against a tree on its side in the middle of blackened stumps and fallen limbs buried in snow. I raked the ground with wild eyes while my dogs yelped and strained to go. My gaze snagged on Dad's limp form. He was lying face-down a few feet below his sled, motionless, arms thrown haphazard above his head. A sob broke from my throat.

Instinct took over. As if some power were pushing me from behind, I let go of the handlebar, ready to plunge headlong down the mountainside to get to my dad. My dogs lunged. The snow hook popped out, and my sled leaped forward.

With a cry of alarm, I dove for it. I caught the handlebar halfway down and landed hard on my knees sending a shock of pain through me. In one superhuman movement, I pulled myself on and up to standing, then stomped on the foot brake with both feet. Beneath me, the claws screeched like fingernails on a chalkboard, slowing the sled, but they couldn't grab hold of the ice to bring it to a stop.

I twisted around and fumbled for the tether streaming out behind us. I caught it, towed in the snowhook then tossed it out again, aiming for the side of the trail. It caught and jerked us to another stop. With the snowhook set and me putting all my weight on the brake, the sled was secure, but the moment I stepped off it, I knew my team would run off—and there wasn't a tree near enough to tie up to.

My body shook with a tremor too deep for cold. *My dad!* He was down there, maybe even dead, and I couldn't get to him, couldn't find out, couldn't help him, couldn't do anything but stand here holding my dogs, scared out of my mind, all alone on top of a mountain, fifty miles from civilization. It was the worst feeling I'd ever experienced in my life, this helplessness. It was as if I'd stepped on a land mine, and the moment I lifted my foot, it would blow.

I leaned out over the edge as far as I could without tipping the sled. When I craned my neck and strained up on my toes, I could just see the wreck. It was directly below me now. My gaze shot straight to Dad.

The breath left my body in a whoosh and I went weak in the knees. Dad was on his hands and knees, head hanging heavy on his neck. At the sight of him up and not dead, my relief was so intense it tasted like hot pennies on my tongue.

Now that my worst fear was past, my thoughts came back in jerks. *Dogs. Dad's dogs!* My attention leaped from Dad to them. All ten were strung down the steep mountainside in the middle of what looked like a giant game of Pick-Up Sticks. Lines were hung up on deadfall, caught in the skeletons of burned out trees and wrapped around body parts. The fighters were fighting, and the biters were biting, while the rest jumped and yowled and spun their wheels in frustration—except for Harley and Goblin. The sight of them turned my blood to ice.

Harley and Goblin were on their backs with lines wrapped around their necks. Every time the other dogs lunged or pulled against their tugs, the lines jerked tight, strangling them. Goblin's legs were flailing in his struggle to right himself. But Harley—my hand flew to my mouth. We'd switched Harley out for the more experienced Patriot on my team when the trail got so treacherous, and now he lay there completely limp, purple tongue hanging out the side of his mouth.

"Dad!" I shrieked. "The dogs!"

Dad's head came up, and he blinked at me. Blood trickled from a long scratch across his cheekbone.

"Their necks!" My voice broke on a sob.

Dad pushed up to his feet, groping for the knife on his belt. It fell from his gloved hand, hit the ground and slithered away on the ice where it disappeared under a burned-out tree tipped onto its side. He dropped back down to knees and stuck his hand under the charred wood. When he drew out his hand, it was empty.

I was hit by another desperate urge to leap off my runners and charge down the mountainside. My dogs were barking up a storm—the noise ratcheting up the panic that was squeezing my chest like a vice. I couldn't seem to draw a breath.

Dad sprawled flat on his belly and peered under the trunk. While he was patting around for the knife, Fitty and Trip bit through their lines. Trip bounded downhill and disappeared into the trees. Fitty, drawn by the barking of my dogs, tried to clamber up the slope to get to us, but he kept sliding back down, unable to get a grip on the ice with his bootied feet.

Harley still hadn't stirred. The other dogs were jumping all over his lifeless body in their urge to get free. "No!" I whimpered, shaking my head. "No . . . no . . . no!" I shot a desperate look at Dad. At the sight of the knife gripped in his hand, my legs nearly crumpled beneath me. "Hurry," I shouted, as he began crawling up to the tangle.

Dad slipped and clawed his way up to the dogs and starting slashing lines. Goblin flipped up onto his feet and scuttled away. Dad moved fast. Dogs sprang away in every direction until the only one left was Harley. His still form was an ugly brown stain on the white slab of earth. Tears spilled out of my eyes and froze on my cheeks, and I didn't even try to stop them.

Dad tossed away the knife, and I vaguely wondered why he'd do something so stupid. He yanked off his mitts, dropping them at his feet. Then he did a thing so bizarre, so unexpected my tears dried up on the spot.

In a quick burst of movements, he knelt beside Harley, picked up his head and pushed his tongue back in. He wrapped one bare hand around his muzzle and clamped the other over his mouth. I watched spellbound as he bent down, sealed his lips over Harley's nostrils and blew in a breath.

From my terrible perch overhead, I could see Harley's chest rise and expand. Then Dad straightened up, locked one hand on top of the other over the widest part of Harley's rib cage and started pumping. *One. Two. Three. Four. Five,* I counted rhythmically in my head as a sudden, desperate hope leaped inside me.

CPR! The parabola night! Dad's recertification course! My stomach twisted. Could CPR actually work on a dog? If there was even the slightest possibility, I knew my dad could do it. *Please, God,* I begged silently as Dad blew in another breath.

Seconds bled into minutes while Dad worked feverishly to bring Harley back, and my dogs kept on jumping and bawling to run. I felt outside myself as I stared helplessly down on them. Drawn by the noise, some of the dogs from Dad's team were trying to get up the hillside to us but couldn't make it on the icy slope. A few danced around him nervously. Trip had vanished completely down the mountain. Fitty trotted over and sat down beside Dad, lolled out his tongue and grinned cheerfully at him. I squeezed the handlebar to keep my hands from rattling off. I couldn't have conjured a worse scenario in my mind if I'd tried.

Then something changed.

In the middle of a breath, Dad's head jerked up from Harley's nose. He sat back on his heels with his hands gripping his thighs. They were a blue-white to his nail beds with frostnip.

He sat that way for a long time, doing nothing but watching the limp dog, his breath billowing white clouds in the frigid air, while I watched them both through my tears, hardly daring to breathe. Dad looked defeated there on his knees in the snow surrounded by burned-out trees standing hollow, skeletons empty of life. They were twisted as if in agony, their naked branches clawing at the sky with gnarled fingers. Others were broken at the waist, bent over in defeat, heads buried in the snow. This was Death's country—black, burned over, ravaged by a forest fire long before I was born, ugly and cursed. The fuzzy sun moved in and out of clouds, turning the ground into a kaleidoscope of shadows and white. The shifting light cast a creepy vibe over the whole foreseeable world. I felt like I was in the middle of a horror film.

Suddenly, Harley's head stirred. Everything inside me tensed. Had it been a trick of the light or had my strained senses played a cruel joke on me? I swiped the wetness from my eyes and lasered every particle of my attention on him. Yes, there it was again! He'd lifted his head off the ground a few inches then dropped it back down. It was the tiniest of movements, but it gave me the feeling of bees in my veins.

Dad wormed his arms gently under Harley and scooped him up. My dog flopped lifelessly there while Dad scooted on his backside down to his sled. He stood gingerly, righted his sled with a foot and laid Harley down in the sled bag. Before zipping him inside, he took out his ax and stuck it through his belt. Why? I didn't have a clue and had no extra mental energy to put to it, because another awful thing had commandeered my mind. How would Dad ever get back up to me? We'd be stranded like this forever. I ran a jerky hand over my salty, stinging face.

Dad pulled what remained of the gangline down to him and wrapped it around his waist. Then he started up the slope dragging the sled with Harley behind him. His foot slipped out from under him, and he fell to a knee with a grunt. I sucked air through my teeth as Dad's face contorted in pain. My gaze instinctively sought out Mojo for comfort. She was calmly staring over her shoulder at me. Our eyes caught and held, and my insides instantly quieted.

When I looked at Dad again, he held the ax in his hand. He used it to drive himself back to his feet. Then, with a swift downward arc, he brought the blade into the ice with a brittle crack. Ice chips flicked up into his face. With a few more swings of the ax, he'd made a little stair. He stepped up on it, narrowing the distance between us by a foot, and my insides quieted some more.

He made slow progress, chopping and clawing and heaving the sled up the slope on his crude staircase until he crested the lip of the road. When at last he set his boots back on the trail, my limbs went all Jell-Oy. The runners clattered against the ice as his sled tottered on the edge. Then with a final heave, it came to rest near mine.

At the sight of Dad, my dogs went nuts. His dogs scrambled up the stairs after him in single file then instantly got busy sniffing and tussling with mine.

I unlocked my teeth and asked in a thin voice, "Is Harley alive?"

Dad stood bent over gripping his knees and breathing hard. "Not very," he said between pants. He lifted his eyes to mine and slowly shook his head. "I don't know, Spence . . . He breathed against my last breath, but his pupils—they're fixed and dilated."

Fixed and dilated.

I moaned inside. Separately, those two words were harmless. *Fixed*: fastened securely in position. *Dilated*: being flat and widened. But linked by a tiny, poisonous "and," they became something altogether sinister. "Fixed and dilated" was a harbinger of brain death.

My chin hit my chest. Harley was a goner.

Chapter 20

Harley was such a happy dog. He always made this funny, very undoglike Chewbacca yowl of excitement when we were gearing up for a run. He psyched up all our other dogs when the going got tough and would yip at anyone slacking on the line. He was our best cheerleader—could get the team to do anything! I loved him so much.

Had been our best cheerleader. I bit down on my trembling lip.

The sun was now glinting through a break in the clouds. Way off in the distance, mountain peaks were so sparkly and clean with new snow they seemed dipped in sugar. I wanted to smash my fist into them, to kick them to smithereens while I threw back my head and howled.

"We can't turn your team around. It's too narrow here." Dad's voice jerked me back. His face seemed to melt through my welling tears. "That's another disaster waiting to happen. We've got to keep going forward."

I stood there empty. I knew there was no use rushing back to the truck anyway. There was nothing more that could be done for Harley, and I'd rather stay out here forever than abandon Trip completely to the wilderness. She might turn up eventually. I nodded my agreement, not trusting myself to speak.

Dad stretched his gangline out in front of his sled. Since we'd started doing long overnight training runs the year before, we'd made a ton of mistakes. But we'd used them all as stepping-stones to get to someplace better. We'd learned more about each of our dogs and their quirks. We ran smarter and packed our sleds for the unexpected. Each run found us more prepared than the last—meals vacuum-sealed by a Food Saver heat up much better in boiling water than meals in plastic Ziploc bags, for example. We'd gotten fast and efficient in readying our dogs to run and in making and breaking camp. We could now do in thirty minutes what used to take nearly two hours. We'd learned better vet care, and how to work a dog through a sore wrist, so we didn't have to carry it in the bag.

As for me, I'd grown bigger and stronger. I'd gotten more capable and hardier, having made a sort of peace with the cold and the sleep deprivation. Mostly, we'd learned to take whatever came and roll with it. Until today—Harley was more than I could bear. It took everything I had not to lie down in the snow and dissolve into sobs.

Dad rummaged around in my sled bag for our stash of extra lines. He unclipped all the chewed tugs and necklines from his dogs and began piecing his broken team back together on the gangline. It was awful not being able to do anything but stand on my brake and watch. I'd have given my prized prehistoric Cerambycidae (longhorn beetle) trapped in amber to be able to press the pause button on my team just this once.

After his dogs were hooked up and ready to go, Dad unzipped the sled bag and peered in at Harley. He zipped the bag back up and stepped on the runners without looking me in the eye. But the grim set to his jaw had told me everything I didn't want to know.

When we pulled the snowhooks and started off again, there were two glaring holes on the line where Trip and Harley should have been. Trip was long gone, Dad's sled bag had become a body bag, and I had the feeling that I would crumple beneath the weight of my sadness. It was a forlorn little band of travelers that eased their way down the backside of the mountain. Even our dogs were a little shell-shocked, I think.

I know I was.

The trail leveled off, and we started across a high-country meadow of snow. At our backs, a big orange sun hovered on the edge of Montana. As it slipped below the horizon, I caught a movement at the shadowy tree line out the corner of my eye. I did a double take, and my heart kicked in my chest. "Dad . . . look!" At the sight of Trip leaping through the snow toward us, I let out a gust of giddy laughter.

Trip bounded up to Dad's sled, stepped right into her place and began running along in perfect pace with the team. She acted like she was clipped on the line, just doing her job like usual—as if the bottom hadn't just fallen out of our world—until Dad got the sled stopped and clipped her back on. It was the craziest thing I'd ever seen, and my smile was so big my cheeks ached. Then the thought of Harley in the sled bag dropped into my head and my smile faded quickly away.

It wasn't long before Dad brought his sled to a stop again. "What now?" I grumbled as I pulled up behind Dad. I wanted to get to our campsite, take care of the dogs, then ball up in my sleeping bag and hide from this horrible day.

"Harley's thrashing around. I need to check on him."

At that, my spirits brightened a little. If Harley was moving, it could only be a good thing, right?

Dad looked back at me, and I saw the pain in his eyes. "I'm afraid he's having convulsions," he said with another slow shake of his head, and I went dark inside again.

Dad pulled the zipper a few inches, and Harley's head popped out. My eyes shot wide. Harley's head bobbed back and forth crazily while I gaped at him, frozen by a jolt of excitement.

Dad pushed Harley's head back down into the bag and zipped him in. "Don't get your hopes up, Spence," he said gruffly as he climbed back onto his sled, "Harley's a long way from being right."

At that, my shoulders slumped, and I stared off in the distance without seeing a thing, wishing hard that life had a rewind button and I could skip us back an hour or two. A few minutes later, another rumble and thrashing began in Dad's sled bag. I was running close enough to hear the crackle and thumps and couldn't keep a lid on my hope any longer. It started leaping around inside me like a hundred little tree frogs.

Dad stopped again. While he was setting his snowhooks, Harley literally ripped through the zipper. He exploded from the sled bag, landed on his feet, and began stumbling around in the snow like a drunk man.

Dad sprang off his runners and lunged for him, but Harley dodged away. They played a little game of cat and mouse while I looked on with disbelieving eyes—the dogs too, we were all completely gob-smacked and riveted on the show. For once, they didn't even try to run.

Harley started to get his feet under him, and it took Dad a few minutes to catch him. But he sure acted like he was going to be all right! Dad kept trying to put him back into the sled bag, but he'd squirm around and lock his elbows and knees and refuse to go in. Finally, Dad looked over and shrugged. The crooked smile he gave me was better than a birthday present! I beamed back at him.

Dad clipped Harley back in his place on the line, and we started off again. I couldn't remember ever being so happy! Harley wobbled and swayed ridiculously as he ran, but he got better and better as we went along. And by the time we stopped to make camp, you'd never have believed that dog had been as dead as a doornail two hours before. He was perfectly fine—and has been ever since.

I know you're probably thinking that this is the biggest fish tale you've ever heard. I don't blame you; I wouldn't believe it myself if I hadn't seen it with my own two eyes. But I did, and it's true. The insatiable need to run resurrected that dog from the dead. Scout's honor.

I told you sled dogs have superpowers.

Chapter 21

That dog's a total screw off," Nico huffed, pointing at Colt through the ranger's windshield. Sure enough, my new white dog with the brown face that looked like it had been shoved into a mud puddle had twisted around on the line and was messing with his brother, Marlin, again.

"Stay ahead, Colt!" I shouted out the driver's side window. But it was too late. He'd already caught his foot over his slack tug, jumbling up the whole team. I stomped on the brake as my leaders, Earl and Jude, ground to a stop then patiently waited for a human to come sort out the mess.

"I got it," Nico said, throwing open the door and bailing out.

Nibbling my bottom lip, I watched Nico gamely dodge the jumping, barking youngsters while he worked to unscramble lines in the murderous wind. After getting burned that first year with everyone selling us their dud dogs, Dad had decided that he would only buy young dogs we could train up ourselves, or we'd breed our own. No more buying dogs from active racers who'd sell us the hand-me-downs they were trying to pass off. So, a few weeks after school had ended in June, we'd driven all the way to British Columbia to pick up "The Guns" from a lady musher who was getting out of dogs because of cancer. The Guns are four brothers named Browning, Marlin, Glock, and Colt. They were so young when we got them, they hadn't even been harness broke yet. Now that September was finally here, me, Nico, and Joey—along with the true professionals, Jude and Earl— were harness training them in my backyard after homework. I narrowed my eyes at Colt. Okay, so maybe only certain sled dogs had superpowers. This one sure seemed like a dud. Perhaps Dad's strategy wasn't foolproof after all.

Nico clambered back into the cab and yanked the door shut. "And that's why you pay me the big bucks!" he declared with a big shiver, rubbing his bare hands together.

"Nope. Friendship dues," I countered with a snort.

Joey snickered as I let off the brake, and the team set off again through the prairie grass. Not five minutes later, Colt's antics had the dogs in another colossal knot.

"See!" Nico said with a disgusted shake of his head. "He's more clown than sled dog."

Joey, squished on the seat between us, bumped her shoulder against Nico's. "Give him a chance," she scolded, then leveled him with a sweet smile. "It just takes some longer than others to become their best selves."

"Hardy har har," Nico said flatly, his voice cracking hilariously on the last *har* and giving me and Joey perfect joke fodder for the rest of the frustrating run.

As we wound our way in fits and starts around the trails in my backyard, we mimicked the heck out of Nico's epic puberty crack. A whole family of spiders was camped out on his upper lip too. *Me*—I didn't even have a single scrawny hair in my pits yet, although I no longer needed a step stool to look Joey in the eye (yay me).

In other news, in preparation for the upcoming race season, we'd decided as a family to call our kennel Skinny Leg Sled Dogs (awesome name, huh!). Mom had our logo embroidered on beanies and blue coats for everyone in our family—plus some extra beanies to hand out to our potential fans. Now that we had a name and official team gear and the *possibility* of fans, I felt legit and full of swagger and itched to race in the big leagues.

"My dad signed up to run the 350-mile Race to the Sky," I told Nico and Joey one frosty December afternoon on our way out to do the dogs.

"How exciting!" Joey said. It was so cold out here, her red cheeks looked painted on her face.

I kicked up a spray of snow. "I want to run the 100-mile so bad!" Dad and I had put a million training miles on our dogs both in our backyard with the ranger and on the snow at either Doug's place or King's Hill, plus we'd done camping runs up the wazoo. My feet were plenty wet from the few little races I'd run during my two seasons of mushing. I was anxious to test my dogs and myself—to prove that I could do it.

"Then do it!" Joey bubbled.

"I can't," I bit out.

"Because he's too chicken," Nico needled with a smirk.

I gave his shoulder a shove. "Shut your face, slime ball. Don't you have an appointment somewhere?"

Nico shoved me back. "Very funny, Boogerman. Why does *chicken* mean *coward* anyway? I've met your chickens. Those things will mess you up."

"I believe Shakespeare used it in that context first," Joey said thoughtfully.

"Are you guys even listening?" I complained. "The Race to the Sky, people!"

"Yeah, you can't run it because you're too chicken," Nico said. "We know."

"No," I said patiently, "I can't run it because of a little thing called my thirteenth birthday. Apparently, rules say you have to be thirteen to run the Race to the Sky. The race is in February, and my birthday isn't until May."

Nico swung an imaginary bat. "I'm sticking with chicken."

"Smart*Asclepias tuberosa*," I shot back.

Nico made another air swing. "What even is *Asclepias tuberosa?*"

Joey giggled into her hand. "The scientific name for a weed."

Enter, Doug Swingley.

Doug wrote a letter to the Race to the Sky board telling them that I was an experienced musher, personally mentored by him, and asking them to make an exception to the age limit and allow me to run the 100-mile race.

"Guess what?" I said excitedly to Nico and Joey at school lunch a few weeks later.

"You like to lick chickens?" Nico suggested around a mouthful of apple.

"No, creepy human, the race board bent the rules for me. Apparently, no one in the mushing world says 'no' to a four-time Iditarod champion. I get to run the Race to the Sky!"

"No way!" Joey squealed over her PB&J.

Nico stole one of my Pringles and flashed me a cheeky grin. "Guess we get to find out if Pepper Boy really is a chicken."

My stomach pitched. *Maybe you are,* whispered the evil fiend. Since I'd gotten the go-ahead, I'd been panicking enough to power a 100-watt bulb and starting to doubt everything. Since Dad would be running the 350-mile race, he'd start before me, so I'd be running without him. Was I ready to handle one hundred miles alone with my dogs and all that Mother Nature and the trail threw at us? I'd only been mushing for two measly years, and Dad had always been there to handle everything that went wrong—and something *always* went wrong on a run. I was just a twelve-year-old kid, a kid with a match-stick leg. The enormity came screaming at me. Could I do it?

I wasn't so sure.

Sure, I'd gotten a lot stronger—gained muscle and balance and endurance. But being physically tough isn't enough in dogsledding; you have to be mentally tough too. This is its thrill, what makes it better than any other sport—fighting through the cold, the pain, the fatigue, the fear, the darkness, the isolation to get to the end of a run. But this is also what scared the heck out of me and kept my eyes stretched wide and fixed to the ceiling until two o'clock in the morning for nights on end. Races are won or lost as much in the mind as they are on the trail, and deep down I didn't know if I had the inner strength—the iron will—to accomplish the gargantuan feat I'd set before myself. Was I a kid with grit?

I'd find out soon enough.

When the bell rang on the second Friday in February, my family was waiting for me out in front of the school with our loaded rig. They were parked beside the *Sacagawea Middle School, Home of the Grizzlies* marquee. Today the block-lettered tiles were arranged to say: "GOOD LUCK SPENCER BRUGGEMAN." The sight of it brought a big, happy jump to my stomach.

I shouldered my way through the river of noisy kids pouring through the double doors. Today was the day—or rather the day before *the day* since it was only the vet checks, the pre-race musher's meeting, and spaghetti feed meet and greet, and the Camp Rimini commemorative run in Helena. But it was close enough. After all the months of training, the endless hours staring at tugs, the long, bone-freezing days and longer nights, ready or not, we were off to the Race to the Sky!

As I scampered toward the truck, the sound of my name cut through the cacophony of a hundred conversations. "Hey, Bruggeman, wait up!" A little electric buzz skittered across my skin. I looked over my shoulder to find Cory weaving his way toward me. His hand shot up above the sea of heads, and he swiped it through the air.

I wheeled around. For once, I didn't have the urge to duck my head and slink away from a cool kid. Instead, I felt about six feet tall as I stood there midstream, bodies flowing around me and converging again at my back. Mushing *is* the bacon of sports after all.

Cory trotted up. I gave him a chin lift, played it cool. Then he grinned at me. "Good luck on your race, man," he said breathlessly, holding out a fist.

I hitched my backpack strap higher up on my shoulder and grinned back at him like a loon. "Thanks!" I said, giving him a fist bump.

He started jogging backward, holding my gaze. "I think it's super cool . . . You know, all your dogs and stuff." Then he turned on his heel and melted into the crowd while I just stood there wearing that big, goofy grin until the blare of Dad's horn jolted me back into motion. Feeling as if I'd been pumped full of helium, I headed for the truck.

Halfway there, Nico apparated at my side. "You ready?"

I flashed him a horrified look.

"If you can't handle the heat, go lick a different pepper," he shot back.

I snorted a laugh. "Smart *Asio otus.*"

He raised a questioning eyebrow at me.

"Long-eared owl."

Nico smiled with his whole face. "You're the biggest nerd on the planet. You know that, right?"

"Not the biggest, Nicoletta," I harrumphed.

"Close enough."

I made a wince face. "Don't tell my sled dogs until after the race, okay."

Nico scoffed. "Like they don't know."

Drugged with happiness and excitement, I yanked open the truck door. "I'll take *nerd* over *chicken* any day. See you guys at the race start tomorrow." Since we'd be gone three nights and four days during part of the school week and living like gypsies as we moved between checkpoints, Joey and Nico were just coming to the start for this one.

Nico grabbed the door. "You know you're the biggest badasteroid in the school, right?"

I felt my heart leap and cower all at the same time. I shot my friend another horrified look.

"Dude, you're an animal," he insisted. "Like a kitten with a bazooka in his pocket!"

"Yeah right," I chuckled as I climbed in next to Chase.

Nico leaned in. "Seriously, Spence, you are . . . You're going to kill it!"

Unless it kills you first, whispered the evil fiend, spoiling it all just a little.

An hour later, we pulled into the fairgrounds at Helena, Montana, where a bunch of vets, each wearing a big green parka covered with race patches and a stethoscope slung around their neck, were busy examining race dogs on small exam tables set up beside the dog trucks. There were dogs everywhere! Of course, there were. Mushers had come from as far away as Minnesota and Pennsylvania to run the Race to the Sky. Eighteen teams in all. Even the vet checks had attracted spectators. A bunch of people were wandering between the trucks looking at the dogs and chatting with the mushers. At the sight of a hot news reporter setting up a video camera right in the middle of the action, my blood leaped. I grabbed the door handle, ready to jump out the instant Dad put the truck into park.

Before any race, each dog from every team has to be checked by a veterinarian to make sure he or she is in good condition to run. Most distance racers have kennels of 50 or more dogs to pick their team from. But since Skinny Leg Sled Dogs was so new, to make up a 12-dog team for Dad and an 8-dog team for me, we'd had to muster every dog in our kennel into service except for one—you guessed it, Colt.

The Guns were turning into great sled dogs, full of talent and heart. But they were still super young and inexperienced, and Colt was definitely the least ready. We knew it wasn't ideal, or even very smart, to use our yearlings in such a big race, untested as they were. But they were all we had. We didn't have a choice if we wanted to run the Race to the Sky—and boy did we ever!

Our first year mushing, we swapped dogs back and forth all the time when we ran—except for Earl and Mojo who were unequivocally (in a way that leaves no doubt) mine. It's really common that one dog will do really well for one musher and not so well for another—not to mention the whole left-handed/right-handed thing, and who likes/hates to run beside who—so, as Doug had advised, we experimented with all sorts of combinations and positions on the line as we worked to build well-oiled machines.

But at the beginning of this training season, we divvied up the dogs for good then each ran the same team and leaders all year long so that our dogs would bond with us as the driver and together as a unit. When harnessed and on the gangline, my team looked like this: Earl and Harley in lead, then Auke and Patriot, Mojo and Tenille behind them, with Charlie and Marlin at wheel.

Marlin—he was really tall and skinny and didn't eat well enough to make it to the finish of a 350-mile race. But he was super driven, so me and Dad were confident he'd finish strong on a 100-miler. Dad ran Browning and Glock on his team. Colt though, he hadn't matured as fast as his brothers. I believed he was a good boy deep down, but sometimes he still couldn't help himself and would turn around on a training run and mess with the dog behind him, causing a little train wreck. He wasn't as confident, or as big and muscly as his brothers either. He hadn't become a sled dog in his mind quite yet, and I wasn't so sure that he ever would.

Dad parked the truck between a couple of rigs ringed with dogs, and I shot out the door, slamming it behind me. A vet tech came over with an exam table and set it up beside our rig while me and Chase started pulling out dogs and clipping them along the trailer. Then a veterinarian with the name Dr. Topham stitched on his parka came over to examine our dogs.

One at a time, I brought my dogs to the exam table, hoisted them up then held them in place while Dr. Topham listened to their hearts with his stethoscope, flexed each shoulder and wrist and checked their body mass to see if he or she was in good enough condition to run. After examining each foot and peeling back their lips to look at their gums and teeth, and reviewing current immunization records, he drew a pink X on their shoulder with a giant, oily crayon. This mark meant the dog was fit to run.

Things were going great until I brought Patriot over to be checked. When Dr. Topham ran his hand down the length of his spine, Patriot gave a little yelp. Dr. Topham's eyes narrowed and a deep V formed between his bushy gray brows. "What's going on here, huh?" he asked my dog in a soothing undertone as his fingers continued to gently probe the area around his hind end. Patriot flinched away from his touch.

Suddenly I had a sinking feeling in the pit of my stomach. I looked around wildly for Dad. He was already on his way over, his brow furrowed up like corrugated tin. He came up beside me and put a firm hand on my shoulder. "Is something the matter?" he asked the vet, leaning in.

Dr. Topham met Dad's intent gaze. "This old gentleman's got a sore back. I want to get him down, walk him around a bit, watch him move."

Good. The vet would watch Patriot walk around the parking lot. He'd see that my dog was moving just fine. Everything would be okay. It *had* to be.

Dr. Topham slid his fingers beneath Patriot's collar and gently pulled to urge him off the table. Patriot balked and wouldn't hop down. The V between Dr. Topham's eyes deepened.

An icy snake of dread slithered into my stomach.

"He ran just fine on our last training run," Dad said. "Showed no sign of distress."

"Sled dogs have such heart and desire, they run through the majority of their pain," Dr. Topham said, releasing Patriot's collar to scratch him between the ears. "A sore back like this would probably show up fifty or sixty miles into the race, and a dog of this caliber wouldn't quit, he'd just not be able to keep pace. There's a good chance you'll end up carrying him in your bag."

The icy dread coiled around my guts and squeezed.

Dr. Topham picked Patriot up and lifted him to the ground. "I recommend he be dropped from the team . . . But it's your call."

Dad gripped my shoulder. "It's Spencer's call."

Dr. Topham's words howled through my head. Besides Earl, Patriot was my most experienced veteran—and straight from Doug Swingley too. Most of my dogs were untested in a distance race situation, but not Patriot. He'd grown up in Lincoln—run the Race to the Sky trail a hundred times. I'd been counting on him to go the distance—to help get me and the less experienced dogs to the finish line. Also, I needed eight dogs for the race!

The rule was that the dogs you left the start line with were the dogs you had to use to run the whole race. You could drop a tired or injured dog, but you couldn't swap in a new dog. I'd never risk hurting one of my dogs on purpose, but I *had* to start with eight dogs to give me the best chance of getting to the finish line. Who knew what the trail had in store for us this weekend and how many dogs I'd have to part with along the way. I shot a panicked look at Dad.

He gave me a reassuring smile and my shoulder a squeeze. "We'll sub Colt in for Patriot. He can do it. He'll be fine. This is why we brought him."

Numbly, I looked over to where our dogs were chained up along the trailer. Earl was lying on the ground with his muzzle resting on his crossed paws watching me through those eerily perceptive eyes. Mojo's ears pricked, and she wagged her tail. Colt was peering out from behind the metal grate on his compartment door. Our eyes connected, and we shared a long look.

I sank my teeth into my bottom lip. I trusted Dad. If he thought Colt could do it, Colt could do it. Dad would never send me to the gallows without a knife in my boot. I knew he and Bill, the race marshal, had discussed precautions to keep me safe and built them into my race. It would be fine, right?

"Okay," I said on a shuddery breath. But even after my private, little pep talk, I still didn't *feel* okay inside—not at all. It felt like my confidence had just been worked over by a sledgehammer. I hadn't even started the race, and I'd already run smack-dab into bad luck.

Dr. Topham fished an orange crayon from his pocket and drew a long, oily stripe from Patriot's forehead down his snout. Cringing, I turned away. That ugly disqualification mark seemed too much like a bad omen to me.

Chapter 22

I still felt off kilter when it was time for the pre-race driver's meeting an hour later. After Randy, the trail boss, introduced himself, he had all the mushers but me draw their starting position from a hat. "We'll send Spencer out right after all the eight 12-dog teams and at the head of the pack of the 8-dog 100-milers," he announced to the motley group of mushers and our entourages sitting around on long, battered benches in the fairground's 4H dining hall. Heads swiveled; all eyes locked on me. "That way he'll be surrounded." He scratched his grizzled gray beard. "So, everyone keep an eye out for the little rookie."

Dad nudged his shoulder against mine as my heart pounded heat into my face. Chase caught my eye and mimicked sucking his thumb. I scowled at him.

Randy held up a small GPS tracking device. "But just to be on the safe side *and* to pacify his momma . . . " He crooked a brow at Mom, and everyone chuckled. "I'm attaching this tracker to his sled, so we'll always know where he is. This is important, Spencer, so pay attention."

I shifted from cheek to cheek, face flaming.

"If you get into any trouble, just flip this up," Randy said, demonstrating, "and press this red button here. Then we'll send in the cavalry."

I felt heavy with the weight of fifty sets of skeptical eyeballs on me. I tugged the brim of my Iditarod ball cap a little lower on my forehead. The racer closest to my age was a girl named Jenny. I glanced at her out of the corner of my eye. She wore cowboy boots, jeans, and a baseball cap pulled on over long brown hair that spilled down her back. She was a whopping eighteen. She'd been born into a mushing dynasty and been on the back of a sled since her Huggies Snug and Dry days, had already run the 100-mile race four times and was running the 350-miler this time around. With everyone looking on, I gave Randy a dignified nod even as my inner voice scoffed, *I'll never push that button,* and I felt a bit of my swagger return.

Randy handed out orange race bibs and maps of the route. "The race starts here." He pointed to a large map tacked to the wall. "You can see the route isn't a straight shot but more like a child's scribble. So, listen up because a missed turn or a wrong turn in the middle of all that wilderness could be disastrous."

Then he proceeded to go over the route, pointing out the checkpoints approximately every fifty miles and spotlighting a few tricky sections of trail. "Right here, about ten miles into the race, the trail hooks onto a county road and follows it for about a mile. If you don't hang a left right here," he said, stabbing the map, "you'll miss the 18-mile Cool Lakes Loop and come out on the state highway way down here." He stabbed another point on the map a few inches below the first. "Once you hit the county road, your dogs will naturally want to keep going straight because it's a wider, straight-ahead trail, so pay attention and don't blow past that turn, or it will cost you an extra ten or fifteen miles with backtracking."

While he talked, I sat there blissfully munching peanuts from a pink plastic bowl and flicking the shells into a tin can which I continually moved further down the table for a bigger challenge. Pretty soon, more shells were landing on the checkerboard tile floor than in the can.

"And right here," Randy went on, tracing a section of the route with his fingertip, "after you come out of the Cool Lakes Loop you'll make a steady uphill climb back over this same ten-mile stretch in the opposite direction. This is when it gets tricky. Once you start going downhill, the turnoff to go over Huckleberry Pass and into the Whitetail Ranch comes up quick, and you'll be going fast around these switchbacks. Step on the brake too much, and you'll get sucked into the corner of a turn and will hit a tree. Gain too much speed, and you'll slingshot around the curve and flip. Either way, *if* you manage to stay horizontal, you'll blow right past the turn if you're not paying attention."

I aimed, flicked, missed. I'd run these trails before with Dad lots of times—except for the Cool Lakes Loop which had been closed for logging until now. The peanut shell clicked on the floor and skittered recklessly until it spun to rest between Jenny's cowboy boots. Mom gave me a disapproving look and scooted the bowl of peanuts out of my reach.

Randy turned back to the map. "So, at the fork in the trail here, veer to the left, and you'll end up back at the start. You want to head west. You'll be whipping around this curve here and literally have seconds to see the marker, recognize the turnoff and make that hard right." He hung his thumbs in his jean's pockets. "Your dogs will have already decided which way they're going and head back to where they think the truck is and a hot dinner, so stay on your toes because that turn to get you over Huckleberry is real easy to miss."

While Randy droned on, invisible scent serpents drifting from the kitchen beguiled me until my mind was blank to everything but food. I folded up my trail map and shoved it into my pocket, ready to move on to the eating, meeting, and greeting part of the agenda.

Instead, a trailbreaker, just off his snow machine and still in grease-covered overalls, got up and strode to the front. I groaned inwardly. "My crew has spent the last couple of days grooming the trail." He held up a wooden stake with a reflective diamond marked with an arrow on one end. "I've put a stake like this before and after every turn and a handful across each lake. These guides are especially important when it's blizzarding, and the wind's blowing, and snow erases any trace of the trail. If you're watching, you won't miss them." He tapped the blunt end of the stake on the floor three times and grinned. "It's a tough race but stay sharp, and you're in for a great run!"

Darkness was falling as we followed a line of dog trucks up into the mountains a few miles outside of town and pulled into historic Camp Rimini in Helena. With my belly full, the excitement from earlier in the day had returned with a vengeance. My insides jiggled with it. Tonight the 350-mile teams would take off on the first fifty miles of their race from the same place that . . . wait for it . . . the U.S. Army trained sled dogs to fight Nazis! *Nazis!* Is your mind blown? I know mine was when I first learned that sled dogs were used during World War II.

The U.S. had a secret plan to invade Nazi-held Norway. The Army needed dog sled teams to navigate the snowy parts of Norway with equipment and supplies for the soldiers, and for covert operations. It was right here at Camp Rimini that the military housed and trained about a thousand sled dogs for this exciting mission!

At Camp Rimini, they developed sled systems that could carry 1,000 pounds or more of equipment for hundreds of miles through snow. They developed a mount that could support a .30 caliber machine gun on a sled! The Army even developed parachute harnesses so dogs, along with sleds and mushers, could be airlifted into remote places.

Dad parked the truck, and I sprang out. A little tingle raised the hairs at the back of my neck. The mountains were already ringing with the yips and howls of sled dogs eager to run, just as they would have done seventy years before when Camp Rimini was in full swing. Vivid imaginings floated before my eyes before fading like smoke among the solid forms moving around me.

I made a quick scan of the area. Now there wasn't a single sign that war dogs and their trainers had ever even been here—not a barrack or kennel, not a landmark, not even a historical marker. From what I'd gathered listening to other mushers talk, most of the record of the life and adventures of Camp Rimini lived in the mind of a retired Army musher, ninety-year-old Dave Armstrong.

As a teenager, Dave worked at Chinook Kennels in New Hampshire, caring for and training the sled dogs Admiral Byrd would take on his famous expedition to the Antarctic. It was an adventure Dave longed to go on but was turned down because he was too young. When the United States entered the war, he enlisted in the Army and, because of his expertise with sled dogs, was sent to Camp Rimini to train war dogs.

A year and a half later, the invasion of Norway was called off—the British took it on instead. So, the sled dogs and their drivers took up a different mission. They were dispersed to remote outposts in Alaska, Canada, and Greenland where they worked as search-and-rescue teams and hauled cargo for the Allied forces in the hardest, most desolate terrain on earth which stretched millions of square miles. Dave Armstrong and his team were sent to Newfoundland.

For the next year and a half, Dave searched for the wreckage of military planes brought down by the Arctic weather. It was grim work. Sometimes he rescued downed airmen, but mostly he just brought in human remains. Can you imagine?

His worst recovery was a B-24 that went down with eleven people aboard. It was equipped with some new and top-secret radar, and the Army Air Force was desperate to get that plane back before the enemy could get their hands on the technology. The race was on. They searched for three weeks with no luck. A trapper who'd been out in the wilderness for a month saw a shirt flapping in a tree. Then he saw a detached leg hanging in the tree too. He'd found the crash site the military was so desperate to locate. Dave was sent in with his team to recover the remains—containers full of them—and the secret radar equipment and return them to the base at Gander Field.

Besides search and rescue work, dog teams were also used to freight stuff during the war. One time in Newfoundland, Dave Armstrong and his team spent days lugging a sled full of critical radio equipment to the top of a mountain too high and snowy for any motorized vehicle to reach. It was grunt work at its finest, harrowing and arduous—but the payoff of that backbreaker is huger than huge. That radio provided key communications in the war effort. You can thank a sled dog you don't speak German.

Crazy thing is, practically nobody knows about these war dogs! Hardly anything has even been written about them. During the war, dog sled teams saved lots of lives, recovered the remains of countless people for proper burial, and salvaged millions of dollars in equipment and supplies. Yet, besides a few stories passed around in mushers' circles and a postage-stamp-sized exhibit in the Montana Military Museum, there is nothing to memorialize these special dogs and the men of Camp Rimini. They've basically been forgotten to the world. Talk about unsung heroes!

As I stood there with feet planted on Camp Rimini soil, I felt a part of something so much greater than myself, part of something both mythical and enduring. See, the story hadn't ended with the end of the war. Twenty years later, Dave Armstrong came back to Montana with his wife, Alice, to stay. Here he mentored the next generations of mushers and founded Montana's Race to the Sky! So, every year, the first fifty miles of the 350-mile Race to the Sky is run through these mountains to commemorate the war dogs of Camp Rimini and their musher-soldier trainers.

Dad shuffled past me dragging his sled to get it set up for his run, and I suddenly felt super glad. Even though I didn't get to run tonight, Dad and the rest of the 350-milers would be keeping the Camp Rimini legacy alive in some small way. Dave Armstrong was my kind of hero, someone I wish I could've known. Those soldiers deserved all the honor they could get.

While Dad and Chase were getting the dogs ready to run, the hot news reporter from the vet check asked if she could interview me for that night's sports segment. My insides were instantly a yin and yang of excitement and nerves.

"How does it feel to be the youngest person ever to run the Race to the Sky?" she asked, sticking a microphone in my face.

I stood so stiff and straight, I almost leaned backward. "Uh . . . pretty incredible." My voice sounded smaller than I wanted it to.

The reporter brushed away a strand of shiny blond hair that had blown across her cheek. "Do you feel prepared for the race?"

I could see my distorted image on the lens of the video camera perched on a tripod in front of me. I ran my tongue around my lips to wet them and cleared my throat. "Yeah . . . um . . . My dad and I have been training hard. We've done lots of overnight runs to get ready."

"Who's your favorite dog, and what makes him or her so special?"

One corner of my mouth quirked up. "Mojo. Because she always puts everything in for me." I tipped my head her way. She was watching me from where she was clipped to the trailer. "And she loves me the best," I added sheepishly, heat creeping into my face.

"That's easy to see why," the reporter chirped, and I thought my face might spontaneously combust.

Behind the reporter, Chase had Fitty straddled between his knees and was slipping a harness over his head. He waggled his eyebrows at me and made a kissy face. I shot him a dirty look.

"Are you worried about tomorrow's race?" the reporter asked.

My heart gave an extra bang in my chest. *Colt would be fine. I would be fine. We all would.* I squared my shoulders and tipped up my chin. "I can't afford to be. You have to be upbeat when you're running your dogs. They key off your emotions, and happy dogs run the best."

Big flood lights came on, illuminating a great swath of forest. A PA system screeched to life then made a loud squawk before mellowing into a continuous sizzle. It was nearly showtime.

"Good luck tomorrow, Spencer," the reporter said, flashing a smile. A little Crest toothpaste sparkle practically pinged out at me from her straight, white teeth. "You're a remarkable young man. We'll all be watching to see what you do."

My stomach fluttered deliciously at her compliment. "Thank you," I mumbled to the yellow knit scarf knotted under her chin.

The reporter turned to Mom. "How do you feel about having a backyard full of dogs?"

Mom laughed. "I'm still not quite used to it, but the sport has done a lot of good for our family." She had to fairly shout above the growing racket. "As a mother, I love it because it's taught my boys to work like men."

"Are you nervous about sending your son into the backcountry alone?"

"He won't be alone. He'll have eight good friends with him who are all loyal, smart, and completely in their element out there."

"But what about the risks?"

Mom gave the reporter the full glory of her smile. "Anything daring has risks. But I'm not a parent who bubble wraps my kids to protect them from the bumps and bruises of life. I embrace any opportunity that lets my boys rise to the challenge and stretch themselves in ways that may be scary and hard but offer life-changing rewards in the end." She put her arm around my shoulder and pulled me against her. "Am I afraid? Of course, I am! But nobody achieves anything great by playing it safe, and I want my kids to face life knowing they can do hard things."

By now Camp Rimini was a bedlam with ninety-six dogs harnessed and ready to run. In the distance, a PA guy's booming baritone was priming the crowd with factoids about the race and Camp Rimini. The first team went past us on their way to the start gate, and the time for chitchat was over.

The next few minutes were a whirlwind of activity, and soon Dad was standing on the runners, and we were at the start gate, and our dogs were impossible to control even with me and Mom and Chase all holding sections of the line. Then snow was flying off Skinny Leg paws, and tails were curling over backs as Dad's team took off beneath the flood of golden light. They flew through the roar of the crowd toward the outstretched arms of the deep, dark woods. In seconds it enfolded them, and they were gone.

While the 350-milers ran their fifty commemorative miles, the rest of us waited around a bonfire, sipping hot chocolate, our faces painted in liquid gold, eyes lit with tiny, dancing flames. For five or so hours, dog people talked dogs into the night while tendrils of wood smoke and mushing lore wove between us, and I stood in the midst ensorcelled by it all. My old life seemed strange now, as if it belonged to someone else, the grassy sideline of a football field a million miles away. My life had become my team, taking care of dogs, standing on runners, staring at tugs or the horizon, a midnight bonfire, rich and full and happy.

Magical hours peeled away, and by the time a handler exclaimed, "Look, someone's coming!" I'd been lured even deeper into the love of this sport, this peculiar way of living.

My gaze snapped toward the forest. After staring into the flames, I was momentarily blinded while I waited for my eyes to come to terms with the dark. Then I saw it, a tiny pinprick of light no bigger than the North Star winking at me through the trees.

The storytellers went silent, and we all watched the glowing, floating orb bob and grow until it became a single bright spotlight boring a tunnel through the darkness and skimming thirty yards of the trail. Then black cutouts of twelve dogs materialized out of the darkness, their cumulative breaths rising like ghosts in the light. It was an otherworldly sight—one I'd never seen from this end at night, and one I would not soon forget.

"Who is it?" someone asked no one in particular.

"Jenny or Laura most likely," someone else said.

Another someone strode away from the group. I stood, rigid with anticipation, gaze locked on the approaching team as the crunch of boots in the snow grew fainter and fainter until it vanished into the crackle and pops of the fire.

A moment later, a disembodied voice called back to us, "It's the dentist!"

Yes! My head fell back, and I grinned up at the sky, savoring a fist-pumping sense of jubilation. This was a good omen for sure!

Dad made the last turn and headed our way. Now the dogs' eyes shown blue-green at us with the reflected light from the fire. It was spooky awesome watching my demon dogs charge toward us and sent a tiny thrill skittering through me. Bit by bit their bodies sort of formed around them until they were fully 3-D, and I could recognize each one. No matter their imperfections and quirks, right then I believed ours were the most spectacular dogs since the history of time.

"Come on, Loverboy! We've got to catch Dad's team and get them to the truck." Chase's bark of command and accompanying shove to my shoulder broke me from my trance, and with a little hop and a skip, I took off at a shambling run after him, feeling as if I was moving a foot above the earth.

Chapter 23

The next afternoon found me smack dab in the middle of the best day of my life. Even the weather was perfect—cold and crisp and clear with a sky blue enough to swim in, except for two small wisps of gray on the far horizon I chose to ignore. There was too much else going on.

Our rig was parked in a massive logjam of dog trucks at the official staging area for the Race to the Sky fifty miles from Camp Rimini in Lincoln. With eighteen teams crammed into the equivalent of a half-block radius, the energy was infectious, the dog factor crazy. Everywhere, dogs were scratching themselves, yawning, scarfing down meat, shaking, peeing, whining, wrestling, drum-majoring their tails. The barking hadn't started yet, but the moment the first dog was clipped to a sled, the noise would be epic.

Then there was the people factor. A couple of hours ago, they'd started trickling into this remote Montana outpost. Now hundreds of them were swarming the lot. With music pumping from loudspeakers, vendors selling food and race paraphernalia, and fans orbiting the dog trucks, the place had taken on a giddy carnival vibe—and I was the main attraction. *Me*—the gimp who'd practically been invisible two years before. Isn't it amazing how something as small as a book can come along and—*Bam!*—change the trajectory of a life?

While Chase got my gear and sled ready, I posed for pictures with Mojo, answered questions, introduced my dogs and handed out Skinny Leg Sled Dog beanies to my fans. Man, the view sure was great from the top! Even the dark clouds slowly stretching and smearing themselves across the distant horizon had a pretty, metallic sheen to them.

Chase bumped my shoulder when he walked by with arms full of harnesses. "You nervous, punk?" he asked.

"No," I snapped.

"You should be," he smirked. "I stuck your teddy bear and a couple extra pairs of your Spider Man underwear in your sled bag. You'll thank me later."

"Ha. Ha," I deadpanned. Nothing could rile me today—not even my brother. I was flying high on self-esteem, and when Doug Swingley turned up to wish us luck, I nearly went into orbit. After our family, all decked out in our Skinny Leg Sled Dog gear, had our picture taken with him, I hovered close, eager for any last-minute wisdom and advice from the champion. All I got from Doug before a race official showed up to inspect our sled bags for the required gear was, "Just enjoy the experience, Spencer." But it was enough. I'd recognized the approval beaming out of Doug's eyes and received the same man's handshake he'd given to Dad.

I felt very professional unzipping pouches and pointing out my stuff to the race official while she marked each item off on a clipboard. When it was all said and done, my headlamp and extra batteries, knife, artic sleeping bag, snowshoes and bindings, ax, first aid kit, cooker and fuel, map of trail, vet communication sheet, arctic parka, a pound of kibble for each dog on the team, a day's rations for me and an extra set of booties for each dog were all accounted for, and I was cleared to run. Then Randy, the trail boss, came over and pinned a GPS tracking device to my sled bag.

Soon after that, the first dog was clipped to a sled. The dog's excited screams ignited the air, raising the hair on the back of my neck. In minutes, the place was complete pandemonium. It was the Rodeo Run times ten—louder, bigger, more thrilling, more intense, one of those rare technicolor, Dolby Surround Sound experiences that tattoos itself onto your mind. When you die, if you're lucky, you'll be inked with maybe a dozen of these kind of days.

At the starting line, the bulge of the crowd had become nearly impassable. Dad was slated to leave near the front of the pack of 350-milers. Just before his turn to go out, he cupped the back of my head and brought me in close. "Keep your eyes on the dogs and the trail." He had to practically yell in my ear over the racket. "You've got this. It's nothing we haven't done together . . . Okay?"

I'd been too busy being the center of attention the last couple of hours to give a thought to the upcoming race. But at the intensity in Dad's expression, the panic that had been lurking patiently inside me foamed over my edges. I took a gulp of icy air. Dad's fingers bit into my skull, and he pulled my head back so that I was looking straight up into his eyes. "Okay?"

Dad's strategy was to beat the other teams with speed—build up enough of a distance that nobody could catch him. My strategy was to do whatever it took to finish the race; I wasn't dumb enough to think I could win the thing. To be the youngest person ever to cross the finish line was what I was shooting for. (Okay, fine. I'd let myself fantasize about beating the pants off everyone. But just a time or two.)

A few yards away, Dad's dogs, harnessed and on the line, were hysterical, in raptures. It was time for him to leave. I went cold from the inside out. This was it—the last I'd see of him until the end of his race two or three days from now. I had the sudden urge to run to the ends of the earth and hide. I'd made a terrible, awful, disastrous mistake! What madness had possessed me to think I could ever do this? Stupid, stupid, insane, and *Stupid!*

My face must have advertised my internal freak-out because Dad quirked a half-smile at me. "Good. A little fear is healthy. It will keep you on your toes."

With Dad looking at me all soft-eyed like that, something more powerful than fear took hold of me. The desire not to disappoint him swelled in my chest until I thought I might explode with it. More than anything, I wanted to make my dad proud. As I stared back at him, my worries unknotted and resolve stiffened my spine. I gave him a real smile in return before he strode away.

"Remember, son, the win is in the try!" he called over his shoulder as he stepped on his runners.

The win is in the try. Everything—noise, movement, color—faded around me for a few seconds while I let that sink in. Then I sprang into action.

After that, everything went by in a blur. It took all of us, plus a few race volunteers and a snow machine holding them back to get Dad's team to the start gate, counted down, and off. Soon, all the 350-milers had disappeared into the vast white wilderness, and it was my turn.

Before I stepped on my runners, I knelt and threw my arms around Earl's shaggy neck. My dogs were barking and jumping straight up in their harnesses—two or three feet in the air. But not Earl. He stood at the head of the team, holding the line out straight, calm and dignified as always. I pressed my forehead against his. "Let's do this, old boy." He gave my face a reassuring lick, his hot tongue bringing me back to center.

I gave each of my dogs a final pat as I strode by. Then I was on the sled surging forward, my dogs nearly dragging Mom and Chase and a couple race volunteers off their feet as we got into position beneath the massive Race to the Sky log arch that marked the trailhead. I gripped the handle with shaking hands, my body coiled tight, breaths bursting out in quick, white puffs.

From where he was holding on to my leaders out front, Chase gave me a big thumbs up. I lifted my chin at him and mouthed a thanks—hoping he understood that it covered everything.

Pressing the stone bear paw through my layers of clothes, I anxiously scanned the spectators lining the trail looking for a cluster of blue Skinny Leg Sled Dog hats. Then I saw them. Cheering louder than anyone, Nico and Joey, together with her grandma, were waving their hands off at me. I managed to shoot them a wobbly smile before my rabid dogs nearly bucked me off the sled. Then I turned inward.

Out past the crowds, the mountains loomed before me like menacing, white giants. I looked out over the heads of my dogs and stared them down through narrowed eyes. Everything had prepared me for this. Nothing had prepared me for this! My moment of reckoning had come.

"Next up we have Spencer Bruggeman, a twelve-year-old student from Great Falls, Montana." The PA guy's voice cut through the ruckus. Colt slammed against his tug then caught my eye and screamed with a pitch that shot straight up my spine and sang in my teeth.

"Easy," I said, rocking from foot to foot.

"Spencer helps operate the family kennel, Skinny Leg Sled Dogs," the PA guy went on. "After reading Jack London's *The Call of the Wild*, he got his dad interested in running sled dogs, and they train all season together. This is his first Race to the Sky. In lead today are Earl and Harley."

The seconds seemed to stretch to infinity. Out front, Mom and Chase were doing their best to keep my team lined out straight. My dogs were hopping back and forth over the gangline, hammering against their tugs, biting at lines in frustration, foaming at the mouth. I could feel the power come up through my feet, into the handlebar, and fill me.

At last, the PA guy started the countdown. My heart dive-bombed out of my chest.

"3 . . . 2 . . . 1 . . . *Go!*"

Someone yanked the snub rope tied to the snow machine behind us. Chase dove out of the way. My dogs exploded forward in unison, and the sled whisked away as if hitched to Santa's reindeer. Suddenly we were flying over the snow through the gauntlet of cheering wellwishers and clicking cameras. My dogs fell instantly silent. I loved that part. Exhilaration sparked all through me.

The exhilaration lasted ten seconds or less.

Not a hundred yards from go, the trail made a steep descent. A county road with three-foot piles of plowed snow on each side bisected the trail at the bottom. My dogs were running like canines possessed. At the sight of the world's largest speed bumps coming up quick, I jumped on the brake, smashing the two metal claws into the ground with every ounce of my ninety-four pounds. "Whoa! Whoa! Whoa!" I shouted.

Yeah right.

I might as well have been trying to stop a moving train by putting out a hand. The icy wind cut into my cheeks and froze little tear rivulets across my temples. I blinked fast to stop my eyelashes from sticking together. The runners slicing over the snow made the sharp hiss of a deflating tire.

I sucked in a sharp breath and held it. My dogs tore down the hill, the sled bumping and skipping over the dips in the hard-packed trail. There was *so much power*, so much momentum, and so little control right out of the gate. I crouched low and braced myself.

The sled launched over the first speed bump. The bottom fell out of my stomach as I went airborne. I gripped the handlebar and hung on for dear life. The sled struck the road in a teeth-rattling blow, tipped up onto one runner and shot forward in a sideways skid. My pack of hell hounds never broke stride.

By some miracle, I managed to right the sled and stay vertical but was still scrambling for balance when we hit the speed bump's evil twin. The sled sailed into the air again. At this rate, I was going to sprout wings. For now, all I could do was try to hang on and stay alive. When the sled hit the ground, the landing jarred my joints in their sockets and sent my sled into a crazy fishtail. But I didn't let go.

I still had zero control of the sled when, twenty yards later, the trail made a hard, ninety-degree turn in front of a fence. Here the track narrowed with lots of soft, deep snow on each side.

"Haw!" I shrieked. My leaders swerved left, smoking around the turn. The sled skidded sideways, spraying out a rooster-tail of snow and nearly whiplashing me into a fence post. I clipped it with my boot as my sled flipped onto its side. Suddenly I was face down in the snow.

We plowed down the trail, my dogs dragging the tipped-over sled with my sorry carcass still clinging to it. My arms stretched above my head until they felt like they were going to snap off.

With my outstretched arms smashed over my ears, the sound of my thundering heart was all I could hear. I bent my legs, digging my knees into the snow to slow us. My forearms burned. My fingers screamed in agony.

My team gradually wound down to a stop. The sled was stuck. I was buried. The only part of me that poked out of the snow were my hands locked in a death grip on the handlebar.

Gasping for air, I lifted my head and brushed snow from my eyes to find my dogs looking back over their shoulders at me in disgust (except for Mojo who appeared concerned for my well-being). Harley made his funny Chewbacca howl and started popping his tug. The sled didn't budge. He stopped and looked incredulously at his teammates and seemed to say, "What—is—the—holdup—here—people?"

An icy trail of snow trickled down the back of my neck. "Thanks a lot, you little turds," I groaned.

My dogs weren't the only ones looking at me. A bunch of high schoolers hanging out at the top of the hill had seen the whole thing. They were pointing and laughing their heads off. A couple of them were wearing my Skinny Leg Sled Dog beanies. *Awesome.*

Chapter 24

After I zombie-clawed my way out of my snow grave, we set off again. Snow down your coat is a great way to baptize yourself at the start of a race, and with a crash out of the way, I settled in for the long run. We all did. My dogs' initial burst of adrenaline had burned off, so now they were all business, focused ahead with tight tugs—even Colt.

We zipped along through the crisp, pine-scented air. Three-minute intervals put racers out of view of each other for most of a race. So now that the noise of the crowd had faded, it was just me and my dogs and the silver spears of light slicing through the trees and bending across the trail. The frozen world was silent except for my dogs' rhythmic breaths, the pit-pat of their feet and the whisper of the runners on the snow. We could have been the only creatures on earth.

I loved losing myself in the backcountry—so far from civilization that it may or may not exist. The backcountry was as comfortable to me as an old pair of shoes—but way, way prettier. Cleaner too—like Clorox bleach clean. The air sparkled with cold. Pine branches drooped beneath the weight of their loads. The whole world was blanketed in white powdery freshness. As we zig-zagged steadily up switchbacks, I watched the sunlight catch the ice crystals drifting down from the heavy boughs and turn them into millions of tiny diamonds and was gripped with the familiar sense of wonder.

Intriguing animal tracks of all shapes and sizes crisscrossed the forest floor. Like always, I passed the time deciphering the stories they told. A ruffed grouse track ended in a pile of feathers next to the imprint of a goshawk wing. The determined prowl of a bobcat intersected with the long hops of a snowshoe hare and veered off into a chase. When we came upon a deer carcass ravaged by a pack of wolves, my musings took a sinister turn, complete with a chill down my spine. A little clearing beside the trail looked like a battlefield. A large patch of snow was trampled down to bare ground and trashed bushes, hair, and smears of bright blood were everywhere.

My dogs sped up and swerved toward it, sniffing the ground with hackles raised. Their lines went all floppy, and they started to pile up. I stomped on the brake. "Stay ahead!" My voice shattered the silence, stabbed my own ears.

Earl veered back toward the middle of the trail, hauling the team with him. On the way past the carcass, Harley reached down and snatched up a leg bone in his mouth. He carried it for a mile or so before finally dropping it. It's an oddball quirk of his, picking up stuff on the trail and carrying it for a while as he runs: a bootie, a patch of deer hide, a 1969 Shelby Mustang GT500. Crazy dog.

We worked our way steadily up the mountain, and soon the wolf kill was well behind us. After an hour of solid running, we crested the top and came out of the trees onto a bare ridge. Below us, the vast white wilderness spread out like a great topographical map. We were high enough to see almost all the way to Canada. I knew these mountains were crawling with mushers, but I couldn't see a single sign of life. I slowed my team to savor the view. I was the lord, and this was my fiefdom. I lifted my arms in the air and whooped, turning a raised hand into a fist pump. Mojo swiveled her ears back toward me but kept running straight down the trail.

"It's all right, Moj. Keep ahead . . . that a girl!"

It was more than all right; it was awesome! Dogsledding had given me a whole treasure trove of wow moments, and up here alone on the top of the world—this was the Hope Diamond.

I let my team fly down the mountain at full throttle. I shouldn't have, but I was just having so much fun, I couldn't help myself. They were too. My dogs' feet kicked up little tufts of snow as they dug in. We whipped around switchbacks, the icy wind whistling through my massive grin, their tongues flying, ears laid back, tails down. Laughing, I played the sled back and forth to miss the larger mounds. Once it flipped onto its side, but I stayed with it, and it bounced back onto its runners, all the time careening down the hill. I was flying high on self-esteem and adrenaline, too caught up in my own coolness and the excitement of the race to play it safe.

I knew better in that "come back to bite you in the gluteus maximums" kind of way.

Near the bottom of the mountain, the snow machine track we'd been following hooked onto a county road. Just for fun, I crouched low, stuck my left foot out and dug the heel of my boot in to carve a tighter turn as we smoked around the bend. This one was just bragging. I marveled at the freedom in my body, what I could do with it. Every part of me felt lit up.

Colt was pulling hard and running perfectly—not goofing off for once. Dad had been right; Colt was just fine. All my dogs were fine—great even. They were all running together as if listening to the same beat of a drum. My heart squeezed with pride. I had the best dogs in the world. Everything was going so well, it was easy to forget all the things I'd been so worried about. Four or five hours from now we'd all be digging into hot dinners at the Whitetail Ranch checkpoint. Then after our mandatory six hours of rest, together we'd blow through the last fifty miles.

The county road was a wide, straight-ahead path of no resistance for my dogs. They chugged along at a ground-eating trot. After an exciting race-against-the-Nazis daydream with Dave Armstrong and our dog teams to recover a top-secret Norton bomb-site from a plane downed on an iceberg in the North Atlantic just in the nick of time, I put in my earbuds and tapped a playlist on my iPod. Music exploded into my skull, drowning out the world. Soon my heart was thumping in time with the heavy bass pummeling my eardrums.

Have you ever heard of the "Butterfly Effect?" Well, it's the idea that the flap of a butterfly's wing in Brazil can set off a chain of events in the atmosphere that, weeks later, spur on the formation of a tornado in Texas—basically, something small can snowball into chaos.

Putting in those earbuds was my wing flap.

My dogs ran down the open road on autopilot. An endless corridor of trees flashed by while I lost myself in my music. Time grew elastic. It wasn't until the sight of a truck moving up ahead struck me odd, like a piano out of tune, that I realized my mistake.

I ripped out my earbuds. "Gaaaaaahhhh!" I shrieked through clenched teeth. "Idiot. Idiot. *Idiot!*"

Heat flooded my face. I'd been mad at myself before but never like this. I had both the urge to burst into tears and to break something. The race was barely two hours old, and I'd already let down my guard. I'd been too busy in La-la Land to notice a little thing like the Cool Lakes Loop turnoff! We'd blown right past it! Seven or eight miles ago!

Somewhere between my crash at the start of the race and that whoop at the top of the mountain, my ego had chased away the healthy fear that had been stalking me for weeks. Shame tasted bitter on my tongue. Dad was halfway around the Cool Lakes Loop by now, and I'd added nearly two hours of time to my run! What's more, if I didn't get my team stopped fast, we'd all soon be roadkill on Highway 200.

I stomped on the brakes with both feet. "Whoa, whoaaaa . . . good dogs."

We came to a halt not ten feet from the stop sign at the highway intersection just as an old Ford truck zoomed by. Standing on the brakes, I looked around frantically, trying to figure out how to anchor the team so I could get us turned around.

The road was too hard packed here to sink a snowhook, the snow too soft and fluffy on the sides to hold it. *How can I do this without losing my team?* I dabbed at the base of my cold, drippy nose with a gloved finger and chewed on my lip.

I glanced up and noticed that the two dark clouds on the horizon had grown and spread up the sky. Bright pieces of rainbow flanked a wide, hazy ring that had formed around the sun. Sundogs. I grimaced. Loved the name; hated the omen. Those pretty prisms of color meant a storm was coming.

Crap. Crap. Crap . . .

The wind had picked up too, but just a little. We still had time. If we hurried, we could be over Huckleberry Pass before the snow got too thick.

I grabbed one of my two snowhooks from its holster. In a flurry of movements, I sprang off the sled, dragged it to the side of the road, and caught the prongs of the snowhook around the metal pole of the stop sign.

My dogs dove into the deep snow and began frisking happily and chomping mouthfuls of fluff. I grabbed the neckline connecting my leaders and pulled the dogs out of the snow before they got into a massive tangle or even worse, a little spat. We didn't have time for that.

Jogging hard, I swung them in a wide arc until they were pointed in the opposite direction. Then I walked backward along the road to stretch out the team. "Stay ahead, Harley!" I called over my shoulder as I hightailed it back to the sled. Earl was already leaning into his tugline, holding the gangline tight behind him.

I sprang back onto the runners and bent to release the hook. "Ready!"

My dogs screamed and jumped into the air, jerking the sled forward. The snowhook hit the metal pole with a loud clank, and the tether snapped taut. I hissed air through my teeth. No way was I getting that snowhook off the stop sign under all that pressure. "Easy," I crooned, feeling anything but *easy*.

They ignored me, of course.

I hopped off, then went down the line petting and calming each dog. When they were all simmered down again, I ran back to the sled, climbed on the runners, and reached for the snowhook. My dogs went berserk. Before I'd even touched metal, the brush bow jerked off the ground, and the snowhook tether was quivering like a bowstring. Pounding the handlebar with my gloved palm, my head fell back, and I growled at the sky.

What followed was the most frustrating, worthless, humiliating half hour of my life. Every time I got my dogs all calmed down and on a stay, and I'd reach for the snowhook, they'd surge ahead so hard, I couldn't get it off the stop sign.

I snacked them. I begged them. I threatened their lives. Nothing worked. They just grinned up at me, tongues lolling, silvery breaths drifting upward until I reached for the snowhook. Then they instantly turned into feral beasts bent on pulling the earth from its axis. I was stuck on a stop sign eight miles from the trail, and the sky was growing darker by the minute.

As I stood on the runners in a frustrated slump, wrestling with a hard decision, a huge gust of wind caught me from the side, lifting my eyelids from my eyeballs and driving needle-sharp points of ice into them from off the ground. The old panic reached up and squeezed off my breathing. We had to get going.

Now.

I took my anorak parka from the sled bag, pulled it on over my Skinny Leg Sled Dog coat then fished out my knife. When I bent to the snow hook, the dogs went wild and the tether snapped taut. With one swift upward stroke, I cut it. Shock waves rippled through the stop sign, and my head whiplashed back as we shot forward.

The dogs pounded up the road pulling hard as if they knew we needed to make up some time. "Easy. Easy, dogs," I called out, encouraging them to drop back to their trots. We still had a long way to go.

Because of you. The dark voice was a low hum in my ear. *And now with only one snowhook, idiot.*

I hunched my shoulders against the wind and glanced at the sky again. Now the sun was hanging over my left shoulder. Beside the sundogs and the soft, white halo, it was giving off some strange new rays. We had under three hours until dark—probably less until snow started to fly.

And at least six to the Whitetail Ranch, imbecile, hissed the evil fiend.

I set my jaw. "That's okay. We still have lots of juice in us. Don't we, dogs?"

At the sound of my voice, Mojo glanced back at me. Her eyes were so full of trust and adoration, I quickly looked away.

You'd better not make any more stupid mistakes, or you'll really be up a creek.

I'm not planning on it, I snapped inwardly. My body was tense, my eyes and ears everywhere at once: the road, the sky, the gangline, the dogs. Stuff happened, but no way would my stupidity be the cause of another setback for us. I'd learned my lesson.

Colt though, he was just getting started. The stop sign wasn't even out of sight when he turned around and started messing with Tenille. His tugline went slack, and with him tripping along all twisted up like a pretzel, the whole rhythm of the team went all out of whack.

"Knock it off, Colt!" I yelled as a new tendril of worry snaked into my gut.

Colt faced forward and went back on his tug. But a minute hadn't passed before he twisted around again to look at me. "Colt, stay ahead!"

It was too late. He'd stepped over his slack tugline with his back leg and started hobbling, slowing the whole team. All the dogs' ears twitched back when I groaned with frustration.

We limped along until I found a spot in the road soft enough to hold a snowhook. I kicked it in then crossed my fingers that it would hold as I dashed over to Colt. It only took a few seconds to sort out his tug. But even that was too long. One hard lunge from Harley was all it took to pop the snowhook. Heart racing, I grabbed the sled as it whisked by and swung onto the runners.

A tense hour of yells and threats at Colt followed. When I finally saw the Cool Lakes Loop trail marker sticking up out of the snow, the rubber band around my chest loosened a little. "Gee!" My leaders cut right, and we swung off the road back onto a snowmobile track. I'd never been so glad to be anywhere in my life.

We headed into a thickly wooded, twisty section of trail. On the steep parts, I pedaled my foot to help the dogs pull, careful not to work up a sweat and get damp. Sweat, of all things, could kill. On a straightaway, I withdrew my insulated water bottle from my sled bag, took a swig and put it back. It was easy to get dehydrated out here. There were so many things to remember, and now they were all shouting at the top of their lungs in my ears.

The wind was really blowing hard now. I ignored it. All I cared about was keeping my dogs on their tugs (I'm looking at you, Colt) and putting trail behind us.

Not very far into the loop, I could tell by the way my dogs' ears perked forward and their increased speed that there was something ahead. They always smelled and heard things way before I did. More canine superpowers I wished I had.

In front of us, the trail disappeared around a blind curve, a thick stand of pines shielding my view. As the dogs took the corner, I bent my knees and leaned out from the handlebar. We skidded, a little fan of snow spraying out from the runners as we sailed around it. The dogs had good speed coming out of the turn, and when we got to a straight stretch, I glanced up the trail, expecting to see an ermine or a deer. Instead, I saw another team coming straight at us.

My head reared back in confusion. It took a second for the smoke from my firecracker thoughts to clear and my brain to zero in on the driver. Suddenly, I had the feeling that the world was slipping away right before my feet.

"You're going the wrong way, buddy!" Dad shouted through the wind.

I squeezed my eyes shut wishing I could simply cease to exist. Who was I to ever believe I could do this? It was too big. Too hard. Too *everything*. And I was too inept in *every single way*. "In way over my head," didn't even begin to describe it. *What* had I been thinking?!

Somewhere deep inside me, a wound I'd foolishly thought healed burst open and spread like poison through my veins. *You thought you could change who you are—that's what. But you were wrong. Once a loser, always a loser.*

Dad was right on us now. Our leaders met in the middle, and our teams began to brush by. Heads swiveled, and our dogs sniffed and took little swipes at each other as they passed. When the fronts of our sleds were nose to nose, I dropped my gaze and studied the miniature mountain ranges of snow that had built up on the tops of my boots.

"It doesn't matter," Dad said as we crossed paths mere feet from each other. "Don't turn around. Just finish the loop."

I swiped angrily at the salty runoff under my nose with a fist. It *did* matter. It mattered so much it felt like a cheese grater shredding my insides because I'd messed up *again*. It mattered because it proved I couldn't do anything right. It was that infamous missed tackle times ten.

"Hey, Spence."

Dad's voice broke through the rush of blood in my ears. I glanced back. He was looking over his shoulder at me. I forced myself to look him in the face. Behind his massive fur ruff, it was ruddy with windburn, yet it glowed like the sun.

"Chin up," he said enthusiastically. "You're doing great!"

Great? I gave a dubious shake of my head, not trusting myself to speak, then pulled my nose down into my frozen neck gaiter to hide my trembling chin.

"You haven't lost your team, and you're not carrying a dog in your bag," he called. Then he flashed me a smile—and it was so genuine, his eyes so sparkly with unmistakable pride, I believed him.

Later, I'd turn to that look in my mind to draw strength from him to keep going. For now, I was so galvanized by his praise, not even having to slink by all those other teams heading the opposite direction could demoralize me.

The wind though, that would prove to be another story altogether.

Chapter 25

About an hour into the Cool Lakes Loop, we glided out of the trees onto the first of the two Keep Cool Lakes. A blank expanse of white spread out before us like milk held in the cupped palms of the mountains. I thought it a really pretty sight. Then we came out into the open, and a gust of wind nearly tore my head off.

There was driving, painful snow swept up from off the ground in that wind. It barged inside my hood, jabbed into my eyes, even blew up my nostrils. Gasping, I tightened my grip on the handlebar and deepened my stance on the runners as I fought for balance.

I couldn't see the front end of my team in the sudden, icy blast, could barely make out Charlie and Marlin at wheel, but I could feel my dogs floundering. When the gust blew past and I got a good look at my team, a sense of dread seeped past muscle and bone and settled in my core. Instead of heading in a straight line across the frozen lake, they were wandering aimlessly, all out of synch with each other while the sled lurched along in fits and starts behind them.

I stomped on the brake and made a quick, desperate scan of the lake. Layers of snowy waves swept across the surface and mingled with the flakes just starting to fall from the swiftly darkening sky. I tried to swallow, but my pounding heart was right up in the middle of my throat. Squinting, I braced myself against another blast and scoured the lake again with mounting horror. But I knew it was no use. The trail was gone—wiped completely away by the wind and blowing snow. We were in trouble. Up a creek without a paddle trouble, and everyone else was long gone.

"Not good. Not good. Not good!"

In a break between gusts, I spotted something way off in the middle of the lake. I narrowed my eyes at the tiny toothpick poking out of the snow. Sure enough, it was a trail marker! *If* we could get to it, I could probably spot another one from there.

That *if* dropped like a big stone in my middle, making it harder to breathe. The trail marker might as well have been the flag on the moon. I couldn't simply point it out and tell my dogs to take me there. They needed a trail to follow.

Oh, that's right, we no longer had one. Because of me. If I hadn't squandered two and a half hours by missing the Cool Lakes Loop turnoff, we would be ahead of this storm instead of stuck out here on the edge of the lake.

I braced my hands against the handlebar and scowled out into the fury. All our problems up to this point had only been a warm-up. The true test of our endurance and our battle against the elements began now. This sudden realization staggered me.

If it's bad, someone who loves me will come along and fix it—I'd lived nearly thirteen years under this certainty. That's how it had always been. But as I stood on the edge of that uncrossable lake ducking my head against wind-driven snow, I knew it had been an illusion. There was nobody to make sure I didn't fall or lose my team, to stop this wind and blowing snow, hold my hand and help me over the next hill, or to get my team to that impossible trail marker out in the middle of the lake.

I was on my own.

Instead of paralyzing me, this truth brought with it a strange sort of power, a weightless sense of freedom. I lifted my face to the wind and dashed snow from my eyes with a shaky hand. This was my life, my problem, my decision. Whatever happened next was up to me. Dad believed in me. Mom believed in me. Joey and Nico believed in me. I needed to start believing in myself too. I was the master of my own fate. Sheesh. Now my thoughts sounded like an inspirational Hallmark card. But really, how amazing would it be to succeed in my own way?

Or fail, whispered the evil fiend, but I turned my back on its ugly face.

The tracker pinned to the sled bag thrashed against the canvas in the wind. They'd have to chip my cold, dead body out of the ice before I pushed that red button. I refused to even glance at it. There had to be a way across this lake. It was in me somewhere, and I was determined to find it. I couldn't let fear take control of my brain. I had to think, and I had to think clearly.

Within seconds I knew what to do. I'd move out in front of the dogs on snowshoes and lead them from trail marker to trail marker until we were back in the shelter of the trees.

But my plan had a flaw—a flaw that wore a hangman's hood.

The only thing I don't like about Montana winters are the super short days, and this one was fading fast. Only a whisper of sunlight was visible behind the boiling stew of low, gray clouds. In the distance, the stand of timber which connected the two lakes appeared as a single black blob. It would be slow going to walk across the lakes on snowshoes, and soon it would be too dark to see.

I ransacked my head for a better plan but came up empty-handed. I'd have to settle for hoping I could find the reflective trail markers by the light of my headlamp. The thought of taking one step in the wrong direction in the dark scared the spit out of me, but I decided I'd rather go out swinging than not try at all.

When I reached down for the zipper on my sled bag, my attention snagged on Earl. His head was raised, and he was surveying the lake. His brain was thinking so hard I could almost hear it whir. My fingers froze on the zipper pull, and I watched him with my whole body, each breath lodged like a bullet in my chest. Then Earl froze too, his nose pointing straight at the marker.

"No way!" I murmured in a rush of ghostly air as I was gripped with a wild new hope.

My dogs were whining and fidgeting and making little nervous growls at each other. But when Earl threw his shoulders into his harness and lugged us forward a few feet, they all snapped to attention.

I scrambled off the brake, and Earl set off toward the trail marker. The rest of the dogs followed while I watched in stunned disbelief. When Earl reached the marker, he paused and scanned the ocean of white. Another trail marker was barely visible in the gloom. He made a beeline for it.

Relentless gusts of wind howled across the lake, doing their best to knock me off the sled. I rode humped up, white-knuckling the handlebar, my down-turned face clenched against the driving snow while the team moved crablike to keep us heading in the right direction and Earl played a living game of dot to dot. The going was brutal, but I didn't care; we were going to make it! I bit back a whoop. Earl's wizardry was going to get us across this lake!

I should have known that it was too easy, too good to be true, that something would happen to ruin it.

Colt happened.

He twisted around to see what Tenille was doing and caught a leg over his tugline. When he began to stumble, Tenille plowed into him and got the gangline wrapped around her ankle. The team instantly slowed to a crawl.

Fury rose in my throat and lodged there like a glowing piece of coal. Dad had been wrong. Colt wasn't fine! He was a screw off! I should never have brought him! He was ruining everything! I'd never been so angry in my whole life. I wanted to launch myself off the sled, grab Colt by his ears and shake the teeth out of his head, shake some sense into him. Didn't he know what serious trouble we were in! I was going to drop him at the Whitetail Ranch and never use him again! Better yet, I would give him to an old lady as a pet. That would serve him right.

The Whitetail. My gut twisted. Twilight was rinsing the last bit of color from the landscape. We would never get to the Whitetail now. No way could I stop the sled to fix tangles out here with a single snowhook—not if I ever wanted to see my team again. So, we hobbled along, my hope fading with the light. My head felt like it was going to blow off my neck.

By the time we reached the shelter of the timber, I could barely make out my leaders. I flicked on my headlamp and found myself in a whirlpool of snowflakes swirling around my head like a colossal swarm of mosquitos. I anchored the team to a tree, untangled their tugs and wrestled the dogs back in place while night mobilized against us. When we finally came out on the other side of the timber, the world had plunged into total darkness. No moon. No stars. No nothing but a thick, cold winter night.

Deadly night.

My range of vision had shrunk down to my headlamp boring a tunnel through the heavy black. Breathing fast, I twisted my head from side to side desperate to catch in my beam the reflective diamond of a trail marker out on the second lake. But all I could see was endless flying snow.

When Earl raised his head to peer out into the darkness, a hollow pit opened inside me. Not even Dog Wonder could see trail markers in this, and if we wandered out on that lake now, we'd get so lost not even aliens could find us. I tried to swallow but couldn't. I was truly and deeply scared for the first time in the race.

But Earl hadn't revealed all his superpowers yet. Why was I even surprised?

He dropped his head and smelled the ground, and I instantly went blind and deaf to everything but him. I saw his ears jerk forward when he got a bit of scent, and the hairs prickled on the back of my neck. Then he started to run.

He ran through the pitch black with his nose down all the time, following the scent of the trail. You know in Star Wars when Han Solo puts the Millennium Falcon into hyperdrive; well, it was like that as we hurtled through the darkness across that big open lake with snowflakes streaking at me in my beam.

Earl ran and ran, sensing with his nose and his feet where the previous tracks lay beneath the new layers of snow. I almost did not believe a dog could do this. But Earl did it! He brought us safely across that lake in the dark. It was his ultimate superpower.

And it felt like a miracle.

Chapter 26

When we came off the lake back into the shelter of the trees, the trail materialized beneath our feet. I ached to throw my arms around Earl, to shower him with pats and scratches, to tell him how amazing he was, but I didn't dare stop for even a minute.

We'd already been running for six hours. We had about an hour back to the fork in the trail plus another hour over Huckleberry Pass to the Whitetail. My dogs needed hot meat, rest, their feet checked and doctored. But the snow was really coming down now, and the tracks were filling up fast. If we didn't push hard to make it over the pass, my leaders would have to swim through deep snow. Breaking trail makes extra work, and my dogs were already running on fumes.

I cast worried glances from dog to dog with eyes half closed to shield them from the flakes pelting my face. Everyone looked good until my gaze landed on Tenille. My heart gave an extra hard bang. *Please, no, no, no!* I strained to see through the snow-choked air. But even though the whiteout made everything hazy and unreal, that rhythmic bob of her head was unmistakable. Tenille was limping.

Panic is like a trick candle. Just when I thought it was out, it sizzled back to life. I whoa-ed my team to a stop, kicked in my snow-hook, then dropped to my knees in the snow beside her. I whipped off my mitts and held them between my teeth while I gingerly felt her right front leg. My hands trembled with nerves. I slowly extended her leg forward to check her range of motion then flexed her wrist, watching for a reaction. I pulled off her bootie and pointed my headlamp down on her paw to check her pads and between her toes. No ice chucks. No cracks. No rubs.

My bare fingers quickly grew stiff with cold. I had to keep tucking them into my armpits to thaw them. While they waited for me, the rest of the dogs rolled around on their backs or lay on their bellies, shoveling mouthfuls of snow. Colt stuck his snout in the crook between my head and my neck and snuffled in my ear, his butt swaying back and forth with fierce wagging. "Go away," I snapped, elbowing him aside as I worked.

When I rotated Tenille's shoulder, she growled and pulled away. I squeezed my eyes shut as my head fell forward. *My fault. My fault. My fault!* That first mountain. Letting them fly on the downhill. She'd injured it then. I knew it in my gut.

I felt sick. I wished I could hit a delete key to wipe away all my mistakes and start over from the gate. It was hard to imagine all that excitement and happy blue sky had been part of this very same day. It seemed part of another life.

Harley yowled and popped his tug to get going again. "Shush, Harley. Settle down," I said, trying to keep my voice light for them. Worry is the last thing a sled dog team needs to hear from its leader.

I rubbed at the knot of pain building between my eyebrows. We were hours off track. This storm was already going to slow us way down, and a dog in the bag would slow us even more. Tired was an understatement. I was starving. My toe warmers had conked out an hour ago, so my feet were big blocks of ice. All the other mushers were long gone over the pass. I was as alone as alone could be out here. It was a "last person on earth" sensation that hollowed my rib cage and squeezed off my air. My whole world had narrowed to the scope of my headlamp with everything around it an endless black void.

A black void with a heartbeat.

A tremor skittered through me, and I shrank in on myself. When we'd first started mushing, night runs freaked me out a bit, but I'd learned to love them right away. At night the woods came alive with smells, sights, and sounds that were missing during the day. Nothing beat streaking through an eternal black and white painting full of shadow and mystery while the world was more dreamscape than real. It was the perfect time to go spelunking in my head.

Not tonight.

Instead of friendly, the darkness felt like a predator. As I knelt there in the snow beside my injured dog, it pressed in against me, was breathing down my neck. The snow squeaked beneath me as I shifted from knee to knee. My breath ran shallow and tight.

A shriek howled through the trees—a ghost from the underworld come to drag me down where demons would tear strips of flesh from my bones. Ba Dum. Ba Dum. Ba Dum. My heartbeat seemed to echo in my ears. I squeezed my eyes shut against the darkness as if not seeing it would make all the scary stuff go away. I had the urge to throw my arms over my head and ball up in the snow.

I was dimly aware of a nudge against my leg. When my eyes came back into focus, I found that Mojo had crossed over the gangline and was wedging herself between me and Tenille. She put her chin on my thigh and gazed up at me. Her foxlike face was tipped in frost. Her eyes shone liquid gold in my headlamp and brimmed with more love and trust than I deserved.

I plowed my fingers into her ruff and greedily tugged her against my body. The rest of the world fell away around us until it was just me and the dog who thought I hung the moon. I clung to her like a tiny piece of driftwood in an eternal black sea while I panted silently into her neck and snowflakes piled up on my back.

Her calm poured into me. The predator backed away a step at a time. When my heart had quieted, and I trusted my legs to hold my weight, with a final scratch behind her ears, I put Mojo away from me and pushed to my feet. It was the hardest thing I'd ever done.

I shoved my frozen hands back into my mitts, unclipped Tenille's lines and gathered her into my arms. "I'm sorry, girl," I murmured against her head as I hustled back to the sled. The words burned in my throat. When I put her in the bag, her forlorn eyes told me exactly how she felt about it.

Truth is, it dejected us all.

Once we were on the move again, everyone except for Earl started fidgeting, looking back, going on and off their tugs as they ran. A teammate in the sled bag always shakes a team's confidence. But it was more than that. It was me. I knew they were keying off my emotions. I scoffed inwardly. I'd been so cocky when I'd told that reporter I couldn't afford to be nervous. We weren't even halfway through the race, and I was already a basket case. I needed to fix this, and now.

Think. Think. Think!

I ran around frantically in my head opening and slamming doors, looking for one that didn't have a Dementor or knife-wielding serial killer lurking behind it. When I saw the door with a golden nameplate that read, "Alphabet Freak Show" in fancy script, I felt a quiver of amusement despite everything. *That's it!* I thought and yanked it open. Light and warmth poured out. I dove inside and pulled the door shut behind me.

I took a deep breath, trying to find some courage in the frigid air. "Take a seat everyone, grab a tub of popcorn and your complimentary packet of Advil for the headache you are about to get!" I called out to my dogs in my best announcer's voice. I was relieved to hear it barely had a quiver despite a thousand terrors ready to detach themselves from the shadowy places and carve out my liver or suck out my soul. "On tonight's episode of Alphabet Freak Show—Words That Don't Rhyme but Should. With special guests—Wacky Words and How to Say Them."

My dogs' ears swiveled back at the sound of my voice, and they picked up a little speed.

"If *womb* is pronounced 'woom' and *tomb* is pronounced 'toom,' why isn't *bomb* pronounced 'boom?' Welcome to the English Language!" Though the air stung my face with the ferocity of a thousand tracker jackers, I went on brightly, "*Cough, rough, though, bough.* Why the heck don't these words rhyme, but for some crazy reason *pony* and *bologna* do? Makes no sense! Don't even get me started on *horse* and *worse* or *busy* and *dizzy.*"

Words had always been my happy place, and they didn't disappoint me now. Even with so much stacked against us, the knots tying up my guts were starting to loosen.

"Is the S or C silent in *scissors*? Anyone, anyone? I've never been able to figure it out. And why do we call it a 'build*ing*' if it's already been built? I'm glad English is my first language because if I had to learn it now, I'd probably paint my naked self in honey and sunbathe on an anthill."

Tenille stared up at me from the sled bag like I'd lost my stinking mind. I probably had. But I'd take crazy with a side of looney wrapped up in a straitjacket any day if it got us to the Whitetail. My dogs were all back on their tugs, facing forward, seeming happier too, so I soldiered on.

"Take the word *queue*. It's spelled Q-U-E-U-E. It means 'a line of people waiting their turn,' and is pronounced, Kyoo. Write down five letters, only pronounce the first. I'm not content with this content!" I huffed a slightly hysterical laugh. "Why can't we just say 'line'?"

"*Colonel* and *kernel*. How can two words spelled so dif—" An eerie howl stopped my sentence as if cut by a knife. The air in my lungs evaporated instantly.

Wolf!

It was close. Like pellet gun close. An answering howl rose up somewhere in front of us. This one had many voices and stiffened the hairs on my arms. My dogs' ears perked up, and they sniffed the air nervously.

I had a strong and undeniable sense of being stared at. I went ramrod straight on the runners, my eyes sweeping back and forth, desperate for x-ray vision to penetrate the dark while that gruesome wolf kill from earlier played through my mind in IMAX.

"Non-English speakers voted 'diarrhea'—" My voice broke on "diarrhea," so I cleared away the Lego that had lodged itself in my throat and tried again. "Non-English speakers voted 'diarrhea' the most beautiful sounding word in the English language," I said in the loudest, calmest voice I could muster. I needed the wolves to know we were here. *Please just be passing through! Please just be passing through!* "J. R. R. Tolkien claimed that 'cellar door' is most pleasing to the ear. He wrote *The Hobbit* and *The Lord of the Rings* series which total 1,187,677 words. I say that makes him the expert."

My eyes were at full stretch. My ears felt like they'd grown points like a cat's I was listening so hard. I hardly registered what was coming out of my mouth. I just kept blabbering on while we put trail in the rearview mirror. Thankfully, we didn't hear any more howls, and when my dogs settled, I did too—one tiny muscle at a time.

We finished the Cool Lakes Loop then wound our way back up the Hope Diamond mountain, cutting fresh tracks in the snow. Our travel was painfully slow. We were practically moving blind in the blizzard, and the low visibility rattled me even more than I was already rattled.

I pulled out my Jelly Bellies, popped a few in my mouth for a distraction and nearly broke my teeth. After that, I held them in my cheek a few at a time to soften while I mumbled through Screwball Plurals and Twenty Tricky Tongue Twisters to keep my rising panic at bay and to urge my dogs along. We still had the Huckleberry Pass to conquer, and it was a doozy on a good day, and now, *this*.

I'd just begun episode five of Alphabet Freak Show—I before E, the Dastardliest of All Double-Dealers when we started on a downhill. I flipped down my drag mat to keep my dogs from gaining too much speed. "I before E except when your caffeinated neighbor, Keith, pulls off a feisty heist, seizing eight counterfeit, beige sleighs from foreign weight lifters. Weird," I said around the frozen candy in my mouth. "See! Treachery at its finest!"

My eyes were peeled for the stake marking the Huckleberry Pass turnoff as I talked. I knew it was coming up fast. "All right, students, remember: I before E except after C. Now it's time to switch subjects. Let's learn about *science*." My little chuckle at my cleverness fizzled out when the front half of my team suddenly vanished around a bend in the trail.

I tried to lead the sled to the outside so that I'd have a wider turning radius, but it's almost impossible to steer a sled with the weight of a dog in the basket. My dogs cut to the inside as the sled whipped around the curve. I stepped on the brake. Big mistake. In an instant, my sled was sucked into the corner of the turn. When I felt the runner sink into mashed-potato snow, icy, liquid metal shot through my veins.

I was toast.

The sled tipped up on one runner. I was so stiff and exhausted, I couldn't correct it. I felt a brief moment of weightlessness as my legs flew up. Then I was engulfed in soft snow.

The sled clattered onto its side. I gripped the handlebar with everything left in me as I started to drag. I tried frantically to right the sled, to pull myself back up and on, but the soft snow, it was like trying to climb Jell-O. My hands were slipping. I was so weak! No matter what, I couldn't let go!

My muscles shook. I was losing my grip! My arms were on fire, legs numb. When I lifted my head to see where we were going, I got a face full of snow, and my grip slipped even further. *Hold on. Hold on. Hold on!*

Snow clogged my nose, packed my mouth. Something sharp gouged my hip, lit it on fire. My back arched reflexively. My cry of pain came out as a gurgle.

I dug my knees into the snow to slow us, but the force of the snow piling up on my thighs just made my grip slip another inch. *Don't let go!*

I couldn't see, could not hang on much longer. The dam burst and the panic rising inside me flooded into my throat, blocking my windpipe. *I can't lose my team!*

The sled bounced, wrenched free of my hands. I clawed after it. My fingers brushed against a runner before closing on air. I glanced up just as my sled was swallowed up in the storm. Then I was face down on the trail.

Alone.

Chapter 27

I raised my head out of the snow to find an utter, spine-chilling black. It was as if I'd been stuffed into a body bag and locked in the trunk of a car. My heart was racing like I'd just sprinted a marathon. I couldn't seem to breathe.

My hand flew up, and I groped for the face of my headlamp with trembling fingers. I tapped it a few times. Nothing. It was dead!

Like you without your dogs, the evil fiend said menacingly in my ear.

Panic gripped me, stringing every muscle in my body so tight it hurt. A scream rose in my throat. I choked it down. I knew if I started, I wouldn't stop. I jammed my hands into my armpits and pulled my knees to my chest. My lips started to tremble. Like a baby, I felt my face crumple. *Get a grip, Spencer!* Crying wouldn't solve anything.

I took a few deep breaths and forced my limbs to unfold, then struggled to sit up in the snow. The black was so thick I felt isolated in a vacuum of darkness. I had the sensation of floating, of being unattached to my surroundings. I longed to surrender to it, to simply fall back and drift away. Then the black hole in my chest swallowed up every thought but one.

Must get team!

I yanked off my glove and fumbled inside my pocket for my spare batteries. I pulled two out. My hand was so stiff it wouldn't close. One of the batteries rolled from my fingers and fell with a gentle *pfft*, sinking into the snow.

Gone.

For a few seconds, I gave in to my fear and let myself shake. Snow was packed solidly up my sleeves, down my neck, and up my nose. I was alone. Without light. In millions of acres of national forest land. In a blizzard. Wet. Freezing. I'd lost my team, my sled, my gear. I had no way of summoning help. Never in a million years would anyone find me out here.

Or your decomposing body next spring, chuckled the evil fiend.

I'm going to die! I'm going to die! I felt a hot wet patch start to spread inside my pants. "Find your team, idiot!" I snarled in self-disgust as I pinched off the flow.

I ripped off my headlamp and fiddled with the latch on the battery compartment. My hands were shaking so bad, it took a few tries to open it. I pried out a dead battery, put it in my other pocket and maneuvered the fresh one in while cold seeped through my snow clothes and into my core. Teeth chattering, I fished out my last fresh battery and snapped it into place. A long beam shot out like a lightsaber, illuminating a great swath of forest. My breath came out in a rush.

I arranged my headlamp back on my forehead, dragged my hood up, then lurched to my feet. Melting snow dribbled down the back of my neck. I pulled my waistbands down a few inches and shined the light on my bare skin. A bloody four-inch gash slashed across my hipbone. I hissed in pain. No vital organs were spilling out, and there was nothing I could do about it now anyway, so I yanked my clothes back in place and put it from my mind. My sleeves had jammed up to my elbows and my arms stung with freezer burn. Every part of me ached as if I'd gone through the rinse cycle. I didn't care. Nothing mattered but catching my team.

I pointed my beam at the ground and quickly swept it back and forth until I found the tracks my dogs had made. They were already filling with snow. I broke into a shambling run. I used my arms and pumped my legs as fast as I could manage, but I might as well have been moving through molasses. I'd never despised my skinny leg more than I did right then. The soft trail and my heavy boots shackled my footsteps, and my awkward gait slowed me even more.

You'll never catch them, gimp!

Instead of discouraging me, that thought shot a big squirt of adrenaline into my system. I ran harder than I'd ever run in my life. The storm was insane, making it nearly impossible to see. I knew it wouldn't be long before I lost the trail altogether, so I ran my awkward, hobbyhorse run until I felt like puking then kept galumphing along through the snow.

I came to where my dogs had swerved crazily into a thick stand of trees. I could barely make out the rabbit tracks that had sent them veering off into a chase. I leaped over downfall and charged through the underbrush after them. My hood was knocked back. Branches slashed across my frozen face. I stumbled, face-planted in the snow, got up, stumbled again. Kept going.

My breath began to tear from my lungs in jagged bursts. I felt a thrum and burn in every muscle. Sweat soaked my base layer. I didn't care. I was dead anyway if I didn't find my team. *Don't think. Just run. One foot, then the other. Keep moving. Must get dogs!*

I half slid/half scrambled down a slope then stuttered to a stop. I whipped to the left. No trail. I whipped to the right. No trail. I pressed my fists to the sides of my head as I spun in a complete circle. The trail was gone! Erased by the storm, blown in by the wind.

Blood pounded in my ears. I went limp to my fingertips. I was so close to collapsing in clamoring, babbling fear. No matter how bad things had gotten today, there'd always been a spark of hope. Now there wasn't one left.

Hands on thighs, I stood there bending forward until my head was practically between my knees. As I sucked great gulps of air, fighting hysteria, I heard something. I held my breath to listen. Suddenly my stomach felt as if I'd swallowed battery acid.

Faint, horrific screaming.

I bolted ahead, my beam aimed toward the terrible sound. I skirted a stand of timber. Then I saw it. The sled was caught against downfall. My dogs were tangled in a knot, and Auke and Charlie were locked in battle. A general panic was skittering through the whole team.

"Stop. STOP!" I shrieked as I lumbered frantically through the snow toward them. "Auke, NO! . . . CHAR-LIEEE!"

Earl was hunkered down on his belly holding the line out straight the best he could. Tenille had spilled from the bag and was dancing around nervously on three legs. Mojo was cowering as far away from the dogfight as she could get while brothers Marlin and Colt bared their teeth and headbutted each other. Harley, he was popping his tug and bawling to go.

I flew at Auke and Charlie. Gasping, I stuck my face down right beside the flashing teeth and shouted into their faces. The bright light of my headlamp and the sound of my voice made them pause long enough for me to break them apart.

I started untangling like a madman, expecting carnage. But by some miracle, I didn't find any blood. I shuddered to think what I would have found even a few seconds later. At last, something to be grateful for.

Oh yeah, and I'd found my team.

But, I was lost.

Lost lost. A desperate lost. A needle in a haystack lost. A never-to-be-found-in-the-ten-million-acre-woods-that-had-sheltered-the-most-dangerous-serial-bomber-in-US-history-for-twenty-years lost.

I walked out in front of my dogs on snowshoes, leading them, trying to get back to the trail. The snow was falling so fast there was barely any space between the flakes. It muted any sounds and closed in on me as if I was in a padded room. Everything was blurred by tiny shards of white. I was so disoriented. The darkness doubled my confusion. I had no idea where we were, which direction the Whitetail lay or if the turnoff marker was ahead of us or behind us. Every direction looked the same. My stomach was lodged in my throat with how lost I was.

My traitorous mind suddenly envisioned Ted Kaczynski creeping up behind me in the silence. I whipped around, heart stumbling. *Stupid! Pull yourself together. He's in jail, idiot!* I edged the tip of my tongue around my cracked lips. "The word 'swims' upside down is still 'swims,'" I murmured as I darted glances left and right. Then I gave myself a mental slap for being such a pansy.

It didn't work.

An endless queue of psychos, masked ax murderers, and wolves with bloody muzzles paraded through my mind as I plodded through the snow, clambered over downfall and jockeyed the sled around tight corners. My shoulders were hunched, neck pulled in like a turtle's. I kept hoping that around the next turn, I'd recognize where we were. But always there was just more tangled mess, swaths of unbroken snow, and shadowy places to lurk. I felt like this forbidden forest was laughing at me, hiding the trail behind its back.

I tried to narrow my focus on my snowshoes punching through deep drifts. My strength was sapped to the bone. The cold was chewing away at me, slow and steady, while the gash on my hip throbbed in rhythm with my heart.

I glanced over my shoulder to check on my dogs. They were jumping behind me like ermine through the snow. Their jaws and eyebrows were shagged with ice. Tenille's eyes glowed back at me from where her head poked out from the sled bag, the zipper pulled up to her neck.

My heart swelled with what a good job they'd done today and how hard they'd worked. I'd asked so much of them. I hated that

I had to ask for more. I was so wet inside from all the running and sweating, my base layer stuck to my skin. To stop meant hypothermia. We had to keep moving. We had to get back on the trail.

Trail! A depth of panic was growing inside me I would not touch. No matter what, I could not allow myself to feel it. "If you're listening, God," I said in a cracked whisper. "If you're as willing to help as Mom says you are, I could use a little right now."

It was as if Dad put his hand on my shoulder. That familiar sense of peace and calm spread through me. Little by little my shoulders inched down from my ears.

It wasn't long before I took a step and something a few feet in front of me popped up out of the snow, startling me onto my rump. The reflective diamond of a trail marker shined back at me in my beam. A smile cut my lips and made them bleed.

While my dogs panted and ate snow, I stood there with my hand on my head scanning my surroundings. I could just make out where three trails led away from me like crooked spokes of a wheel. I could feel the mountain peaks looming all around me but couldn't see anything through the darkness and whiteout to help me get my bearings. I knew we needed to go west but had no idea which way that was anymore.

I pulled the trail marker from the snow, trying to puzzle it out. It had either been knocked down by a sled as it came around the corner or a gust of wind. When I touched the diamond at the top, it spun loosely on its nail. The arrow rocked to a stop pointing down at my feet.

"*Augh!*" With a roar of frustration, I hurled the stake like a javelin as hard as I could. I throw about as well as I run. It skewered a snowbank not ten yards in front of me, and it only went in halfway.

I couldn't think past not finishing, but we were up against a wall with no way over that I could see. As I paced in a little circle, a thought sailed into my skull like a Hail Mary Pass: *Let Earl have his head.*

My gaze shot to my leader. He lay on his belly, chin on crossed paws, watching me closely. Earl had been born and raised in these mountains. He knew these trails. He'd run this race lots of times. He could scent the other dogs, follow their tracks and take us to them. Hadn't I just watched him do it at the Keep Cool Lakes? *Yes!* He could use his superpowers to save us again!

Feeling fifty pounds lighter, I lined out my dogs, unstrapped my snowshoes and climbed stiffly on the runners. "Earl, go home!"

Earl stood and shook, dropped his nose to the ground and sniffed around for a minute. Then he raised his head and stared down one of the trails. He took a long look over his shoulder at me before turning back to the trail and staring down it again. Just when I thought he was going to go that way, he dragged the team over and started off in the opposite direction.

I felt ridiculously triumphant. I'd recovered my team. We were on the move again. We'd taken a beating today, but we weren't down yet. After everything we'd been through, I was more determined than ever to make it to the Whitetail. One more hard push, and we'd be there.

Now that I was standing still, it wasn't long before the shivering started. Soon my muscles were wracked with uncontrollable spasms that came from deep in my core. My teeth chattered so hard it was a wonder I didn't bite off my tongue. My skull felt stuffed with cotton, eyelids weighted by bricks. The dogs plodded on while my body drifted into a peculiar lack of sensation. I was working so hard to stay on the runners, it didn't register that we were going downhill more than up and that the forest was starting to thin out.

Time slid sideways. For the briefest of moments, I forgot where I was. Then the edge of my beam glanced off something other than trees. I came back to awareness on a sharp gasp and pointed my head-lamp at it. I blinked hard a few times against my mental clumsiness and looked again.

My knees nearly buckled beneath me as I burst into violent tears.

Chapter 28

The Race to the Sky arch loomed before us like a giant, gaping mouth. "Whoa!" I shrieked through the sobs lurching from my throat. "Whoooa!" I threw myself on the brake.

Earl had brought us back to the Start. It was dark and deserted without a sign of life in sight.

I stumbled blindly off the runners, and in a crazed frenzy, kicked in my snowhook and got the team turned around. Tails weren't wagging anymore; doggie smiles gone.

My brain fog had evaporated. Now I felt maniacal. While Earl held the line out straight, I tore through my sled bag for the trail map. Wiping my frozen tears and snot on my forearm, I studied the map by the light of my beam through swollen and stinging eyes while Harley gave the team a pep talk and calculations buzzed in my head. *Ten miles over the pass. Approximately five miles per hour with Tenille in the bag going mostly uphill in a storm.* "Two hours," I said through clenched teeth, stuffing the map into my pocket.

I understood exactly where to go now, how to bypass the Cool Lakes Loop section of the race route, cutting out the forty miles I'd already covered, and head straight over Huckleberry Pass. The marker sticking out of the snowbank, the trail to its left would take us to the Whitetail. Thanks to my terrible throw, no way would I get lost now. *Unless you lose your team again, stupid,* the evil fiend huffed, and I threw him out of my head for good.

Jaw set, I yanked out the hook. "Hike, hike!" I called out frantically. The team started off without their usual oomph. I could feel their disappointment. They'd expected the truck would be here where they'd left it with hot food and warm beds. As I watched them trot dejectedly back the way we'd just come, my eyes burned with shame for getting them into this situation even as I used words as a whip and drove them back up the mountain.

The wind blew knives. Another violent shiver took hold of me. The pain in my fingers and toes was so intense, it left me gasping. I knew I was in serious trouble. Deadly trouble. I needed to get out of these wet clothes and get dry, but our clock was running out. *Just two more hours!* I jumped off the runners and began to push to get warm.

Looking back, I truly thought we could get to the Whitetail, that I could run all the way over Huckleberry Pass in that storm. The early stages of hypothermia, exhaustion, the need to prove to myself that I could do it, and the desire to make my dad proud had all made me a little insane. Wise, old Earl though, he knew better. He'd known it at the fork in the trail.

He stopped dead in the wind.

"Earl! Hike, hike!"

He didn't move.

I started slamming the handlebar with my mittened palm. "Earl! Come on! Let's go!"

My leader laid down on the trail.

Red fireworks exploded in my skull. I shoved away from the sled and staggered down the line. No need for a snowhook now. When I reached Earl, I grabbed him by the collar and yanked. "Get up!" I growled through clenched teeth.

He wouldn't budge.

Anger gave way to desperation. Fresh tears blurred my vision. "Please, buddy," I begged as I pulled him with all my might. He stared up at me with big, solemn eyes and calmly refused. Behind him, the rest of the dogs sat soberly down in the snow.

My legs gave way, and I crumpled onto my leader. "Please, Earl, take me to the Whitetail. Just a little bit longer. I know we can make it," I sobbed into his icy ruff while he gently licked the tears spilling down my cheek. I felt a warm, comforting body burrow against my heaving back and instinctively knew it was Mojo. That's when I knew I had failed.

Something inside me broke. Every muscle in my body contracted savagely, pulling me into a ball as all the anguish and loneliness and failure of twelve years ripped and clawed and tore its way out. "I'm sorry, Dad. I'm so, so sorry," I choked through the terrible, grinding sobs. I'd thought I could change who I was, but now I knew I'd only ever be a big disappointment.

This wasn't the end of the world, but it felt like the end of mine. Sandwiched between my best dogs, I cried and cried as I'd never cried before, not caring to quit until I decided I had no choice. Then my sobs gradually came to a shuddering stop.

I lay there limp and spent while I suffered a moment of deep sadness and surrender. Nico was wrong: I wasn't the biggest badasteroid at school. Not even close.

When I got so cold I knew I had to move before I couldn't, I cleared my eyes with a few swipes of my hand and pushed shakily to my feet. The twenty steps back to my sled was the longest walk of my short life. I felt faint-headed and empty. I'd done lots of hard things today, but what I did next was the hardest of them all.

I flipped up the latch on the tracking device and pushed the red button.

My ears throbbed. My eyes stung. My throat burned. My chest felt like it had been trampled. I'd thrown myself the pity party of all pity parties, but the punch bowl was empty, and confetti littered the floor, so I turned to my dogs. They were each curled up in the snow looking at me expectantly. They grabbed my heart and squeezed. They needed meat. I had no idea how long it would take for the cavalry to come, so hot water over kibble would have to do for now.

I put a bucket of snow on the alcohol cooker. While it melted, I visited with each dog, petting and whispering in their ears. I checked pads and between toes and rubbed balm into feet. The cold got a hard grip on me again as I worked, and soon my body turned in on itself with ache. My fingers quit cooperating, brain too. It was all I could do to toss out eight tin bowls and slosh a scoop of watery kibble into each of them before crawling into my sleeping bag more dead than alive. I was shaking so violently, I felt strangely warm.

Time slid sideways again. Through my ventilation hole, I saw a speck of light floating toward me. *Oh look, there's a firefly*, I thought drowsily before giving myself a mental shake. The growl of an engine a few seconds later confirmed that my mind was definitely playing tricks on me. I struggled into a sitting position in my bag and screwed up my eyes against the blinding light coming at me like a holy angel descending from heaven.

A snow machine roared up and stopped beside us. "You the lost little puppy?" a man's voice called out over the idling engine.

I blinked dumbly at him.

"I just got a call from Bill that there's a mom who's pretty worried about her boy."

I followed his gaze to my dogs and saw their outlines nestled in a row beside me, eyes sixteen shiny, blue marbles in his headlight.

"Let's get you and your dogs to my place, out of this storm," the snow machine man said, tipping his head in the direction he'd come. "Cabin's just back up there in the trees. It'll take us five minutes if you follow me with your team. You can warm up there while your crew drives around the mountain to pick you up."

Mom and the race people had been watching my blip on the computer screen from the Whitetail for hours, the snow machine guy named Jerry told me as I sat in front of a roaring fire suffering the long and excruciating process of thawing out and my dogs rested cozy in his kennels outside. They could see that I was lost, but I was moving around so much they couldn't risk leaving their pocket of Wi-Fi to come after me until they were sure I'd stopped for good and they'd know exactly where to find me. When my distress signal came, Bill, the race marshal realized my blip was practically in his friend Jerry's backyard. So, he called Jerry up and asked him to go and fetch me.

Now I was bundled up in Jerry's favorite recliner, a mug of steaming hot chocolate in my hand, telling the solemn, old musher about all my troubles. I could practically feel the energy seep back into me with each scalding sip, while the slow return of blood to my skin drove stinging needles of heat into my limbs. By the time the ding dong at the door an hour later sent my heart into overdrive, I felt almost human again.

I hauled myself up out of the chair as my mom swept through the doorway like a hurricane wind, her eyes wild and hollowed by worry. At the sight of her, a humiliating lump grew in my throat. I had to bite down on my bottom lip to stop it from wobbling like a baby's.

Then she was there, wrapping me up in her arms and smashing me against her. She seemed to cave in around me from her hips up. "Oh, honey," she said on a whoosh of air that ruffled the hair at my temple. "Are you all right?"

For a second, I let myself melt into her, bury my face in her neck. "I'm okay." I was horrified to hear a tiny quaver in my voice muffled against her coat.

She cupped the back of my skull and pressed her cheek against my greasy hair. "Let's get you home."

A deep breath was required, followed by another. Home sounded so good. Too good. I forced a smile, then pulled away and looked up to show it to Mom, hoping my eyes weren't still red and puffy from my earlier cry. I wonder what would have happened to me—to my spirit—if I would have quit then. I easily could have. Probably should have. So glad I'll never know.

"No, Mom," I said with a small shake of my head. "Get me back on the trail so I can finish the race."

Chapter 29

The race marshal trucked us to the Whitetail Ranch in his dog truck while I dozed against Mom's shoulder, hot air from the heater blasting in my chapped face. An hour later, we pulled up to the team of vets waiting to descend on my dogs.

Chase came running over from a big bonfire that lit up the sky, his breath puffing out in little jet streams. "You look like something the dogs barfed up," he sniggered as I half-climbed/half-toppled out of the truck.

"You're hilarious," I muttered dryly, ignoring the urge to knuckle-sandwich the annoying smirk off his face since it *was* nearly eleven o'clock at night and he *was* out here in the deep freeze waiting to help with my team.

It was still snowing away grimly, but the storm wasn't raging with the same ferocity over here as it was on the other side of the mountain, and there was no wind to blow away the smell of hot meat and straw clinging to the air. All the 350-milers had already left the checkpoint (theirs was a four-hour mandatory layover versus our six), so there was no chance of seeing Dad, who Mom had told me was still in the lead.

The 100-miler teams were all bedded down on their lines in long, even rows across a snowy field in what weirdly looked like a giant garden of dogs. A few dogs poked their heads out of their straw nests as we banged compartment doors open on the race marshal's truck and dropped my dogs. Besides our noise, all was perfectly still.

While Chase divvied out hot meat, I went with Dr. Topham from dog to dog, looking over every part of them inside and out and answering his questions.

"What happened to this little lady?" he asked in a quiet voice when Tenille flinched away at his rotation of her shoulder.

Heat sprang into my face. "I let her run on the downhill," I mumbled.

"Shoulder sprains happen to the best of them," the vet said, way too kindly. "We'll give her some Rimadyl (doggie ibuprofen) to make her comfortable and put her to bed. She'll be just fine in a week or so." He reached into his pocket. Even though I'd seen it coming for twenty miles, the sight of that big orange crayon still caught me in the gut. Tenille was out of the race, but at least she'd be okay. My relief was bone deep.

In the middle of our examinations, the first of the 100-mile mushers strode out of the ranch house to ready his dogs for the next leg of the race, his six-hour layover nearly up. A couple of race volunteers with a timer and a clipboard left the bonfire and followed him. Within minutes, the enthusiastic barking of his team shattered the stillness of the night. I was amazed at how the other fifty-six dogs asleep in the dog garden hardly stirred through all the ruckus. They were pros.

Dr. Topham put his stethoscope to Earl's chest, and we bent over him together. When I saw that deep V form between the vet's brows as he listened, the icy snake in my stomach stirred. "There's a little wheeze in his lungs."

Just then, Colt nosed between us. "What is it?" I asked Dr. Topham anxiously as I dodged Colt's kiss attacks. "In Earl's lungs, I mean?"

"Might be nothing. We'll check him again before you leave."

"How'd Colt do?" Chase cut in as he passed by with the poop pan and rake.

My sudden flash of anger eclipsed my unease for Earl. Shoving Colt away from me, I thrust out my chin. "Terrible! He was a pain in my neck the whole day. I'm going to leave him with you."

Once the dogs were examined, fed and put up, Mom towed me by the arm toward the ranch house which glowed like a jack-o-lantern in the night. When I stepped inside, the warm air heavy with tempting smells wrapped me in a big ole hug that elbowed all other thoughts away but one: *Food!*

The dining room was crammed with mushers and handlers and race volunteers sitting around an assortment of tables. My eyes went straight to the feast crammed along the kitchen bar. I heaped a paper plate with turkey, mashed potatoes and gravy, and two pieces of cake (carrot . . . because, *vegetables*). As I slunk, head down, to an empty spot, I was greeted with encouraging words, slaps on the back, and a few thumbs up. My lips tried a brave smile. It was weird. I'd screwed up a lot that day, hadn't even made it over Huckleberry Pass, yet somehow it was then I knew in my heart, I was a genuine musher.

I swear there was magic in that food. I shoveled it in until my body and soul were back on speaking terms. Then Mom whisked me into a warm, dark room where a crackling fire was the only source of sound and light. Bodies were sprawled out across the floor, others conked out in chairs. Wordlessly, I shucked off my damp clothes and handed them over to Mom, who spread them out before the fire to dry.

"I'll wake you in four hours," she whispered near my ear as she swiped some stingy stuff on the war wound slashed across my hipbone. Seconds later, I was toes-up on a couch clad only in my underwear. The instant Mom pulled a quilt over me, I went blank.

In what felt like one minute, my mom was shaking me awake. I shot up like Dracula from a coffin. Okay, I'm a big, fat liar. I slowly peeled my gritty eyelids open to find that the fire had burned down to tangerine embers and the room was empty except for us. I longed to burrow back down into the quilt and sleep for another five years, but the realization that all the other mushers were practically to the finish line at the Seeley Lake Community Center spurred me into action.

Stifling a groan, I sat up with all the finesse of an old man. There was pain in every muscle and joint of my body, way worse than I'd ever had, and my head was full of cobwebs. The simple acts of standing and dressing took a merciless toll on my body. But bodily suffering was the least of my problems I was soon to find out.

When I zombie-walked out to the truck ten minutes later, I was assailed with the worst possible news. "Earl has pneumonia," Dr. Topham announced in a grim tone.

For a moment I was struck dumb by his words. "Give him some medicine?" I sputtered.

"I've already started him on antibiotics. What Earl needs most is rest."

I was instantly Big Gulp Mountain Dew awake. "He can't!" I cried. "He's my leader!"

"Not today, son. I'm sorry."

Suddenly, I felt turned all back to front. I groped for the edge of the truck. "But . . . but I can't finish without him!"

The vet put a hand on Earl's head which was hanging out of his open compartment. My lead dog was looking at me, his eyes filled with apology. "You'll have to use another dog," Dr. Topham said gently.

Another dog! I wailed inside. I didn't have another leader! My gaze flew to where Chase had picketed my group of misfit dogs along the edge of the truck. I swept my headlamp over them while my mind scrambled.

Not every sled dog could lead. Only the best and brightest knew the commands. Some wouldn't even run at all if they had dogs behind them. Too much pressure. As I looked from Marlin to Auke to Charlie to Colt, I realized how much I'd depended on Earl's intelligence, experience, and skill. He was my Gandalf, my Yoda, my Dumbledore. I didn't know what—if anything—we could accomplish without him at lead. I'd never run a single mile without him, and to lose him now before the fifty most important miles of my life felt like a knockout blow.

My gaze landed on Mojo. Her ears perked up and she gave me a cheerful wag of her tail. My heart reached for her. She was so small and sweet, had the least commanding presence of all our dogs. Not once had I put her in lead. But I was her human. In two years of running dogs, she'd never once complained, quit on me, or let me down. She was my hardest worker, tougher than she looked too. I dug fists into sore eyes. Mojo wasn't a sure bet by a long shot, but our little team mascot was probably my best bet and giving up now was not an option.

I squatted down stiffly in front of her. I took her head in my hands and rested mine on hers. "What do you think, girl?" I murmured. "Can you do it?"

She put a paw on my knee and gave me a little lick on the chin. Sighing, I scratched her behind the ears. "Put Mojo next to Harley, Chase," I said, then cast a sideways glare at my canine nemesis as a truth rubbed like sandpaper in my armpit. "And put Colt the Dolt next to Auke."

Someone snorted. It was probably Chase but could have been Satan. Colt cocked his leg and peed on a tire. With a frustrated kick of my boot, I sent up a spray of yellow snow. I didn't dare attempt this run with less than six dogs, so not only was I out my main leader, I was stuck with that bonehead too.

Talk about a double-whammy.

With Mom and Chase's help to massage, bootie, and clip my dogs on the line, exactly six hours to the second from the time we pulled into the Whitetail, I struck out for the Seeley Lake Community Center with Harley and Mojo in lead, Auke and Colt behind them, Marlin and Charlie at wheel, and another rubber band around my chest making breathing a chore.

After only a few hours of rest, my dogs were fresh and raring to go. Me, not so much. Agony was pulsing through me like a drumbeat. While I rolled my stiff shoulders to work out the kinks, my dogs' enthusiasm was traveling back to me like electricity down a line. Show-offs. That thing about a sled dog's ability to recover quickly— it's *the* superpower of all canine superpowers. Truth is, dogs are superior to humans in so many ways.

For a mile or so, the trail followed the county road that led out of the Whitetail. My fingers were death-gripping the handlebar while my eyes bounced between Mojo and the side of the road. I knew a trail marker signaling a right-hand turnoff was coming up fast and was terrified I'd miss it. I was even more terrified that Mojo wouldn't respond to my vocal command and my team would fall apart this soon out of the gate.

When I caught a flash up ahead, my heart did a roundhouse kick in my chest. I pinned the beam of my headlamp on the reflective arrow and pressed lightly on the brake. "Easy, easy . . . "

Forty yards. Thirty yards. Twenty yards. Ten! I sucked in a sharp breath. This was our make or break moment!

"Gee!"

Harley instantly cut hard to the right. My eyes went wide, and I huffed a disbelieving laugh as Mojo swerved in perfect step beside him. No hesitation. No glancing back. *Like a ninja!*

"That a girl, Mojo!" I whooped.

Dog after dog made the turn in the manner of synchronized swimmers until, skidding wildly, the sled jumped off the road onto the groomed trail. I was so riveted on Mojo, the hard jolt of the runners against hard-packed snow nearly bucked me off the sled.

Most dogs in lead for the first time squat or sit down, unsure of themselves without a dog's butt to follow. Not my spunky little Mojo. As we headed across twenty miles of flat ranchland, her tug was perfectly tight, and she was facing straight ahead, leading with the authority and determination of a dog who'd been running at point their whole life.

I huffed another little laugh. Being vertically challenged hadn't stopped Napoleon from conquering most of Europe, and it clearly wasn't going to stop Mojo either. The rubber band cinching my chest snapped, and it was suddenly easier to breathe.

At the devil's own hour of four thirty in the morning, it was still perfectly dark out and would be for three more hours. But thankfully last night's storm had sheathed its claws. The clouds had even parted to reveal a moon all soft and soupy around the edges like a melty lump of ice. The air was crisp and biting, the conditions great for a run. This section of the route was way less complicated than yesterday's too.

First of all, it was a straight shot to the finish line with no more chances to miss turnoffs or go the wrong way. Two easy hours across these flats would get us to the wooden bridge on the Blackfoot River— the almost halfway point. Once we crossed the bridge, an effortless stretch through marshy river bottoms and willows would slowly metamorphose into the timbered foothills of McCabe Creek Summit. The long, steep climb up that behemoth stood to be the only hard part of today. After a breeze down the other side, we'd have just a final five-mile push through roller-coaster terrain to the finish.

"Good dogs," I called out on the rise of a yawn. I stretched one arm in an arc over my head, then the other. At this rate, we'd be to the community center before the kitchen volunteers even put the breakfast burrito fixings away. My stomach perked up at the prospect. *Today's going to be cake!*—thought no intelligent person ever who didn't want to be jinxed.

I was clearly an idiot.

For an hour we chased the moonbeams and shadows playing tag along the trail with only the jingle of the dogs' traces and their rhythmic pants and footfalls to interrupt the calm. My brain was blissfully empty of all worry and fear. The dogs were firing on all cylinders as they loped across the moonlit flats. It was a beautiful thing to see—a spectacular way to be, this flying blissfully under the silvery moon. I wanted to stop and still the world, to smash the master clock and make time stop. There was nothing better than this, and it was easy to forget all the hard stuff and my screwups from the day before or any troubles that may lay ahead.

But Colt was there, so of course my euphoria couldn't last. Just when I was feeling like all was right with the universe again, he turned around to bug Charlie.

"Stay ahead, Colt!" I yelled.

It was too late. He'd already balled up the team. "Quit being a . . . a . . . *blight*, will you!" I growled through clenched teeth as I worked to untangle his leg.

Not ten minutes after I'd stopped to fix Colt's mess, he did it again. "You are disgrace to God's creative powers, Colt!" I shouted as I stomped on the brake.

Wash, rinse, repeat for the next infuriating hour. By the time my plastic runners hit the bridge's bare wooden slats, instantly cutting our speed in half and nearly pitching me over the handlebar, I was so mad at that good-for-nothing dog, I had a burning desire to find out if all dogs really do go to heaven. Though I seriously doubted it.

I jumped off and began pushing the sled to help the dogs pull it across. Toward the middle of the bridge, my attention was drawn to the team as a unit. Everyone was peering straight ahead into the darkness, ears pricked. Even Colt. A cold shiver gathered at the base of my neck. When the runners hit snow on the other side, I swung back on, my body alert in every limb and cell.

My dogs picked up pace. We whipped around a corner. My eyes were looking everywhere at once. Nothing moved. All I could see were gauzy shadows hulking across our path and the flickers of a few lazy stars.

Suddenly, a dark hole in the willows that caught no light, didn't seem to have any form, detached itself from the spiky black backdrop and drifted toward the trail. Fear hit me like a hammer. My dogs exploded forward, rocking me backward. I fought for balance while my feet instinctively scrambled for the brake. I angled my heels inward and desperately dug them into the snow. "Whoa! Whoa! *Whooooa!*"

I watched in horror as the whole night and all the darkness in the world seemed to coalesce on the trail right in front of us. My dogs were fighting against me, gunning for a chase with the fervor of ten million years of predatory instinct pumping through their veins. It took everything I had to muscle my team to a stop.

It towered over us barely four team-lengths away—an immense black paper cutout in my beam. All the blood seemed to drain from my body; the spit dried up in my mouth. *Moose!* a thousand voices shrieked at once inside my head.

It was nightmare huge. At least six feet at the shoulder. Fifteen hundred pounds of pure danger with razor-sharp hooves that could tear a dog to bits. No antlers. Female. *Worse.* She turned her massive head back and forth as if using her ears as a nature-made radar system.

This can't be happening! This can't be happening!

I'd never encountered a moose on the trail, only heard stories—horror ones. Ugly, bloody tales of trampled dogs and death and carnage, of grown men leveled by tears. Two years of mushing, all my experience, had not prepared me for this.

Out front, my dogs were barking and hitting their harnesses to get at her. The long hairs on the moose's rump raised as if electrified. She blew snot out her nose and stared at us, her eyes two hot coals in my beam. Dazed by terror, like a rabbit panting beneath a circling hawk, I was pinned in place with only my white puffs of breath showing life.

The moose twisted around and peered into the willows for a few seconds before turning back to us and snorting again. I watched the dewlap hanging beneath her chin sway back and forth as if standing outside my body. Then her ears flattened back, and she put her head down and charged.

Chapter 30

The moose barreled toward us like a runaway train. She was charging at a gallop, but it felt like Time itself had applied its brakes putting everything into slow motion. Steam billowed from her nose. Snow sprayed up from her gangly legs in her wake. I could feel the pounding of her hooves in my molars. My dogs had gone quiet. A scream was lodged in my throat.

The moose was bearing down on us. Ten yards away. *Five.* I couldn't unlock my body. I'd lost the power to move.

She was so *big. So close!* I could see the whites of her eyes. Could smell her too. Musky. Pungent. Her stench snapped me out of my trance.

I gasped, and my lungs filled with fire. Battle blood surged in my veins. I whipped off my parka in one lightning move, feeling reckless and desperate and bold.

The moose took the team, hit my leaders head on. She began striking at them with her hooves. "*Nooooooo!*" I bellowed, waving my parka over my head to make myself look bigger.

It only ticked her off.

She spun around, snaked out at Harley with her hooves, started stomping him into the snow. Harley's screams ripped through the night, the most harrowing sound in the world. The rest of the dogs were trying to make themselves disappear into the snow.

Rage exploded through me. Made me strong. Fearless. Ten times my size.

I leaped from the runners and ran toward her with a blood-curdling scream, flapping my parka in front of me. I felt feral. Out of my mind. Herculean. I wanted to ruin and wreck and destroy.

The moose faltered, tossed her head, then wheeled around and galloped a little way back down the trail before turning to face us again. Her long ears rotated like satellite dishes. She blew another blast of steam out her nose.

Shrieking like a banshee, I made a false charge at her. The moose swayed a little on the trail as if indecisive then looked toward the willows again. She seemed to think about something while I yelled even louder and stomped my feet and shook my parka at her.

She turned back at me and gave me a look of loathing and spite. We stared at each other. Threw daggers with our eyes. The stars vanished. The snow beneath my feet, the trees, willows all disappeared from the universe until all that existed was me and this living, breathing threat to my team.

My heart was thumping so hard it felt like my ears were about to explode. My Skinny Leg jacket crackled with the up and down pumps of my chest. She was less than twenty paces away. Refused to give up the trail.

Behind me, one of my dogs began to bark. The moose's nostrils dilated, quivered. When she looked past me to my team, my brain lit up like the Fourth of July. Two sideways steps put me between her and my dogs. "*Git!*" I shouted, widening my stance and squaring my shoulders and jaw at her. The hump on her back appeared to rise like a big, brown moon as she began to lower her head.

Oh heck no you don't! I thought savagely.

Before I'd left the Whitetail, I stuck a bottle of Gatorade in an inside pocket to keep it from freezing. I didn't think—just pulled it out. *"Go away!"* I roared, chucking it at her as hard as I could. *"Leave my dogs alone!"*

The bottle streaked end over end through the air, a silver wraith in the moonlight. For the first time in my life, my throw met its mark. The Gatorade hit the moose square in the face. The dull thud was shockingly loud in the crisp dawn air. She reared a little, shook her head, then spun around and lolloped away.

All my air came out in a rush. Everything just went limp. As I stood there, fist pressed to my heaving chest, watching her melt into the darkness, I saw a calf dart out of the willows and totter after the moose on knobby, broken-toothpick legs. Seconds later, it was gone too.

It had all happened so fast. Less than a minute had passed since the momma moose stepped on the trail, and it was over. I came back to a sense of the greater world on a quick gasp. *No, it isn't!* I thought frantically, whirling around.

I skimmed my headlamp over the team as I dashed back, met each set of eyes. My dogs were whining, pacing around nervously, seemed okay—except for Harley. He lay on the snow like a limp rag. The sight of him was so horrible I could hardly look.

Nausea swept over me. Splatters of blood around him appeared blue-black in my beam. I sank to my knees beside him. "Oh, Harley." The words were more breath than sound.

I felt completely different than I had the day before—Life before? Eons before?—as if I were in someone else's skin. Could it really have been just yesterday I'd strutted like a peacock around our dog trailer chatting with all our fans? I pulled off my mitts. I no longer seemed part of the normal world, a world where the most important question of the day was whether Mom had packed BBQ or Sour Cream Pringles in my lunch. School, home, my bed—none of it seemed real anymore. All that was real was here—reaching for my trampled dog, the unbearable sting in my chest as if my heart had been skinned with a knife.

With tears spilling down my face, I laid a trembling hand on Harley's side. Whimpering, he lifted his head and looked at me with dazed, pain-filled eyes. "Hey, buddy," I croaked.

His front leg was bent at an odd angle with his paw tucked up underneath his rib cage. My throat worked, felt blocked by a shard of glass. I shot a glance at the tracker still hanging from the sled. Narrowed my eyes at it while my heart hammered away in my chest.

Mushers just handle it, said an internal voice more Dad's than mine. I swiped the tears away, squeezed my eyes shut and pressed my thumb and forefinger into the hollows above my nose while I came to grips with what needed to be done, what *I* had to do.

When I finally looked back down at Harley, everything inside me quieted. Like sunlight through a magnifying glass, all my focus narrowed to a single, brilliant point.

My hands were steady as I began tiptoeing my fingers over his body searching for other injuries. I spoke quietly to him while I gently probed. His ears were down, a sure sign of pain, yet he made no struggle or sound, just watched me calmly as I worked. I knew that he understood I was trying to help him.

Even when I discovered an ominous, three-inch gash on his broken leg, he barely flinched. Feeling as if a giant had put his boot on my throat, I followed the muscle from his shoulder to his elbow with my fingers. When I felt a tendon tremble against my bloody fingertip, I loosed a breath through my lips. No internal damage to the ligaments. Once his leg healed, he'd be able to run again.

The other dogs had recovered from the moose attack, and by their demanding barks, I knew they were antsy to get out of this place. Working quickly, I anchored the sled to a tree, cut a couple short lengths of willow, then dug out my first aid kit from the sled bag before dropping back down next to Harley.

Sweat sprouted up across my skin. I'd come to the part I'd been dreading the most. Teeth clenched, I gently pulled his paw out from under his body. Harley's howl of pain sliced through me like a buzz saw. When I straightened out his leg, he bared his teeth and growled low in his throat. Breathing heavily, I swiped my hot face with the back of my hand before gathering a handful of snow.

I used the snow to clean away the blood from the gash then snipped away the matted fur for a better look and to wash out germs and debris. The torn flesh gaped like an open mouth. It was leaking a steady trickle of blood. I could see ugly bruising under his fur, and the swelling had already started.

I packed the gash with another handful of clean snow as a make-shift ice pack and to staunch the bleeding until Dr. Topham could stitch him up, then laid a willow on each side of his leg to make a splint. By now, Harley was panting as if he'd just finished a sprint. "Almost done, brave boy," I said on a shaky exhale as I began wrapping an Ace bandage tightly from ankle to shoulder to hold it all in place.

After I'd secured the bandage with a clip, I smoothed the fur on Harley's muzzle then buried my face in his neck. I needed a minute. We both did.

Slumped against my dog, the adrenaline slowly fizzled out of me until I was drained of all energy. Now that the crisis was over, a reaction set in. Each movement, almost each thought seemed an effort. But I knew I couldn't let this trauma take over everything else. There was no place for weakness now.

Harley's warmth and the steady beating of his heart against mine was comforting. I drew a huge breath as if sucking it up through a straw. It was all I could do to stand. My legs wobbled, and the world seemed to sway. I felt about as strong as a wet noodle and could barely pick up my dog.

It was just coming on daylight as I loaded him clumsily into the sled bag. A faint glow was spreading across the mountain peaks at my back and painting the snowcaps in pastels. The pretty pinks were in contrast with my ugly mood. I was down to five dogs. We still had a behemoth to climb with the added weight of a dog in the bag. Then there was the little matter of being out another leader with thirty miles to go.

I scrubbed my frozen hands over my face before taking stock of my remaining dogs. The slim pickings didn't improve my spirits, but I refused to let the dark thoughts win.

First, I tried Charlie at point with Mojo. The instant I whistled up what was left of my team, Charlie sat down in the trail and cowered as if she were being dive-bombed by a squadron of sparrows. The other dogs mowed right over her causing a huge tangle. Strike one.

My attempt at running Auke in lead was even more of a disaster. She growled and shot dirty glances at Mojo before trying to rip off her face. Strike two.

I called a time out. Busted out the snack bag. Threw a little hissy fit inside my head.

While the dogs ate frozen salmon steaks, I watched the sun lick the sugar-spun world with long swipes of its pink tongue and brooded. What the heck was I supposed to do now? I was down to nothing. Harley was in the bag. Charlie and Auke had both bombed at lead. I had to have Marlin at wheel.

I flung a pinecone in one hard, sharp movement at a trail marker. Missed. Turned a dark look on Colt. He'd worked himself into such a frenzy when I'd tossed him his salmon, he had it between his feet and was panting over it before starting to gnaw.

Stupid dog.

My glower deepened when I clipped him unceremoniously in beside Mojo a few minutes later. The other dogs jumped and barked to go while Colt looked back at me with a befuddled expression on his muddy brown face. I stepped heavily onto the runners. "Ready . . . " I called out looking him in the eye and injecting all the enthusiasm in my voice I could manage. "*Hike, Hike!*"

Chapter 31

Colt ran with an awkward, sideways gait and shot nervous glances back at me while Mojo tried her best to drag him along. His tail was standing straight up like the flag on the back of an old-fashioned bike announcing his insecurity, and his tugline was totally slack. But on the bright side (and by bright, I mean like Cassiopeia—the furthest star we can see with our naked eye whose brightness at 16,308 light-years away is barely above the 6th magnitude limit), he hadn't sat down on the trail.

We were moving at a crawl. The earlier traffic punching through the freshly fallen snow had carved a crisscross of deep furrows in the middle of the trail, which added a ton of resistance to the runners and made for very hard pulling for my dogs. Without every bit of strength on the line plus a dog in the bag, I knew with a growing hopelessness that it was impossible to make it the last thirty miles. But impossible is for sissies, so I hopped over and started to pedal.

The next time Colt looked back, our eyes met and locked. I kicked off with my right foot sending up a little explosion of snow behind me.

"Come on, Colt!" I called in a hard and flat voice. "I need you to be more!"

A mile caterpillared past, then another. The landscape was pure and sparkling white, the air still with the silence only fresh snow can bring. Sweat trickled down the divot in my back as we slowly worked our way out of the marshy river bottoms and into the foothills of McCabe Creek Summit which loomed above us, slashed and bald, like Azog, Chief of the Orcs.

We were deep into the trees when I felt Colt put a little pressure on his harness. There was the tiniest uptick in speed. My head came up sharply. At the sight of his tug snap, a ragged hope began to form within me. "Atta boy, Colt!" I whooped. "That's what I'm talking about!"

Once Colt felt the resistance of a tight tug, his muscle memory kicked in. Once his muscle memory kicked in, his confidence began to grow—and my hope right along with it. He looked back at me less and less until his head was continually oriented forward. His tail lowered. His ears straightened. As his body language relaxed, mine did too. Soon he was banging on his harness, and I felt almost gleeful, like I was still hanging on to some small luck by my fingernails.

Just as I was taking back every murderous thought and bad name I'd ever called him, in true Colt fashion, he started messing around. Instead of running in a straight line, he was wandering back and forth across the trail like a drunken sailor. I suddenly felt so exhausted I could hardly stay upright. "Stay ahead, Colt," I called out dully.

The imbecile ignored me and cut toward the side of the trail. Mojo tried to steer him back to the middle, but being so much bigger and stronger, Colt pulled her the other direction. Growling through my teeth, I made to stomp on the brake.

Before my boot hit metal, I felt a subtle shift beneath my weight. When the hiss of the runners rose slightly in pitch, I stopped moving, stopped breathing, everything about me stopped—except for my lips, which were breaking into an incredulous smile. The sled had started to float.

Remember near the end of *Return of the Jedi* when Darth Vader hurls the evil Emperor Palpatine to his death just in time to save his son and the galaxy? Yep, the villain in this story became the hero too.

See, the side of a trail is a lot firmer because less traffic has passed over it. A sled doesn't bust through the ground as much on the edge so there is better footing for the dogs. When I thought he was screwing off, my brilliant, awesome, clever Colt had been looking for the trail's sweet spot. Once he found it, he held the team there, cutting the workload in half and doubling our speed.

Mom says the annoying troublemaker at school is usually just bored and needs a challenge. Dogs too, apparently. Colt the Dolt killed it at lead. He became Batman to Mojo's Robin, and together they saved the day—the part that they could, anyhow.

Not even a superhero can hold back the sun.

The sun got bigger and brighter and hotter as we wound our way up through the thick timber, and the sky got bluer and bluer and bluer until it was the friendliest blue you can imagine—yeah (*scoff*), if kryptonite is friendly. It was hard to fathom we were even on the same planet as the day before. Typical Montana.

Mid-morning, my dogs' breath quit blowing white, and I knew we were in for it. I stripped down to my base layer, but the dogs couldn't take off their heavy coats, so for every minute running, I had to let them spend equal time cooling off in the shade.

To beat the heat (by "heat" I'm talking thirty to thirty-five degrees here) we tackled the mountain in little, frustrating bites. Despite Mojo's determination and Colt picking out the best trail, our climb up McCabe Creek Pass was agonizingly slow. When the trees finally thinned out to nothing and the switchbacks smoothed out into an impossibly steep, straight-shot to the summit, the sight of that final half-mile ascent nearly leveled me. I got off and started to push. It was either that or sit down and bawl, and I'd already done enough of that to swamp a ship.

The dogs were barely trotting, their shoulders rounded in exertion, their bodies slanting down toward me at a sharp angle. My feet hurt so bad. Soon I was waddling beside the sled more than pushing. My head pounded. My heart felt as if it was going to explode out of my chest. My skinny leg buckled, and I collapsed half on the runner.

The dogs stopped, looking back. Mojo popped her tug and wagged her tail. Her gaze was steady, burning into me with the intensity of our bond and injecting me with strength. Willing my arms to obey, I reached for the handlebar and pulled myself up.

The sun beat down on us from straight overhead, determined to bend us to its will. With every step, the trail got steeper and steeper, and massive rock formations reared up around us threateningly. All of us were weaving now, staggering up the slope. Every footstep, every push was an effort of supreme willpower. My gas tank was empty. I could hardly hold myself up. All the dogs' ears were down, every tail tucked. There was no way we'd ever make it to the summit.

"Ewuuuauuahhhhh . . . " The guttural sound broke through the thundering in my ears. Grumpy walrus? Angry bear? It was a wild, far-out noise not quite covered by words.

I raised my eyes to the sled as another excited Chewbacca yowl burst from the bag. Colt started barking in, then Marlin . . . Auke . . . now Charlie! I watched in wonder as Harley's strange pep talk went through the whole team, firing up each dog one by one. Soon every dog was hammering on their harness, every head back in the game. Including mine.

It was crazy how that sound made us all suddenly believe we could do anything. Harley's enthusiasm and cheerful spirit is a superpower not to be underestimated. In action, it's a bona fide jaw-dropper. You should have seen us pound up the slope to the tune of his strange song, and when the land finally started to level off, we all collapsed in the snow.

While I sucked air and the dogs rolled around on their backs to cool off, awareness of my surrounding dawned a little at a time. Black on white. Burned over. Death's country. Ugly and cursed. When I realized we were in the exact spot Dad had resurrected Harley from the dead long before, the slow shake of my head made a little divot in the snow. The Happiest Dog Who Ever Lived was riding in the bag again. This fact was a bleak one, but in a weird way it inspired me too. Mushing had challenged us at every turn, had pushed us way beyond our limits, yet with persistence we'd always made it through. That thought drove me to my feet.

Harley's makeshift ice pack had nearly melted again, and his splint was starting to loosen. No more bleeding, thank goodness, and he seemed comfortable enough, though forlorn. After I packed another ball of fresh snow on his gash and rewrapped the Ace bandage, I gave him extra special attention—nuzzling him, murmuring in his ear what an awesome, brave dog he was and how we never would have made that climb without his encouragement. "Don't worry, boy. We're almost there," I told him with a final pat to his head. "We're going to get you to Dr. Topham soon, and once he's fixed you up, I'm going to give you a great big steak."

I'd said the "soon" part so convincingly, I practically believed it myself.

We slowly wound our way down switchback after switchback. The sun had turned the snow sticky, making it hard for the runners to glide. I helped pedal, but it killed. The reflection of the sunlight off the snow straight into my face was another huge torment. It burned my eyes and made my face stream with hot, stingy tears.

Time lost all meaning. My eyes swelled to slits. The silence had grown so heavy, I thought I might buckle under the weight of it. An electrical storm of pain was lighting up my lower back from hours of standing on my uneven legs and the jolting of the runners. My legs felt like jelly beneath me, my arms like big blocks of wood. My brain was so fried from sleep deprivation and bone-deep exhaustion, I'd come to the edge of hallucinating and the ability to think clearly, so I narrowed my mind to everything but the sight and sound of the endless white ribbon of trail and the patter of little feet, focused on an inner resource and kept going. We all did.

On and on my dogs ran, following Mojo and Colt. By mid-afternoon, we weren't running so much anymore as barely moving forward. Surely, we had to be getting close. *Please, let us be close!* I *had* to get Harley to the vet.

When the sun cracked over the mountains like an egg, sunny side up, and we *still* hadn't come to any sort of an end, hadn't even seen a sign of civilization, I completely lost heart. We'd been on this trail for what felt like years now. Had we somehow missed the finish? Made a wrong turn in my haze? The whole world seemed empty of people but for me.

I stifled a moan. We'd overcome so many obstacles, made it this far, only to be broken at last by the heat. The sun had sapped my superheroes' strength. They needed meat. I wanted to cry at how drained my dogs were, at the missing sparkle in their eyes. They'd worked so hard, had given me their all. Love for them swarmed my throat. It ached with gratitude for their loyalty, with pride that I got to share my life with these amazing animals. For their safety, I knew I couldn't let them go any further—and that ached most of all.

As I fought to draw a full breath, through the trees, a splash of red against the white backdrop blazed in the sinking sun and caught my eye. My tired, sluggish, hungry brain was having trouble keeping up, and when it registered that it was my mom's red hair making all that visual noise, my breath caught to see her there.

No, wait. That couldn't be right! I shook my head to erase the mirage, but, yep, she was still there, standing halfway up a little rise, and my dogs' heads were turning toward her too, all ears pricked at once. When her cheer punctuated the air like an exclamation point at the end of the long silence, I smiled so big I tasted blood from the cracks in my lips.

"Go home, Moj! Go home, Colt!" Mom whooped as she broke into a run toward us.

Go home. That command was the key to unlocking a final surge of power. It was as if an electrical pulse zinged down the line. Adrenaline shot through me and blew out all the stuffing from my head. Pain vanished. Something in my bones reset. The dogs instantly picked up speed, running like kids on the last day of school.

Mom intersected us on the trail, eyes bright with proud tears. "One more mile!" she cried.

One more mile. A little laugh/sob broke from my throat. "Eat your heart out *cellar door*!" I called to my dogs. "Tolkien was dead wrong!"

I swear Mojo looked back and grinned.

Mom jogged alongside, galvanizing us with praise and by the upbeat tone of her voice. Soon I started catching glimpses of log buildings through the trees. Ahead disembodied voices began to cheer. "Is that real?" I breathed.

The dogs' tails stiffened; their ears cocked as Mom gave me a huge smile.

We came around a shadowy bend to find a small crowd of race people waiting for us along an orange stripe sprayed across the trail. At the sight of them, relief took me directly in the knees, and I struggled to hold myself up.

The instant we slid across the finish line, Chase appeared out of the camera flashes and grabbed the neckline between my leaders. "Took you long enough," he said through a massive grin as he jogged us toward the parking lot. Everyone followed.

When we reached our truck, my dogs flopped down beside it, pink tongues working furiously. I stumbled from the runners. The world tilted and swayed. It was almost impossible to walk.

Everything around me was a discombobulating kaleidoscope of movement, color, and noise. When Dr. Topham materialized out of the chaos and put a steadying hand on my shoulder, it was as if a thousand pounds fell from my back.

I went straight for the zipper on the sled bag and was waylaid by a fifty-something guy I'd never seen before. "That was some feat you just pulled off," he said enthusiastically.

I made a preoccupied grunt, anxious to get Harley out.

"I'm Kim, a reporter for the Missoulian newspaper."

Suddenly, the guy was no longer background noise. My hand froze on the zipper, eyes snapping to his.

"How do you feel after your first distance race?" he asked.

Everything stopped for a beat, and the broken shards at the end of the kaleidoscope tube settled into a dazzling pattern of color and light. As I stood beside my injured dog, my body wrecked and held up by sheer force of will, stood in memories of attacking moose and murderous wind, of a raging blizzard and lost team, of fear and despair, and a villainous sun, of mountains too steep to climb, I allowed myself a shy smile of pride. "Sore, but accomplished," I said to the man. "I'm glad we got it done."

The reporter's smile stretched clear up to his eyes. "You're quite a kid. I'd like to write a story about you for tomorrow's paper. Can we talk?"

My blood suddenly felt like it was carbonated. "Sure," I said, yanking down the zip. "As soon as I've seen to my dogs."

Chapter 32

Dogs, two double bacon cheeseburgers, interview, bed—in that order. Those things accomplished, I fell headlong into the mythical sleep of the dead in a rental cabin not far from the community center. Mom had tucked me in with the promise she'd look in on me between dog handling duties for Dad who wouldn't be finished with his race for another day or so. Everything else was a blur.

My shrieking bladder woke me up. When I shuffled through a tunnel of fuzz into the bathroom, I found a newspaper sitting on the toilet seat. When I picked it up to lift the lid, the headline struck my comatose brain like a bell: *Great Falls Father, Son Find Calling at Race to the Sky.* The smile that cut my face made me wince.

Ringing with wonder, I ran my thumb across the blurry picture beneath the headline. *Mojo. Colt. Me. Us.* I tried to scrub the sleep off my face and couldn't. "Spencer Bruggeman was ten when he read London's *The Call of the Wild,* and he heard the call loud and clear," was all I took in before folding the paper and tucking it under my arm. I'd save the article for when I was more human than zombie. I wanted to feel the full impact of it my first time through. I also relished showing it to Nico and Joey over Oreo towers and big glasses of cold milk when I got back home in a few days.

On my way back to bed, I caught a reflection in the mirror above the sink and was surprised to see a familiar face staring at me through swollen eyes. I stared right back, feeling so strange to myself, it was hard to believe it was me.

My first awareness was pain. My head ached, and my shoulders ached, and my lungs ached, and my hip joints ached, and the ankle bones of each foot ached excruciatingly. Even the warm air blowing against my skin was painful.

Someone was calling my name from the other end of a long tunnel. I opened my lids in treacherous little slits. It took a moment to place my bearings. Dark room. Dim light. Bed. *Not my pillow.* And then I remembered.

I turned my head, and my neck hurt too. A face slowly pulled itself together at the side of the bed and became the nose, jaw, and upturned lips of my dad. With a ballooning of happiness, I settled on his eyes.

They were filled with fire.

Epilogue

I fork another big bite of cake into my mouth. The inch-thick, electric blue frosting is so sweet, my teeth threaten to explode from my jaw. Humming with pleasure, I reach for my Sprite, and my elbow bumps the red lantern sitting by my plate. I lunge to steady it as it bobbles and clanks, then hide a goofy grin against my collarbone. Funny how a stupid lantern can make you feel like you could leap a small building in a single bound.

But this one does.

The last finisher of a dog sled race is presented the red lantern as a symbol of perseverance. Mine is going on the shelf above my bed—right next to the trail marker I'm gonna nail on my wall when I get home tonight from the awards banquet.

You know the one.

The trailbreaker guy went out on his snow machine this morning and fetched the trail marker sticking out from the snowbank at the base of Huckleberry Pass. Then all the other mushers (100 *and* 350-milers!) signed it before the race marshal presented it to me in front of the crowd an hour ago along with the red lantern. I've never smiled so hard in my life.

I give the reflective diamond a quick spin, and all the signatures meld into a pinwheel of squiggles and loops. I feel so light inside as I watch it teeter and reel on its loose nail, it's a wonder I don't float straight up to the ceiling and bob there for the rest of the night.

When the arrow wobbles to a stop, I lean the trail marker against the wall, then slide the red lantern to the middle of the table right up next to Dad's. I shoot another grin at my armpit. Yep, a matched set. Dad got the red lantern too.

Dad's sudden burst of laughter from across the room sets off a little firework in my chest. It's a throw-the-head-back laugh made of teeth and tongue and that mini-rib-cage-looking-thing at the roof of a mouth. I study his face. It's totally ravaged by wind and cold and sun, yet I've never seen it more incandescent with life. He says something to the pair of mushers he's standing with, and they laugh too. To see them now, you'd never know Dad finished last and the other two didn't even finish at all.

I drag my finger through the thick frosting, and pop the blob into my mouth, giving my molars another something to squawk about. Dad went out hard and fast in the first leg of the race at a pace he couldn't maintain—a rookie mistake. Then the sun reared its ugly head. While heat was dropping the other teams like flies and I was struggling up McCabe Creek Summit with Harley in the bag, Dad played it smart and camped his dogs in the shade, then only ran at night after that. He hadn't built up enough of a cushion though to keep his lead or have enough gas left in the tank for a hard push at the end, and first Huggie's Snug and Dry Jenny, then Laura, who'd both ran their teams at a smarter/steadier pace, passed him in the last few miles of the race.

I snort around my finger. Beaten by a couple of girls—me and Chase are gonna get years of mileage out of that one. Seriously though, every other team scratched. *Every. Other. Team.* Seven of them. Many of them race veterans too. The race conditions were *that* tough. Some guy even broke his leg when he got whiplashed into a fence post. So, when you see it from this angle, the red lantern looks pretty darn good, huh?

A breath leaks out of me as I take in the room full of dog people talking dogs and swapping trail stories over crumpled napkins and piles of greasy paper plates. Everything around me feels so soft and friendly, it's a short jump in my head from this room to the gridiron chalked onto Jaycee Park's faded grass. With happy chatter and laughter lapping at my ears, my mind slowly works its way from then to now, and when I get to this moment, in this room, with these people and my red lantern, I realize that I don't mind having a skinny leg at all.

"Hello there."

I come grinning out of my reverie to find practically the oldest man I've ever seen standing beside me. I'd been so busy playing in my mental sandbox, I didn't even notice him come up. I blink owlishly at him.

Age has whittled him down to my level. His eyes are heavily bagged and pinked around the inner rims, but twinkles shine out twin keyholes of a bright and lively mind. I know instantly that I like him.

I grab my napkin and make a quick swipe across my mouth. "Hello, sir."

"Not sir," he says with a wink in a voice that could sure use a few shots of WD-40. "Just Dave."

Old and Dave. I sit up a bit straighter as my heart throws an extra beat.

He eases down into the chair next to mine. "I used to run dogs in these hills for the United States Army when I wasn't much older than you," he says, and my heart is suddenly galloping away in my chest, and the little hinges on my jaw are swinging open.

"I'll tell you about it sometime. But not now. It's *you* I want to talk about." His eyes light up even more, if possible. "I hear you're a boy with spirit!"

Author's Note

It's been said that a mother is only as happy as her most miserable child. I was an exceptionally sad mom the year I watched my son, Spencer, slowly dying inside as he stood alone on the sideline of the Grid Kid football field while everyone around him got to play. So of course, this cat lover would say "yes" to anything after that—even a backyard full of sled dogs. And what an adventure those dogs have been!

Of all the exciting, harrowing, triumphant, and heartbreaking experiences we've had running sled dogs, twelve-year-old Spencer's first Montana Race to the Sky ranks at the top. From the moment he slid across that finish line with his beleaguered little team, I knew this was a story that needed to be shared with the world. It happened almost like I described it in the book. Yes, Spencer has a skinny leg. Yes, four-time Iditarod Champion Doug Swingley became our mentor. Yes, Spencer made all those mistakes during the race. Yes, Earl brought the team back to the starting line in the middle of the night. Most notably, instead of quitting the race, Spencer said to me, "Mom, get me back on the trail so I can finish the race!" And yes, Spencer and ninety-year-old-plus retired Army dog trainer Dave Armstrong shared that sweet exchange at the Race to the Sky awards banquet.

I fudged timelines a bit for brevity. For example, not all of those little calamities happened during Brett and Spencer's first overnight camping run, but they did happen at various times during their training runs, including their run-in with a mountain lion. All the characters in the book are based on real people, except for Nico and Joey, who I created to flesh-out the bullying subplot. The dogs are all real too. In the picture of Spencer and his team above, you'll recognize little Mojo as the lead dog on the left and husky Earl as the lead dog on the right. The dog running at wheel next to Spencer on the left is Colt, and the dog right behind Mojo on the line is Harley. I made up the moose too, because what story doesn't need an exciting moose attack? None that I know of. Oh, and Spencer's dad really did do CPR on a dog and bring it back to life. How cool is that?

About the Author

A native of southern Nevada, Suzette has somehow found herself living in Montana's land of ice and snow where she and her swashbuckling husband, Brett, a competitor in Alaska's famous Iditarod, own and operate Skinny Leg Sled Dogs. Their three fine sons have sadly given up their poop-scooping duties for the greener pastures of college.

Although Suzette cheerfully runs herd on forty rambunctious sled dogs and a basset hound, she is unequivocally a cat lover. A lifelong songwriter, she is the author of several stage musicals, most notably, *Symphony of Life*, on which she collaborated with Emmy Award-winning arranger Kurt Bestor.

You can follow the adventures of Skinny Leg Sled Dogs on Instagram and Facebook and learn more about Suzette's writing and music at www.suzettebruggeman.com.

Scan to visit

www.suzettebruggeman.com